Look what people are

Julie Elizabeth Leto

"Julie Elizabeth Leto does it again with another great read! Danger, mystery, suspense, romance and, well, lots of hot sex."
—*The Best Reviews* on *Brazen & Burning*

"Sizzling chemistry and loads of sexual tension make this Leto tale a scorcher."
—*Romantic Times BOOKclub* on *Chasing Charlie*

Kimberly Raye

"Kimberly Raye is hot, hot, hot!"
—*New York Times* bestselling author
Vicki Lewis Thompson

"A red-hot, sizzlin' read."
—*Heartstrings Reviews* on
Sweet as Sugar, Hot as Spice

Leslie Kelly

"*Don't Open Till Christmas* by Leslie Kelly is a present in itself where the humor and the sizzling sex never stop. Top Pick!"
—*Romantic Times BOOKclub*

"Leslie Kelly has penned a story chock full of humor sure to bring a smile across even the Grinch's face and lots of steamy sex scenes so hot you will need to turn on the air conditioner to cool off."
—*The Romance Reader's Connection*

Julie Elizabeth Leto
Kimberly Raye
Leslie Kelly

BOYS *of* SUMMER

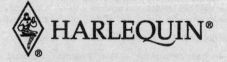

HARLEQUIN®

TORONTO • NEW YORK • LONDON
AMSTERDAM • PARIS • SYDNEY • HAMBURG
STOCKHOLM • ATHENS • TOKYO • MILAN • MADRID
PRAGUE • WARSAW • BUDAPEST • AUCKLAND

ISBN-13: 978-0-373-79268-9
ISBN-10: 0-373-79268-9

BOYS OF SUMMER
Copyright © 2006 by Harlequin Books S.A.

The pulisher acknowledges the copyright holders of the individual works as follows:

FEVER PITCH
Copyright © 2006 by Julie Leto Klapka.

THE SWEET SPOT
Copyright © 2006 by Kimberly Raye Groff.

SLIDING HOME
Copyright © 2006 by Leslie Kelly.

This edition published by arrangement with Harlequin Books S.A.

® and TM are trademarks of the publisher. Trademarks indicated with ® are registered in the United States Patent and Trademark Office, the Canadian Trade Marks Office and in other countries.

www.eHarlequin.com

Printed in U.S.A.

CONTENTS

Dear Reader,

I've had a love/hate relationship with baseball since I was about nine years old and realized that if I wanted to spend any time with my family, I had to either learn how to play the game or spend my life in the bleachers. You see, my older brother was one of the best shortstops in Little League. My dad was his coach. My mother was the park's player agent and often umpired. My two little brothers were standouts in peewee ball. Our doorbell—no lie—played "Take Me Out to the Ballgame."

So I played softball (made the all-stars, too, when I was twelve, by the way). I also kept score and called games over the loudspeaker during tournaments. I was a begrudging fan, but a fan nonetheless. Once I hit my teenage years, I learned the most important thing a girl should know about this particular sport—the guys are hot. I mean, no athlete looks better in tight pants than a baseball player. Nobody. Trust me on this.

And yet, when I chose a hero for this novella, I decided I wanted to write about the team owner. I don't know what it is about guys with endless power and loads of money, but for some reason, I find them intriguing. Enter Donovan Ross. Poor devilish, sexy playboy Donovan. He's on the brink of losing everything that matters to him when his ex-wife comes back into his life with an offer he can't refuse. Will he strike out or hit one over the wall?

In August I'll have my first full-length Harlequin Blaze novel out in two years. *The Domino Effect*, an Extreme Blaze title, is a follow-up to last month's Signature novella "Driven to Distraction" in the *A Fare To Remember* collection. If you like your heat with a little intrigue, then please take a look! There are excerpts up at my Web site, www.julieleto.com.

Happy reading!

Julie Elizabeth Leto

FEVER PITCH
Julie Elizabeth Leto

To the Leto family.
My love for baseball came solely from
the love for my family. In the game of life,
we're World Series champs. Love you all!

To Tim & Alyssa
My love for football, soccer and horseback riding is
because of you. Thanks for broadening my horizons!

1

Mid-March, 2006

"TELL ME AGAIN why you divorced him?"

Callie Andrews held her gaze steady on the reservations computer, not needing to look up to see who had crossed the polished brass threshold of Diamond, the only four-star restaurant in Louisville's sports-entertainment district. She'd only divorced one man in her twenty-nine-year life and no one—her starry-eyed waitresses, fawning busboys or unflappable maître d'—could understand why she'd dismissed such a prime cut of a man. No one seemed able to comprehend how the marriage of a sharp-minded beauty like herself from the wrong side of the tracks and the wealthy Prince Charming from the castle on the hill couldn't have been glorious together—the stuff of romance novels and fairy tales. And even after six years since the ink on the legal papers had dried, Callie didn't have the heart, or the stomach, to explain.

Again.

Instead, she gave her hostess a sharp, humorless grin and gestured toward the computer screen so her employee could forget about Callie's ex-husband and call the next group to dine.

With a haughty roll of her eyes, the hostess grabbed a stack of menus and stalked away. Taking a fortifying breath, Callie looked up, expecting to see Donovan Ross strolling up to her, shaking hands, signing autographs and posing for pictures, as if he were the star player of the Louisville Slammers baseball team rather than the team's owner. But instead, she watched as the crowd spilled from the bar and waiting area to close in on him. A loud crowd. An angry crowd.

Callie instantly ducked around the gleaming reproduction of the Slammers' World Series trophy and barreled through the tightening throng. Though Donovan looked as unflappable as ever in his crisp burgundy polo, finely cut blazer, worn, scruffy jeans and two-thousand dollar boots, the man jabbing his finger mere inches from her ex-husband's face was not so cool.

Callie did a double take.

The man taking her ex to task was the normally soft-spoken, even-tempered mayor.

Callie slipped between the two men. "Mayor Davidson. Party of three, yes? I'm afraid your usual table won't be available for a while, so I'd like you to take my private table, if that's all right with you?"

Her gregarious tone, gentle but firm touch and subtle scans around the room broke through the mayor's bluster.

"Callie, yes…that would be lovely."

But he glared back at Donovan before leaving, jabbing his finger one last time. "I'm not through with you, Ross. You're tearing apart the fabric of this community and I won't allow it."

Cecil Boudreux, Callie's efficient maître d', suddenly appeared, his slender arm extended graciously toward the restaurant. His slightly affected French accent—Cecil had been born and raised in Kansas City more than fifty-six years ago—soothed the mayor.

"Please, Your Honor," Cecil crooned. "You prefer the aged, single malt Scotch, yes? I've already sent your server to fetch it."

With a gruff apology to Callie, Mayor Davidson followed Cecil to Callie's private table, which was always set for emergencies such as this one.

She glanced at her ex-husband, who had the audacity to wink at her, despite the fact that the crowd wasn't milling in stunned silence or breaking up now that the show was over. Antagonistic whispers flowed and several men, judging by the bulging veins and tightly clenched jaws, were considering taking up where the mayor left off. And for once, the women were scrunching up their noses at Donovan as if he carried a foul odor rather than his signature combination of heady musk and spiced sandalwood.

"May I show you to your table?" she asked him.

Donovan quirked a half grin, bringing the scar on his lower left cheek into sharp relief. It looked like a dimple and, God knew, few women could resist a man with dimples.

Luckily, she'd had practice.

"You just gave away our table," Donovan said, his voice husky, deep and heated with sensual sizzle.

She stiffened her spine with enough ice to keep his tone from melting through to those sensitive spots he knew so well. She led him away from the crowd before she responded. "That table was never ours, Donovan."

"More's the pity."

She bit her lip to keep any sharp retort to herself. She'd just averted a major disruption to her restaurant's legendary relaxed atmosphere and she wasn't about to let Donovan or his drama, flirtatious or otherwise, disrupt her business. She'd worked too hard to rise to the top of Louisville's business community to allow some tiff between the mayor and the city's favorite son to derail her success.

As she led Donovan through the main dining area, she smiled and greeted her guests with grace and ease. But about halfway through the room, she realized her ex's presence was giving everyone a serious case of heartburn—even customers who hadn't yet been served. When she met his eyes, he merely grinned. What the hell had he done? She clearly couldn't seat him anywhere in the main dining area without starting a riot.

"Did you trade Cody Cameron right before the start of the season or something? If looks could kill…"

"I'd be the main ingredient in steak tartare. You must be in heaven."

She winced. Despite her long-lasting antagonism toward her ex, she couldn't lump him in with the same unappetizing dish she refused to put on her menu. She didn't despise him. She actually still liked him, arrogance and all. And, God help her, the man's sexiness had only increased since their breakup. Their marriage had been relatively short and in the subsequent divorce, she'd received the seed money to finance Diamond, her lifelong dream, and Fever Pitch, the adjacent bar she'd designed to look more than a little like the place they'd met seven years ago. And since he'd taken it upon himself to treat his entire team to dinner or lunch at her establishments after every home game, the restaurant had built a reputation as "the place to be" from April to September—baseball season. Her exquisite food, extensive wine list and efficient staff took care of luring customers the rest of the year. She owed a great deal to Donovan, but certainly not enough to let him disrupt the dining experience of this evening's customers.

She gestured toward her office.

Surprisingly, he followed with no argument.

The minute she shut the door behind him, Donovan slid into the red leather chair in front of her polished mahogany desk. He gazed around, nodding, as if impressed with her taste. Funny, but she suddenly realized that in the year they'd been married, they had never set up house together. They'd either lived in the guesthouse of his father's grand estate or had been on the road with the team. Her office in her restaurant had been one of the first spaces she'd been able to call her own—and she couldn't help but feel defensive as he perused the furnishings with such scrutiny.

"What was that all about?" she asked, gesturing toward the restaurant.

"Don't you read the papers?" he replied, brushing an imaginary wrinkle out of his jacket.

God, the man was too handsome to be real. Thick, dark hair. Sparkling blue eyes. Lashes that, by all rights, should belong to a woman, and yet stirred the heterosexual in her completely.

"I get deliveries on Tuesday morning, you know that," she replied. "I'm lucky if I have time to slurp down a cup of joe."

A thrill—half sexual awareness, half warning—skittered up her spine. Donovan was watching her too closely. With too much intensity. She remembered that expression from the first time they'd met seven years ago, when she'd served cocktails to his table at After Bern, one of the many hangouts of the rich and famous in Tampa, Florida, where she'd been living at the time. She'd effectively fought off the groping hands and lewd suggestions of his tablemates and put the overstuffed, overmonied Major League team executives in their place, thus sparking the interest of the young, hotshot team owner who'd managed to treat her with respect, even though his eyes had blazed with unbridled lust.

But she couldn't afford to surrender to that lust again—no matter how much she also lusted for him. Not when she knew from personal experience that she and Donovan Ross, while electric in bed, didn't have the staying power required to make a relationship work while fully clothed.

Callie moved to her file cabinet and picked up the clipboard with the forms for tomorrow's produce order. She had a million things to do, and yet she couldn't let her ex go without finding out what had turned him from Louisville's favorite son to Kentucky's most wanted.

"Donovan, what's going on? Somewhere underneath that arrogant grin, you look like you've just lost your best friend."

His chuckle was more like a sniff, as if he were trying to find the humor. He came up empty-handed. "Lost her a long time ago. Tonight, I'm losing the team, and there's not a damned thing I can do about it."

2

UNTIL THE WORDS sunk in, Donovan watched his ex-wife move with utter efficiency but with a dancer's grace. God, she was amazing. With very little effort, he could imagine her undressed, seductive, wearing nothing but his shirt, unbuttoned to her navel, driving him crazy with want even if they'd made love only moments before. Time hadn't dulled his memory of what they'd had. And what he'd so foolishly tossed away.

He didn't know why he'd come to Diamond tonight. His craving for the chef's amazing oysters Rockefeller aside, he knew going out in public probably was not the wisest strategy. But sequestering himself in his penthouse, staring down at the darkened baseball diamond in the stadium and knowing he'd essentially gambled away his lifelong dream didn't hold much appeal, either. He'd saved one institution—his father's business and reputation—at the sacrifice of another. His dream.

Damn, it had been a great run, but it was over now. Best to accept the inevitable. But for some reason, he needed to tell Callie about it himself, even if he couldn't explain the extenuating circumstances that had led to his downfall.

"You? Lose the team? You're such a liar."

"I'm not lying. I made a deal with Douglas Baxter that means he'll get majority ownership of the Slammers if the team doesn't generate a relatively impossible amount of revenue this year. The whole thing was supposed to be a secret, but word got out this morning. By the end of the year, the Slammers won't be mine and they probably won't be in Louisville."

She laughed. Not the uncomfortable twitter he often got from the women he dated who were either too young or too flaky to understand his jokes, but the deep-in-the-belly guffaw that belonged only to a woman who could read him like a book.

Only this time, whatever she was reading was dead wrong.

"Better check your calendar. April Fool's Day is still a few weeks off."

"I'm not kidding. It's in all the papers from the *Gazette* to the *New York Times*. I spent the entire day on the phone with *Sports Illustrated* and ESPN. I made a very unwise business decision. Unfortunately, that means that by the end of this season, the Slammers will likely be moving to Las Vegas."

"Las…?"

He hated how her skin turned from rich, healthy olive to cold, pasty white. He hated how her hazel eyes rounded into saucers. He had no issue with the way her pouty, pink lips dropped open, but he would have preferred if the pose was in anticipation of a kiss rather than an expression of unadulterated shock.

"Vegas? You can't. You wouldn't!"

"I won't have a choice."

"I don't understand. Donovan, what were you thinking?"

Donovan cleared his throat and took a deep breath. He hadn't yet told anyone the entire truth, and he wasn't sure he could get the words out now. He'd taken a calculated risk a year ago when he'd approached his old friend Douglas Baxter about a supersecret loan. He'd needed a quick cash influx to bail out the retirement fund at Ross Industries, his family's company. Donovan was rich, but since his primary business was industrial real estate, his assets weren't liquid. He needed cash fast and delivered in a way that wouldn't arouse the attention of auditors or the press.

If the citizens of Louisville had caught wind of the corporate crisis, his father's legacy, his love, his reputation, would have been ripped to shreds. It had taken every persuasive bone in Donovan's body to convince his father to replace the lost funds with a loan from his ne'er-do-well son. At the time, Donovan couldn't admit that he didn't have enough disposable income to simply hand over several million dollars without sacrifice.

So he'd gone to the one man he'd thought could both keep a

secret and part with a huge amount of cash in a quick transaction—Douglas Baxter, a Las Vegas hotelier who'd been trying to lure a team to Sin City for years. He and Donovan had gone to college together—albiet briefly, since Baxter dropped out to pursue the American Dream out west—but they'd remained friends due to their mutual love of baseball.

And now, because Ross Industries hadn't rebounded quite enough to repay the loan to Donovan, he'd sealed the Slammers' fate. The team he'd built, nurtured and turned from an expansion team into World Series winners would be moving to Nevada. The entire population of his hometown would think he was a greedy, double-dealing snake.

Even his ex-wife, the woman who'd once looked at him as if he'd hung the moon now looked as if she wanted to kick him there.

"I didn't plan to lose the team," he said, with more edge in his voice than he'd intended, "but, if that's how it works out, there isn't anything I can do about it."

Callie slowly lowered herself into her chair, scooted herself in, then slammed back out and nearly tipped her seat over in the process.

"Douglas Baxter? Isn't he that gambler you went to college with? The one you told me you'd lost a whole semester's tuition to until you figured out he'd marked the cards during Thursday night poker? No wonder everyone in Louisville hates you! How could you do business with him?"

Two-point-four seconds of calm. More than he'd expected.

"You've always despised the team," he said calmly, which was a feat in itself. He hated what he'd been pushed to do, but he'd had no other option. The choice between losing his baseball team and losing the pension fund at Ross Industries, which employed hundreds of Kentucky residents, had been a no-brainer.

"I've never hated the team, Donovan."

He shifted in his seat. "You never loved baseball, that's for sure. I thought you'd be the one person who'd rejoice at my decision."

She threw her arms out and did a quick spin. "Hello? Have you looked around at my decor lately? Read my menu? Checked out the clientele? It's all Slammers, all the time. And I'm not the only one. What about Babe and The Sweet Spot? Janie's Round The Bases? Hell, even Fever Pitch! I just plunked down a huge investment in that bar so it would bring in a clientele beyond the people waiting for tables in the restaurant. And it's not just me— what about every other business owner who has hitched a ride on the tail of your arrogant, self-serving, greedy star?"

Maybe coming to her for a little sympathy, if that's why he'd come, hadn't been such a good idea.

He frowned. He might have asked for it, but he certainly didn't need a dressing-down from Callie Andrews. "A little paint, new carpets and art, and you're still the best restaurant in town."

Her eyes narrowed to sharp slits. Clearly, his compliment hadn't gone as far as he expected. He didn't make her place a regular, weekly stop only to see her. He really did think she'd built a first-class establishment, better than many he'd visited in New York and Los Angeles.

Not that seeing her wasn't a perk.

The way her nostrils flared and her eyes blazed with keen indignation reminded him of how she looked when they were on the verge of hot sex. Callie did nothing halfway. She threw her entire body, soul and spirit into every activity that required passion—from working out at the gym, to planning the menu for a private party, to orchestrating a seduction for her husband. God, he missed that. A woman who took charge. A woman who'd put his pleasure first, knowing he'd return the favor tenfold.

Maybe that's what he missed. Maybe that's why he'd lost his mind and ended up at her place, staring at hazel eyes that brimmed now with unadulterated anger.

She stood perfectly still, except for a barely perceptible quiver in her bottom lip. In another woman, he might have thought she was on the verge of tears, but with Callie, he knew better. She wanted to say something, but was holding back. Why? He had no idea. Everyone else in his life, from his top management to the batboys, had cursed him for his decision. He'd met with everyone associated with the team late last night, breaking the news to them before the press releases reached the media. He'd never experienced such concentrated hatred in his entire life. Donovan liked being liked. But sometimes, a man had to do what a man had to do.

"You look like you want to ask me something?"

Her eyes reflected myriad emotions, none of which Donovan could read. He hadn't been married to her long enough to figure her out, but luckily for him, Callie had an honest streak a mile long and no compunction about telling someone exactly what she believed they should know—if she felt inclined to open up, which she was often reluctant to do. When she shut down, no amount of coaxing could break through the walls of ice she could immediately and efficiently erect. And the temperature in the room had definitely dropped several degrees since she'd shut the door, so much so that he thought they'd slipped into the wine cellar rather than her office.

"Why'd you come here tonight?" she asked.

He shook his head. "Habit?"

Her mouth thinned into a severe line. "Or to gloat that you've finally found a way to destroy what I've built."

Donovan stood, his hands instantly fisting. He might have expected that response from another divorced woman, but not his Callie. He'd gone to extreme lengths to ensure that their split had been amicable. Despite his disappointment that their marriage had failed, he hadn't been willing to lose her friendship over the mistakes they'd both made. Sure, things had been tense. But never nasty.

"That's a low blow, Callie. You know I've always supported you here."

She looked askance, combed her hands through her straight, red hair, cut stylishly so that fringes of bangs framed her round, greenish eyes. She was such an exotic combination, thanks to an Italian mother and a father who, by her mom's best guess, was a redheaded, green-eyed good old boy she used to run around with at the minor league ballpark in the small Florida town where Callie had been born. A player? A coach? A fan? Minnie never could remember, but her daughter had long ago come to terms with not knowing that part of her heritage—something that showed Donovan her ceaseless capability to forgive.

Could she, then, with a little coaxing, turn that generosity on him?

"You're right," she said with a sigh. "I'm just so damned shocked. You love that team."

She dropped into her seat and only six years of estrangement from his one-time lover kept him from sliding around behind her and massaging the tension from her shoulders and neck—body parts whose flesh he could still taste, still feel, despite the passage of time. "I still love the team, but I had to make some hard choices, and well, things didn't turn out the way I planned. I figured you already knew. I shouldn't have been so flippant. I apologize."

She started, as if those words had never crossed his lips before.

"Don't look at me as if I've never said I was sorry to you before, Callie."

"I don't believe you ever have."

"Bullshit."

She cracked a smile. "Okay, maybe once. Like that time that you accidentally threw away my favorite pair of earrings."

"You'd wrapped them in a tissue!"

"They needed cushioning."

"You could have put them in the two-hundred-year-old antique jewelry box I'd bought you in New York instead of leaving them on the shelf above the bathroom sink."

"And risk breaking a hinge that cost more than my first car? That thing scared the shit out of me."

"You can be such a brat."

"And you can be an impossible ass." Her shoulders dropped, and the tension in her jaw loosened. "But you're not a guy who goes around throwing apologies away like confetti, so I appreciate those words when you say them."

Had her gaze really softened, or was the stress of this day finally pressing in so close that he was imagining things?

"I don't have the energy for regrets anymore," he told her.

"How can you say that? Whatever your reasons for dealing

with Baxter, you're stripping your hometown of its pride and joy. You'd better regret it, or those people out there are going to eat you alive."

"Baseball is just a game."

"To me? Yeah. To seventy-five percent of my patrons clamoring for the steak Diane that your second baseman orders every time he comes here, no. They love the Slammers as if they were their own sons. They love my restaurant. They love you, at least they did. I figured between your team and my restaurant, we'd finally found a way to make a marriage work, in a sense. Now you're hitting me up for another divorce."

He sat up straighter. "Excuse me, but who hit whom with divorce papers?"

She arched a brow. "My lawyer was faster than your lawyer. Don't try and pull any you-broke-my-heart crap. I know better."

"Do you?"

He watched her cheeks deepen to a bright, telling pink. He shouldn't be toying with her about something so emotional, something he suddenly realized was a raw wound between them, even if they had spent the last six years pretending that the dissolution of their marriage hadn't mattered much. He shouldn't have come here. He was dead serious about not having regrets. Not a single one. For all his money and power and celebrity, regret was the one thing he couldn't afford, especially now.

He stood. "I'm sorry I disrupted your restaurant. I thought a show of normalcy might calm the storm, but clearly I was wrong."

He walked to the door and paused, hoping for some odd reason that Callie would stop him. But why should she? He'd given up on their marriage without a fight. Over the past six years, they'd managed to be polite to each other, which had been relatively easy since nearly all their interactions had happened under the watchful eyes of his management team, her employees and dozens of restaurant patrons. But despite the legalese and settlements between them, he'd never stopped noticing how sexy she was, how beautiful and confident and capable. Until today, when his phone had started ringing to the point of insanity and his condo, his office, his parents' house and his other businesses had all been staked out by the press, he'd been able to sufficiently fight the urge to act on his simmering feelings for his ex-wife.

Then his entire world had been ripped out from under him. Now, the sensations of wanting her again, needing her again, had been unleashed.

"I've got to go," he insisted. "Thanks for the chat."

"Wait." She stood, smoothing her hands down the sides of her sexy chiffon slacks that taunted him with flashes of her bare legs underneath, making him ache low and hard. "If you want to hang out, I could bring you dinner back here," she offered.

He couldn't tamp down a grin. "Will you share it with me?"

She matched his smile tease for tease, completely unaware of the fire she was stoking. "Donovan Ross, are you flirting with me? You'd think you would have learned about the danger of that activity a long time ago."

He shrugged. "I like danger, risk, adventure. Remember?"

She crossed away from her desk and sidled up close to him. The enticing blend of her perfume—a subtle mix of lavender and vanilla, only enhanced by the spiced aromas emanating from the kitchen—taunted him with equal power to the gentle swell of her breasts beneath her sleek, black halter with the winking rhinestones at the curve of her luscious neck.

"And I wanted stability, home and safety. Remember?"

Yeah, he remembered. How could he forget when their differences—so basic and so intrinsic to who they were and where they'd come from—had cost them their marriage?

"I remember, Callie. It's probably the one thing in my life I've ever wanted to forget."

3

"WAS THAT Donovan? I can't believe he had the balls to show up here."

Callie turned in time to see Babe Bannister exit through the back door leading from the alley, a garbage bag fisted in her grip, her arms and shoulders clearly tense with disdain for Callie's ex-husband. Funny how just twenty-four hours ago, she would have been A-OK with sharing a little animosity toward her former husband with her best friends. In fact, dishing on Donovan had occupied a good portion of her late night tête-à-têtes with Babe and Janie. Tonight, she was suddenly feeling oddly protective.

And from the look on the Babe's face, Callie would have bet money that the buxom beauty who owned The Sweet Spot, a specialty ice-cream shop adjacent to her restaurant and one of a trio of Slammer-themed businesses operating in the growing sports and entertainment district, would have preferred lobbing the refuse at Donovan rather than throwing it in the Dumpster. Luckily, Donovan was already out of sight, having ducked down the alley rather than antagonize her customers again.

"I take it you heard the news?" Callie asked.

Babe wiped her hands on the back of her jeans and gave a sniff that was half from derision and half from the unique and pungent odor that festered in this alleyway. "No one is talking about anything else but the Slammers' moving at the end of the season, except of course, how my business is surely going down the toilet once my best customers take off for greener pastures. Or should I say drier pastures? The damned desert. Who plays baseball in the desert?"

"Phoenix," Callie quipped. "Besides, I bet they eat a lot of ice cream in the desert."

Babe replied with a wet, tongue-vibrating raspberry.

Callie chuckled and gestured to the door. She couldn't argue that the players, coaches, entourages, groupies and hangers-on made up the bulk of the customers on game nights. Donovan had a standing reservation for twenty after every home game. A huge fan contingent headed over to The Sweet Spot nightly for sundaes and malteds concocted with Babe's amazing talent for pairing all the right ingredients with the name of the player the flavor best fit. Those who hadn't visited before the first pitch usually made their way after the game into Janie's Round The Bases, where Janie sold everything from Slammer T-shirts and caps to signed pennants and rare, collectible memorabilia.

The three of them had created a mutually beneficial business triumvirate. They'd done cross-promotions. Callie had bought much of the restaurant's memorabilia collection from Janie and all of the ice cream on her menu came from Babe's shop.

And as three women working hard in an industry that regarded female entrepreneurs with suspicion, they'd forged a friendship Callie treasured more than anything else. Babe's irreverent sense of humor often coaxed Callie out of her overly serious, single-minded moods and Janie, so unsure of herself and oftentimes fragile, brought out protective instincts Callie never knew she had.

With Babe and Janie, Callie felt balanced. And damn if she couldn't use a serious shot of equilibrium right about now.

She had hated sending Donovan down that dark alley to his car in the valet lot when he'd clearly sought her out tonight for some weird reason, but she figured dealing with sticky ground and putrid odors behind the building was a lot better for him than getting his face pounded in by irate baseball fans incensed that their favorite son had made a business deal that could potentially send their winning team to another city.

"Our businesses are stronger than baseball loyalties, Babe. We'll both make it through. We'll just have to get a little creative."

Her friend's dubious look made Callie's stomach dip low and heavy. When the new stadium had been built, the entertainment district had blossomed around it. During the season, baseball fans drove the economy. In the off-season, the group that owned the sprawling field brought in concerts and trade shows and anything else they could think of to keep the money flowing. She had to hope that the powers that be would come up with some idea to keep them all from sinking.

But hope was hard to come by when her dreams seemed to be slipping away.

"Have you spoken with Janie?" Callie asked.

Babe took a deep breath and sighed. "She had to close up early. There was a run on memorabilia and now she's glued to the Internet, trying to figure out what fair market value is. Right now, she's thinking the hype will die down quick and she'll be stuck if she orders too much, but this could also be her last shot at moving a ton of merchandise."

"Is she shopping for new digs in Vegas?"

Babe winced. "As if. She's just worried her brother won't have a business to come home to now."

Callie paused, her teeth suddenly aching. Janie wasn't one to follow the team. She didn't even like baseball. But her brother had opened the store in pursuit of a dream, shortly before shipping off to Afghanistan with the Reserves. Janie had been holding his place for so long now that Callie and Babe considered her one of the team. And Janie had done a pretty good job with the store, despite the fact that she thought an infield fly was a particularly pesky insect.

Babe, on the other hand, had grown up with the sport and had even been named after the Bambino by a sports-obsessed father cursed with three daughters instead of sons. Her family had had the ice-cream shop for years, but it had been Babe and her specialty flavors that had turned the mom-and-pop shop into a raging success. Even if the Slammers left, she'd do okay.

They'd all do okay.

Right?

"Let's go check in on Janie," Callie suggested. "I'm sure she could use a break."

On their way down the closed hallway that connected the restaurant, ice-cream shop and memorabilia store under one roof, Callie checked in with Leona, her bar manager, and Cecil, the maître d'. They reported all was smooth sailing now that Donovan had left, so she decided a few more minutes on break wouldn't hurt. From behind the bar, she grabbed three longneck beers emblazoned with blue, green and black labels. Team colors.

Oh, jeez. The brewery! Well, she suspected they'd just go back to pushing the Derby on their signature label instead of the team. Donovan's questionable business choice, which she realized now he hadn't even begun to explain, would affect so many Louis-ville entrepreneurs, not to mention the fans. Suddenly, she wished she hadn't sent him away in such haste.

In the hall, Callie gave Babe one of the beers.

"Damn," Babe cursed as she opened a twist top with the corner of her T-shirt. "I finally find something I'm good at and your pampered, son-of-a-bitch ex-husband decides to mortgage the team or something. What the hell was he thinking? How could he need money?"

Callie eyed her brew with more enthusiasm than she would normally on a night where she still had five hours until closing. Alcohol wasn't going to get her out of this new mess. But it cer-tainly wouldn't hurt.

"I didn't get the details," she replied. At the time, she'd been too shocked to wonder why Donovan had gone to Douglas Baxter for money. Now, she couldn't stop thinking about his choice.

Babe wiggled her blond eyebrows. "Not that there's anything wrong with having more money. Beats the hell out of having less. But just how much cash can one man have?"

Callie twisted the top off the beer, opting for the burn on her skin than chancing snagging the hem of her new blouse. "Donovan always was a man who wanted more than his fair share. Of money. Of fun. Of women. I used to find it attractive."

"And you don't anymore?"

Callie avoided answering by taking a long swig of the slightly sweet, yeasty microbrew. Since finding out that Donovan might soon leave, her attraction for her ex-husband seemed to have ratcheted to dangerous levels. How could she just let him go?

"God, this tastes good." In an unguarded moment, she shifted back to her old habits and wiped her mouth with the back of her hand.

"You didn't answer my question," Babe pointed out, rapping hard on Janie's back door.

"Really?" Callie asked with a sniff. "I hadn't noticed."

Janie came to the door almost immediately, her light brown hair tied in the remnants of a ponytail and her deep, chocolaty eyes slightly drooping with exhaustion behind her plain-rimmed glasses.

"I've already started on the wine," she said, lifting her own glass in response to Callie's offer of beer.

Callie kept the longneck. She'd probably need it.

"Curse Donovan Ross! I could wring the man's neck with my bare hands," Janie said with a frown, sounding not so much angry as discombobulated.

"You almost had your shot," Callie answered as she and Babe slipped into the workroom behind Round The Bases. Piled high with jerseys in various sizes and surrounded by stacks of foam fingers declaring the Louisville Slammers perennially Number 1, the space under any other management would have been messy and claustrophobic. With Janie at the helm, Callie always found the spot frantic and warm. There was something about Janie that made Callie smile, probably because she'd taken on this store on account of her great big heart instead of the capitalist ruthlessness that drove both her and Babe.

Janie's eyes widened. "He showed his face here?"

"Momentarily."

"Callie ran him off," Babe explained.

"I did no such thing," she denied. "I simply suggested that if he didn't want to pay the medical bills of all my patrons who would end up with indigestion tonight because of his presence, he might want to scoot out before things got ugly."

Janie grinned. "You didn't!"

Callie swallowed another swig of beer. "No, but I wanted to."

"What did you say?"

"What could I say? It's his team. His toy. He can do whatever the hell he wants with it."

"Never mind that he's ruining the livelihoods of those of us who've built our businesses around his," Babe said sharply.

Janie finished off her paper cup filled with wine, then frowned. "Maybe that was our mistake? Besides, the reporters said the move wasn't for sure. If revenues go up dramatically and Donovan repays the loan to that Vegas guy, the team could stay."

Babe smirked. "How many people are going to come out to support a team that's moving? Ticket sales are going to plummet. I hear there's already a line outside the office because season ticket holders want their money back."

Callie's chest tightened. Donovan was losing his dream. How could he have risked something so important? Heck, they'd divorced because of the team, hadn't they? He'd put that damned team above his marriage, and now he was letting it go without a fight?

"I don't think Donovan's holding out much hope," Callie offered. "But you know, business is always a gamble. We've all been doing pretty well and we can keep going. We just have to adjust, Donovan included. This isn't the end of the world."

After downing half her beer in one long swig, Babe eyed her warily. "Then how come you look like you just saw the Four Horsemen of the Apocalypse?"

The three of them pulled chairs around Janie's worktable, surrounded by the baseball cards and team-emblazoned whistles that were part and parcel of her business. This wasn't the first time they'd gathered here for a female bitch session. But damn it, Callie thought, it could be one of their last. What would happen to her if she lost her two best friends?

Growing up as a nomad thanks to a mother who had no desire to put down roots, Callie hadn't learned how to make friends. She'd stumbled onto Babe and Janie quite accidentally and they'd filled a void in her life she never knew existed. Losing them would rank up there with losing her restaurant. And, frankly, losing Donovan.

She swilled her beer until the liquid almost made her choke, then answered Babe's question. "Because of all the people in his miserable, superficial life—and you ladies know that Donovan is rarely without an entourage—my ex-husband came to the restaurant tonight specifically to see *me,* and only me," Callie said, her voice a hoarse whisper.

"What?" they asked in unison.

"Where were his usual hangers-on?" Janie asked.

Callie shook her head. "Deserted him, more than likely. He was clearly freaked out by everyone's reaction to the team moving. And think about it—all of his friends are connected to the team in some way. He's probably playing this one solo."

"Clearly," Babe muttered.

Callie ran her hand on her hair, noticing that more than a few artful tendrils had escaped free. "Not clearly. He seemed to need to talk, and this from a man who isn't great at showing his emotions unless he's winning by twelve runs against the league's leading team or he's losing because of a bad call. It's extremes for him. Huge highs. Intense anger. Deep lows."

"Undeniable passion?" Babe asked.

"Shut up," Callie snapped.

"Ooh, hit a nerve," Janie said, her delivery a singsong meant to annoy.

"My last one," Callie snapped.

"Should we back off?" Babe asked.

"And change your normal behavior?"

Janie and Babe laughed and Callie couldn't help but join in. Yes, her life was about to undergo some serious changes. Now, when she was finally starting to feel settled, when she was finally starting to accept that her marriage and divorce from Donovan were things of the past, all hell had broken loose. But there had been something in his eyes tonight—something more than the dreamy sapphire blue that could set her heart racing at breakneck speeds. Something that told her they were nowhere near over.

Callie finished her beer and started on the one she'd brought for Janie.

"You know," Janie mused, her voice slightly dreamy, as if their entire lives hadn't just been turned upside down by one man's selfish decision. Or it could have been the wine. "I've been thinking."

"Uh-oh," Babe quipped.

Janie stuck out her tongue. "Things like this happen for a reason."

"How philosophical," Babe said.

"No, I'm serious," Janie said. "We're always sitting around here or over at Fever Pitch, making fun of the groupies, watching them take what they want from those hot players. But deep down…haven't you ever wondered what it would be like to do the same thing?"

Callie turned toward Janie and looked carefully at her neck, wondering if she'd sprouted a new head—one without a brain that allowed her to think rationally.

She frowned. "Okay, maybe I'm the only one who thinks that."

"No, you're not," Babe admitted. "Maybe we've all got the hots for someone associated with that team, but we've got too much class to go for them when we know we'll just be the flavor of the week."

"But is there really anything wrong with that?" Janie ventured, still sounding almost as if she were trying to convince herself as well as her friends. "Being the flavor of the week? At least it's a flavor and not bland, boring guys with no color, no taste, no sense of fun."

Callie shook her head and toyed with the edge of a banner draped across the table. She couldn't deny that the last few guys she'd dated lacked…excitement. They were nice enough, polite enough, but they didn't spark anything within her except the irrepressible need to yawn. A lot.

Unlike her ex-husband, who, even when he was only annoying her, at least made her life interesting.

"What's made you so *carpe diem* today?" Callie asked.

Janie merely sighed. The answer was obvious.

The team was probably moving at the end of the season. Their lives were about to change. For better or for worse had yet to be determined, but the outcome would most certainly be decided by them.

"So, what are you proposing?" Callie asked, intrigued.

Janie shrugged a little, but not with the dismissive quality that would have told Callie this was all some lark. Her friend was serious. A little tipsy, perhaps, but serious. No matter what crazy thing she was about to propose—and no one could propose craziness quite so well as Janie—Callie had to seriously consider what she proposed. After all, they were friends.

Janie and Callie lived pretty much at their jobs, and Babe often brought them into her large, extended family, so Callie valued these relationships more than she'd ever imagined she would. Her whole life, she'd lived hand to mouth, moving with her mother's newest job or boyfriend, making do the best she knew how, which usually meant keeping to herself at school so she could focus on working rather than on social events and friends. Now that she finally had the luxury of bonding with women her own age, she took their interactions seriously, even when one of them was about to propose something she might not ever do. Normally.

The least she could do was listen, right?

"I think we need to adjust our attitudes," Janie said.

"I have a great attitude," Babe offered.

Callie snorted. Janie smirked before digging into the refrigerator underneath her desk and pulling out the bottle of merlot she'd apparently been working on. She found two more paper cups and filled them, along with her own.

Gratefully, Callie accepted hers. Yeah, nowadays, she tended to prefer a long-stemmed, handblown bowl wineglass, but her past wasn't that far removed from her present. There'd been times when she'd drunk right from the bottle.

"We have one season left, right?" Janie asked, sipping her wine daintily.

Babe nodded. "That's the story I heard. If Donovan can't come up with enough money this season to pay back the loan, Baxter moves in and will likely use his clout to move the team."

"Then," Janie said with a toast of her paper cup, "let's make this season count. Who says the guys should be the only ones to make it to home plate?"

Callie and Babe hesitated. Home plate? The naughty look in Janie's eyes said it all.

"Home plate as in first base, second base, third base…home?" Babe asked.

Janie grinned. Ah, the ever popular, juvenile but ingrained baseball metaphors for sex.

Sex?

Callie choked on her wine, slapping her palm across her mouth to keep from spitting merlot all over Janie's clearly valuable jersey.

"You okay?" Babe asked, patting her on the back as she stifled her laughter.

Callie skewered her with a look of death. Yeah, ha-ha. Somehow, Callie didn't find the humor in discussing sex when her ex-husband's cologne, penetrating eyes and, God help her, vulnerable smile were still so fresh in her mind.

4

CALLIE HAD no idea if Janie was entirely serious, but just the idea of doing something so deliciously wicked, so undeniably unlike the woman she'd become—cool, efficient and invincible—made her heartbeat accelerate and her skin sizzle with forbidden fantasies.

Forbidden fantasies about a man she'd already tossed aside. A man who, even in their short time together, had touched a part of her she'd practically forgotten she possessed—her heart.

"Are you proposing what I think you're proposing?" Callie said, refilling her paper cup with the tasty merlot.

"We're not talking about seizing just the day anymore, are we?" Babe asked. "You're talking about grabbing something a little lower on the male anatomy."

Callie covered her mouth to contain her laughter. Clearly, the possibility of forfeiting the popularity and theme of her restaurant had caused her to lose her mind. That she was even putting sex and her ex-husband in the same sentence—even if only in her mind—was enough to verify her undeniable insanity.

"Look, we've all got our fantasy guys associated with the Slammers, right?"

Suddenly, Babe and Callie weren't quite meeting Janie's eyes.

"Oh, you've got to be kidding me," Janie said at their silence.

"Okay," Callie admitted, unable to lie to her best friends. "Yeah, we all have our fantasies. There's no law against it."

"No, but the three of us have had an unwritten law about acting on those fantasies, haven't we?"

"We don't want to look like groupies," Babe said.

"That's true," Janie replied.

Babe added, "Most of the guys are real dogs, cheating on their wives, coming in with a new supermodel wannabe on their arm every night. But some of them aren't bad, right? I mean, some of them are pretty damned hot."

Callie shifted in her seat. Trouble with her fantasy was that, well, he wasn't really a fantasy. Only six short years ago, he'd been her reality. He'd swept her off her feet, swung her into a magical world of wealth, power and pleasure. But she'd left him. For good reasons—reasons she'd had to remind herself of more and more often lately. Especially tonight, when he'd made a decision she simply couldn't understand—to seek her out in a moment of weakness. A time of need.

Why?

"What are you proposing?" Callie asked.

"Nothing formal. Nothing binding. It's just that after this season, we really don't know what's going to happen to us, do we? The stadium will be empty. Not only are our businesses directly tied to the Slammers, but we don't even know if the entertainment district will survive without regular games, right?"

Callie nodded. No one could argue with Janie's business sense. She'd made a go of the memorabilia shop despite the fact that she knew nothing about sports and showed no desire to learn. But her man sense? Well, none of them were exactly experts in that department.

"So, you're saying we should go for what we really want while we have the opportunity?" Callie guessed.

Callie would have loved to find out more of what Janie meant exactly, but sirens and flashing lights out front drew her attention. All three of them dashed to the window and peeked between the advertising flyers to see the ruckus outside.

Callie immediately recognized the car at the center of the trouble. A red Porsche Cayman S.

Donovan's car.

And an ambulance.

Without thinking, Callie shot to the door. She struggled with the dead bolt for a second, but before Babe could help her, she'd worked the mechanism free and dashed down the stairs onto the sidewalk and then out into the street.

Donovan sat on the hood of his car, a white cloth pressed to his lip. Between the streetlamps, the twirling red lights on the ambulance and the flashlights held by police officers who were now directing traffic, she saw the distinctive dark streak of blood on his face.

"Donovan!"

Once she was face to face with him, she pulled up short. He was trying to swallow a half grin, at once brimming with an infuriating mixture of apology and wry acceptance. She glanced at his car, which had distinctive dents from baseball bats on the hood and windshield. His headlights looked as if they had exploded, but the bumper was pretty much untouched.

"What happened?" she asked, fists thrust on her hips.

A paramedic approached with an ice pack. "Looks like someone did to Mr. Ross's car what the whole city of Louisville would like to do to him."

Callie eyed the man narrowly until he cleared his throat, mumbled a vague apology and then went back to his work.

"Why didn't you go the back way?" she asked.

"Road was blocked by your valets. You really should supervise those boys better."

Callie glanced quickly at the front of her restaurant. From the sniggering glee of her valet staff, she wondered if they weren't responsible for the damage themselves. She'd look into the matter soon. Very soon.

"Did you see who did it?"

"Well," Donovan said, moving the cloth he'd held to his lip to look, wide-eyed, at the impressive stain of blood there. "I couldn't give you a very detailed description as I was covering my face from the shattering glass, but at the risk of sounding vague, I'd say it was a former Slammer fan."

"This is not a joke, Donovan," Callie chastised.

He only shook his head. "Sweetheart, no one knows that better than I do."

The cops approached soon after, followed in quick succession by the news media. Callie tried to blend into the background, but too many reporters knew her history with Donovan Ross, so she had to fight through the throngs herself. But in the ruckus, she learned that national news trucks had set up shop in front of the stadium and the Ross mansion, all to cover the fan-led protests that had taken root across town.

With police cooperation, Callie grabbed a moment to speak to Donovan alone. "Looks like you're the person to hate right now."

"Just what I always wanted to be."

She rolled her eyes. "The sad part is, I don't know if you're serious or not."

"Yes, you do."

His gaze turned intense. Intimate. Suddenly she was transported to the past—not six years, to their divorce, nor seven, to their whirlwind wedding, but four months prior to that, to when they'd first met.

As if his hand was touching her now, she relived the charged sweep of his flesh over hers. She remembered how his gaze, so bold and inviting, had sparked a hot fire within her from the first moment he'd spoken. And she could never forget how, only hours later, his hands and lips and tongue had turned that flame into a full-out four-alarm blaze.

She wanted that again. God help her, but she did. Whether Janie's suggestion or the beer and wine had pushed her this far, she didn't know. What she did know was that she couldn't let Donovan leave town and leave her without feeling him inside her one more time.

"You can't go home," she said, her voice breathy and deep.

He stepped closer to her, and the perplexed look on his face mirrored the confusion raging through her brain. God, she'd drank the beer and the wine too quickly. She should know better than to mix her booze. She was light-headed and overheated, with a thin sheen of perspiration suddenly developing between her breasts and at the small of her back, her favorite places for Donovan's luscious kisses.

"I'll go to a hotel."

Callie swallowed hard. "You're hurt. You shouldn't be alone."

"It's a few scrapes and bruises. You should have seen the other guy."

She smirked. Donovan was a lover, not a fighter. He had fairly good sense when it came to confrontation, and she was certain he'd stayed in the car until the cops had run the mob off. Not that he wasn't big enough and strong enough to fight off an attacker if he had to, but after running around with hooligans and thugs most of her childhood, Callie had a deep appreciation for a man who'd rather negotiate with his brain than his fists.

"I don't give a damn about the other guy," she said.

"But you give a damn about me?"

"Can you believe it? I'm shocked myself. Besides, your parents would never forgive me if I let you bleed to death in some lonely hotel room."

"Thank God they're out of the country."

"Why don't you go to their place until this all blows over?"

He winced. "The press is already camped out there and I'm hoping if I don't show up, eventually, they'll leave. Mom and Dad are coming home soon, and I don't want them in the middle of all this mess."

"Then it's settled."

"What is?"

Emboldened by the combination of how much she'd imbibed, her conversation with her friends and the warm sandalwood scent of his cologne, Callie snagged Donovan by the collar and tugged him close. Flashbulbs sparked behind her and she didn't care. For all the press knew, she was threatening to thrash him for moving the team, just like everyone else.

But Donovan's eyes flashed with surprise, then warmed to a liquid blue, brimming with promises she thought she'd never see again. Which was appropriate, since she was about to speak words she definitely thought she'd never say again.

"You're coming home with me."

5

RIDING SHOTGUN was not Donovan's favorite position in a sleek sports car like Callie's souped-up 1965 Ford Mustang fastback, but since his Porsche was unsafe for the road, he didn't have much choice. Besides, not having to pay attention to stop signs and traffic lights gave him a chance to steal long glances at Callie. She really was beautiful, exotic in a way only girls who didn't grow up valuing their appearance over their brains could be.

Over the years, he'd silently noticed each and every change she'd made to her appearance. Her shortened hair. The bolder red color. The disappearance of the extra set of piercings in her ear. Her body shape had even shifted, fuller and rounder in some places, toned up and slimmer in others. She clearly worked out on a regular basis, but wasn't denying herself the delicacies at Diamond. He also noticed that her skin, usually only sun-kissed during the season when she treated her staff to a Monday afternoon game, now seemed to sport that healthy look year round. Was it spray? A tanning bed? Regular vacations, maybe when the team played away?

Damn, he hated not knowing the details of her life—and having no right to ask. Ever since he'd met Callie back when she was wrangling a table of rowdy team owners at a bar in Tampa into smitten passivity, Donovan had wanted to know everything about her. She'd fascinated him in ways no woman had up until then—and none had since.

But despite his fascination—or perhaps because of it—she'd bailed on their marriage after only a year. She'd claimed then that the constant traveling and entertaining and glad-handing of his team owner's lifestyle didn't suit her, that she felt useless and left out. But judging by her current choice of profession, she hadn't been entirely honest. She was now Louisville's premiere hostess. She'd glad-handed everyone from the president to the city council. Sure, the travel he'd offered had been extensive, whirlwind and constant, but he'd always figured that a girl who grew up living hand to mouth would cherish a permanent first-class ticket on a private jet bound to the country's most exciting cities.

But just as with so many other things, he'd guessed wrong.

"Still live in the apartment on Main?" he asked.

She flicked her gaze at him from the corner of her eye. "I moved out of there over two years ago."

"Oh. Find something better?"

She cracked a small grin. "It's a place to hang my hat."

The small talk ceased and in all honesty, Donovan was somewhat relieved. The air between them crackled with electricity, the kind that could spark into either a full-out argument or a wild make-out session.

What had he been thinking? Seeking out Callie tonight had probably been the worst decision he'd made in a long time, short of his deal with Douglas Baxter. This whole day had been hell since last night when his attorney had called to tell him that the details of his supposedly confidential deal with Baxter had been leaked to the press. He guessed his luck and golden touch had been bound to run out eventually.

He'd anticipated the anger, betrayal, outrage and out-and-out hatred he'd fielded from his star players, his coaches, his rookies and his business associates. And he had known the fans would be fit to be tied. He didn't blame them. He'd spent a lot of time and money selling the team to the city and he'd accomplished this in ways even teams like the Yankees and the Red Sox envied.

But now, the fans hated him. He'd struck a deal with the devil, and fans were going to make sure there was hell to pay. He deserved it. Their disappointment tore at his gut like a jagged-edged knife. Louisville wasn't a big town, but it had bled baseball from the first moment he broke ground on Bluegrass Stadium. He'd worked his ass off to draw first-class players to his mid-sized hometown and then, in only three short years, his coaching staff had turned the ball club into World Series winners. The ride had been like so much in his lifestyle—hard, fast, furious and fabulous. Yet as much as he'd tried to prepare himself for the ire of his city when word of his deal hit the press, he'd never really expected that someone would try to knock his head off with one of the city's signature baseball bats.

And he'd never expected Callie to run to his rescue. Seemed to him that if anyone deserved to smack him upside the head with a maple slugger, it was her. On his behalf, she'd ventured into dangerous territory.

Donovan glanced sidelong at his ex-wife. Without deviation, her gaze was glued to the road ahead, ignoring both him and the scenery outside. As they passed Cherokee Parkway, he noticed her eyes flick to the right for a split second, but she exhibited no expression. No wistful smile. No romantic sigh.

Sweet Surrender—a Louisville landmark, providing decadent desserts for every mood. He couldn't help but chuckle. Hell, that place held memories he was sure neither one of them would ever forget.

At night, the place opened only for dessert. During their first year of marriage, before she opened the restaurant, the two of them would sneak away and share a rich chocolate torte with raspberry sauce, feeding each other sinful forkfuls until they overdosed on sensual delight—at least, until they got back to his penthouse and indulged in sensual delights that had nothing to do with sweets.

"I'm not thinking about it," she said, her voice flat and sharp.

He cleared his throat to cover a grin. "If you're not thinking about it, then how did you know I was wondering if you were?"

"Because I knew *you* were thinking about it."

He scoffed at her claim, even if she was dead-on. "I have no idea what you're talking about."

"Right. Just like you had no idea that the whole city of Louisville was going to want your head on a platter for cutting a deal with a creep who you know will move their beloved team." Her gaze finally left the road, and when it did, the greenish slits revealed her anger. "What the hell were you thinking, Donovan? You have more money than God. Your father has more money than you. Why would you take a loan from a shark like Douglas Baxter?"

Donovan pressed his lips closed. He wanted to tell her. He wanted to trust her. He needed someone who would understand not only what the team meant to him, but what his family meant to him. He and Callie hadn't been married for long, but despite the fact that she was neither from Kentucky nor from a well-bred family that shared box seats with his parents at the Derby, Callie had won the admiration of his mother and father almost instantly. His mother, who like Callie, hadn't been born with a silver spoon in her mouth, particularly liked her. Peggy Ross understood not only what it was like to have a ramshackle childhood, but also the culture shock of marrying a wealthy man. If only Donovan could have comprehended that.

"What I'm doing will be better for everyone in the long run."

"Oh, right. I forgot. It's giving me a chance to change my decor."

Her voice dripped with sarcasm. Callie wasn't one to mince words and so far, she'd kept herself fairly under control.

"There's always a silver lining."

"Who are you now, Jiminy Cricket?"

Her condo was within walking distance of trendy Bardstown Road, right off Douglass. She pulled up to the gate and rolled down the window to key her security code into the mechanism. Judging by the way she jammed her fingers on the numbers, he wondered if he would be better off getting out of the car now and possibly escaping with his life yet again. But even as his fingertips danced over the door handle, he couldn't bail. He wanted to be with her tonight. Needed to be. And to that end, he had to tell her the truth.

Probably.

Possibly.

When he found the right moment.

The gate slid open and Callie tore through, racing toward her garage at a scary speed. The garage door was barely all the way up when she vaulted over the driveway. She shrieked to a halt, threw the car into Park and flipped off her seat belt at the same moment.

She got out of the car in such a rush that he sat there stunned. Behind them, the garage door grumbled closed. He wasn't entirely surprised when Callie crossed behind the trunk, ripped open his door, grabbed him by the sleeve and hauled him out.

"Okay, hotshot. You want a place to stay tonight? You tell me the truth. All of it. Right now."

"NICE place."

Despite being irked that he'd somehow, again, managed to dodge her insistence on coming clean, Callie experienced a shiver up her spine as she turned on the light. As with her office, Donovan had never seen her condo. Until tonight, he hadn't even known where she lived. Seemed odd to her, since during the baseball season, they saw each other two or three times a week, depending on whether or not the team played at home. Win or lose, he hosted some sort of party at Diamond. Sometimes, he invited the management team. Sometimes a few players and coaches. Sometimes his latest morsel of arm candy. Sometimes all of the above. Only now, with him standing so close—injecting his cologne into her personal space, perusing the art she'd carefully hung on the walls and touching the knickknacks she'd scattered through the room—did she realize how empty she'd felt during those weeks when the Slammers were playing away or in those dread weeks immediately following the end of the season.

"Thanks," she said. "It's home."

"Did you hire someone?"

She glimpsed the half grin on his face, knowing he could have cared less about who had painted her walls in the soft, soothing blue or who had tossed the space with a varied collection of pillows and afghans over her buff leather couches. Donovan had been raised in such a way that complimenting a hostess's choice in furniture and accessories was an automatic response. As a guy with a bottomless bank account, he knew all the best interior designers from Louisville to New York City.

But she could distinctly remember the first night she'd taken him home to her old apartment just off Kennedy Boulevard in Tampa, the one with the "bedroom" behind the recycled shower curtain and the kitchen that was the size of a phone booth. In fact, it hadn't been a kitchen, more just a space with a microwave and a hot plate she'd bought at the Salvation Army store. Her carpets had been a mismatched collection with every imprint from seashells to horses, but on the upside, she didn't vacuum so much as shake the dust out of the second-story window, right over the rusty fire escape and the trash cans below. She'd taken Donovan home as a test and despite her obvious lack of funds, he'd still sincerely complimented her on the apartment.

He wasn't the type of man a woman such as her should have married, but otherwise, he was pretty close to perfect. A fabulous lover. Funny. Smart. Ambitious. And tonight, without the added pressure of trying to figure out if he was "the one," since she already knew from personal experience that he wasn't, Callie imagined pursuing him the way Janie suggested, rather than trying to find out why he'd put the team in jeopardy. What if she didn't like his answer? What if his reasons were unjustifiable? She certainly wouldn't want to sleep with him with the same urgency that she felt right now.

What was the saying? Ignorance is bliss?

"Want a drink?" she asked.

"God, yes."

She slid over to the bar and mixed his favorite drink, scotch with a splash of water. For herself, she switched the ratios. She needed to keep a clear head, especially since having Donovan alone with her in her condo made even the air seem dangerous. He'd always been the risk-taker, the thrill-seeker. Back when she'd been a poor waitress trying to make a living on tips while she learned the high-end restaurant business from the inside out, she'd proceeded with as much caution as she could with Donovan. He'd been, after all, completely out of her league. Rich, educated, savvy and suave. In the midst of their whirlwind affair, she'd constantly anticipated the moment when he'd cast her off for someone prettier, someone smarter, someone with a more desirable pedigree.

But instead, he'd married her. He'd tried damned hard to give her the fabulous life he insisted that she deserved. She expected that any other woman would have jumped at the chance to be a pampered trophy wife to a powerful man—hell, she'd thought she'd died and gone to heaven when he'd first slipped that four-carat ring on her finger. But after a few months, the novelty of being a pampered woman wore off. She'd lived her entire life working hard, improving herself, making a difference, even if it was just to her own bank account. Turning from an industrious entrepreneur wannabe to a pretty piece of fluff didn't cut it. She realized now that she'd never fallen out of love with Donovan, but only with his lifestyle—not that the distinction made any difference.

She gestured toward one of the couches. Donovan hesitated. "I'm still pretty beat up."

"You're a big baby. Bruised looks good on you...and you can always take a shower. Later."

He accepted the drink and speared her with a look so sexy that on any other night, she would have stepped away from the heat. But not tonight. Not after the suggestion Janie had made. Janie was right. If Callie's world was about to be turned topsy-turvy, the least she could do was grab what she so obviously wanted.

"If I shower, I won't have anything to wear after."

She quirked a half grin. So many responses danced on her tongue, with *you won't need anything to wear* being the first on her list.

Nah, too obvious. She opted for choice two—humor.

"You can borrow one of my nighties."

He chuckled, sat down beside her and took a long sip of his scotch. "If you promise to wear a matching one, I might take you up on that."

"If you wear anything remotely resembling a nightie, you can bet the whole effect will be lost."

He leaned closer to her. "And what effect is that?"

She licked her lips. God, she'd always wanted to do that at precisely the right moment, driving a man wild with such a simple gesture. Judging by the flare of Donovan's nostrils, she'd timed this one perfectly.

In the interest of a good tease, she pulled back. "My neighbor's husband is about your size. I'm sure he'd be willing to part with a pair of sweats and a T-shirt until tomorrow."

She nodded her head so that he'd scoot over far enough to give her room to sit and still have a little personal space. She sat there, sipping her scotch-flavored water, wondering just how crazy she had to be to go through with this madness.

"You still want to know why I made the deal?"

No. "Is the deal done?"

"Yeah."

"Your lawyers can't get you out?"

"The lawyers? No, the lawyers can't do a damned thing."

That surprised her. Donovan wasn't a fool when it came to business. He was savvy. A force to be reckoned with and respected by his colleagues. "Then I guess you're screwed. And tomorrow, a lot of people will need to know the truth. Most more than I do."

"Most people can't know the truth, Callie. In fact, no one can but you. I'm serious. Whatever I tell you has to stay between you and me. Promise me."

Now she wished she'd poured more scotch into her glass. The intensity in his eyes bordered on desperation, though she knew Donovan too well to think he'd ever cross that line. She recognized the wild look of fear—not fear for himself, but for someone else. Who was he protecting? Who was he sacrificing his dream for?

She took a deep swallow from her glass, then put the drink down on the beveled glass table in front of them. Now more than ever, she wanted to grab this moment—the one brimming with heat, emotion and intensity—not a moment where angst over his choices stood between them.

She held out her hand toward him. "Whatever is said…or done…here tonight is between you and me. In the morning, we won't even speak of it again."

He eyed her hand skeptically.

She thrust her fingers closer, once again sliding her tongue over her lips so they were moist. Ready. Eager. "Isn't that a deal you can't refuse?"

When his gaze slid from her knees to her thighs, then from her breasts to her eyes, heat raked over her body. "Yeah, but you're not supposed to know my weaknesses. My vulnerable spots."

Her hand started to shake. Damn him, but he'd better take her offer soon or she'd back out. "I like your vulnerable spots."

He hesitated for what seemed like a century. Couldn't he see what she was offering? Or was he just trying to come up with a way to say no, despite their clear and present desire? She was just about to withdraw her offer when his hand shot out and grabbed hers.

"Deal."

He used their hand-to-hand connection to yank her toward him and kiss her. She didn't have time to react, to protest, to rejoice, to push or pull as the sensations of his skilled lips shot through her.

He tasted new. He tasted familiar. His scent teased her with its heady musk, a scent she couldn't have forgotten, even after one hundred years. When he coaxed her lips apart with his soft, moist tongue, she surrendered to her need to devour him fully, no matter how their connection could burst into flames in the morning.

She wanted the here. She wanted the now. And tonight, Callie Andrews was going to get everything she wanted—and more.

6

DONOVAN'S SHOULDERS and chest ached from tight, hard tension. Was Callie going to haul back and sock him for being so bold, or was the worst day of his life about to morph into a night of ultimate fantasy? He had only physical clues to judge by and since Callie responded to his kiss by stroking his cheeks with fingers that then speared through his hair and tugged him closer, he had to believe he'd hit the jackpot.

Either that, or she was seriously screwing with him.

He pulled away. "What's going on?"

She eyed him dreamily, her hazel-green gaze glazed with lusty need. "God, Donovan. Isn't it obvious?"

"You were supposed to push me away," he explained.

She arched a brow. "Is this some new fantasy you've developed since we were married? I guess I could try to play the sweet little virgin in need of masculine coercion, but I'm not an actress and frankly, what you're asking would be a stretch for me."

Her sarcasm was one hundred percent Callie. Sure, she'd been sending him signals he couldn't help but respond to, but he'd never dreamed that the ex-wife he'd parted with more than six years ago would be interested in a romp tonight, particularly when his actions with the team could spell potential damage to her beloved restaurant. What was she up to?

"You know what I mean, Callie. We've been interacting for six years since our breakup and despite the undeniable sexual tension between us, you've never wanted another go-round."

"Of marriage? Bite your tongue! But sex, well…" she purred, closing the distance between them like a cat on extended claws.

"We were great together, Donovan. You can't deny how amazing it would be to feel that way again. So pleasured. So satisfied."

Every muscle in Donovan's body tightened to the point of pain, from his jaw to his dick. Especially his dick. But being the owner of a Major League Baseball team gave him one big advantage over other men—he knew a player when he saw one and he knew when he was being played.

He pressed his hand gently but firmly on her shoulder. "What's your scheme, Callie? You're going to get me all hot and bothered and then pull back so that I'm suffering like I deserve?"

She clucked her tongue. "Donovan Ross. Have you ever known me to be a tease?"

"Women change."

"When they're children like the ones you've been dating lately, yeah, I suppose they do. Like the diapers they should be wearing. However, we older, wiser models don't mess around with the head games. Life is too short. And life is what changes. Look at today. Here I am, minding my own business, catering to a full house of hungry, thirsty restaurant patrons who don't mind paying premium prices for great food and service, and then you walk in and turn my world upside down. Our mild-mannered mayor nearly asks you to step outside, and when you do venture beyond my doors, someone tries to kill you with your team's weapon of choice. Makes a girl think that the time to take what she wants is now, not after the object of her naughty dreams is in the hospital. Or dead."

Her diatribe was filled with lots of interesting tidbits, but that one at the end made the hair on his arms stand on end. Would have had the same effect on other parts of his anatomy, but a man's body could only stretch so far.

"You dream about me?"

She bit her bottom lip, holding the pouty flesh between her teeth until he thought he might groan from unrelenting frustration. "Occasionally."

He scooted forward. They'd been arguing, right? About…? His ability to form a coherent thought fizzled, sputtered and died. The only part of his brain still working wanted nothing more than to know how deeply he'd invaded his ex-wife's sleep.

Once again, they were nearly nose to nose. He could feel the warmth of her breath against his lips, could see the distinct dilation of her pupils encased in irises that seemed to grow greener, more intense, more exotic, with each fired moment.

"Tell me."

She breathed in deeply, her mouth shut tight, but with a Mona Lisa smile dancing on her lips. "I'm not the one who has secrets to reveal tonight."

"Your secret is better than mine, trust me."

Her gaze darkened. "I do trust you, Donovan. That's the whole damn point, isn't it?"

Finally, he understood the sudden turnaround in his former wife. No matter how the dissolution of their marriage had been typed out in neat fonts with precise signatures and tidy seals, Donovan and Callie had never lied to one another. Perhaps that had been why their marriage had been so easy to end, because when she'd told him how unhappy she was, he believed her. He'd also understood that the very aspects of his lifestyle that made her feel small and insignificant were things he couldn't change. The team had been his business. His baby. He'd been perfectly willing to share the experience with her, but he couldn't force her to love the baseball industry just because he did. So he'd let her walk away without a fight.

Now, that dream was teetering on destruction and for the first time in a long time, Donovan had cared more about something else than he had about his team. Was Callie asking him to move her higher on the list, as well?

"Lay it on the line, Callie. What do you want from me?" he asked, then amended, "Besides sex."

"There's nothing else."

He leaned back, hating how it broke the spell of seduction weaving them together. "You've never been one for casual sex."

"Maybe that's my problem."

"Who says you have a problem?"

She grinned at his protective reaction. "I say so, Donovan. Earlier, when you told me about the team, I felt like the world was a carpet ripped from underneath my feet."

He opened his mouth to protest, but she silenced him with a single finger across his lips.

"I know I was overreacting. I can make my business work without you and your team." Her voice rose as she forced confidence into her tone. "But I can't change the fact that when the team leaves, you will, too. How I can face another day knowing that all those sexy dreams I have about you stripping naked and sitting on my couch allowing me to have my wicked way with you will never come true? Pure fantasy doesn't work for me. I need to know there's an element of reality or I can't suspend my disbelief long enough to enjoy the ride."

Donovan didn't bother with the buttons on his shirt. The damned thing was already covered in blood and dirt. He ripped the fabric free and shrugged his sore shoulder out of the sleeves. Callie's wicked grin spurred him further, until he was sitting on her couch wearing nothing but an equally sinful smile.

She stood. "This is for one night only."

"What?"

She closed her eyes tight. "I can't give any more, Donovan, not without risk. So one night. Together. No regrets."

He shook his head. How could he make such a promise when he'd been wanting her so badly since the moment she'd walked out?

Still, if he argued, it could all end here and now. He couldn't live with himself if he didn't at least take a shot at winning her back.

"Whatever you want, Callie."

She smiled. "Wait here."

He braced his hands on the edge of the couch. "If this is some sort of joke—"

Callie reached around the back of her neck and undid the clasps fastening her halter. The dark material spilled down like a midnight waterfall, exposing breasts that captured the dim light with their delicate, ivory flesh and dusky, fully extended nipples. She slid the blouse down over her slim hips, then shimmied out so that she was wearing nothing but the gauzy black slacks that fluttered around her long legs like a storm cloud.

She braced her hands on his thighs, leaned forward and kissed him with all the depth and intensity of a woman dead serious about the seduction she wanted as much as he.

"No jokes, no lies, no tricks. It's just you and me, Donovan. But first, I have to set the scene."

CALLIE SCURRIED into her bedroom, shut the door as quietly as she could, then leaned against the cool wood and tried to make sense of what she was doing. She closed her eyes tightly, but when she opened them, she caught sight of her reflection in the full-length mirror across the room. She recognized the emotions coursing through her. Fear. Arousal. Determination. Lust. She wanted him. She had for a long time—longer than she'd ever admit to anyone. Now, she had a chance to once again experience that fabulous, bone-melting sexual pleasure that only Donovan could give her.

And with him leaving soon, she needed closure. The season officially started in a few weeks, but she was sure with the cloud of the team's imminent migration hanging over Louisville, the season had come to an unofficial close following Donovan's announcement. With Donovan no longer Louisville's favorite son, she couldn't even entertain the idea that he'd return for holidays and in the off-season to tend to his other business ventures. His business would no longer be welcome in Kentucky. Once he left, he'd be gone for good.

The time to act was now.

She stripped out of the rest of her clothes, dashed into the bathroom and gave herself a quick wash with a wet cloth, followed by sweet, lavender-scented lotion. She loosened her hair, freshened her makeup, then changed into a negligee she found buried at the bottom of her pajama drawer. It was wrinkled, but it fit. Nicely. Black satin. Peekaboo bodice.

Yes, this would do.

On her way out, she dashed back into the bathroom and found the carton of condoms she'd had there for entirely too long. Callie had had a few lovers over the years—very few, but she'd always played things safe. Even tonight, some things were nonnegotiable.

In the kitchen, she found a bottle of wine, two glasses and a corkscrew. Too predictable? She put them away, then opted for two shot glasses, lime and a shaker of salt. The tequila was in the other room. Yes, definitely naughtier.

She found Donovan standing at the window, nude in the moonlight. He had his fingers through the slats in the blinds, so if anyone looked up, they'd see nothing more than his eyes.

Gingerly, she approached from behind, placing her bounty on the bar right beside him. "See something interesting?"

"The stadium lights are on."

Perplexed, Callie slipped into the space beside him and parted the blinds herself. She had no idea the lights from the ball field could be seen from her condo. "I'll be damned," she muttered.

"For associating with me?" he quipped.

She glanced up at him, a smile teasing the corners of her mouth. There were few naked men she would feel comfortable trading barbs with. In fact, there was only one.

"If that's the case, my fate was sealed a long time ago."

"You could always ask for forgiveness," he offered, turning so that his muscled torso and hard thighs were inches away from her.

"You have to really want forgiveness for that to work, and I don't regret one minute of what we had together. Do you?"

"Only the minutes we missed because I was too busy working or you were too angry to stick around."

"I was never angry."

He arched a brow even as his hands snaked out and encircled her waist. "Don't start lying now."

"Then let's stop talking."

She grabbed his face and pulled him down, then kissed him with every ounce of longing she had for the freedom she sought. The freedom to do what she wanted tonight, feel what she needed to feel, without a moment of fear, without an instant of regret. She knew this man. She trusted this man. She understood that in the morning, there was no chance they could stay together beyond a bite of breakfast and a cup or two of coffee. Their paths would soon take them on entirely different roads.

But in the meantime, she intended to enjoy this one last pit stop. Donovan smoothed his hands over the silk of her negligee, groaning as his fingers pressed hard over the cool material. He slipped under the lacy hem that tickled the curve of her bottom, and possessively cupped her. Donovan always was an ass man and the thrill of remembering how she used to flash him surreptitiously to get him hot and bothered made her sex pound with excitement.

"I remember this," he murmured.

"Me, too," she whispered, her lips brushing against his chest.

"No, this outfit."

He toyed with the thin, spaghetti straps on her shoulders. With one yank, they popped away, released from the teeny snaps holding them in place.

"I've had this for years," she said, amazed at how the boning in the bodice held the top in place.

"I bought it for you," he said with a growl.

Good God, he had. She'd kept it all this time?

"I can't believe you didn't toss it."

Neither could she.

"I haven't worn it since you bought it for me."

"I don't believe you wore it for very long then, either."

She pushed away from him softly, turning as she slipped over to the bar. "Then maybe this time, I'll stretch it out."

"To torture me?"

"Don't you deserve it?"

He licked his lips. "Most definitely. Is that what you dream about with me? Punishing me?"

She dipped into her private stock and pulled out a bottle of her best tequila. Callie wasn't a big drinker anymore, though she'd imbibed her share in her wayward youth. But her suppliers loved to stock her liquor cabinet every Christmas. Tonight, she figured a little liquid courage could go a long way.

"Not exactly," she replied cryptically.

"Then what, exactly?" he asked.

She twisted open the tequila, then grabbed a knife from the drawer. "Sit over on the couch and I'll show you."

7

WITHOUT HESITATION, Donovan did Callie's bidding. He took the tequila bottle she'd uncapped, but didn't have the least desire to drink. For this, he wanted to be stone-cold sober. He wanted to remember every detail, every nuance, every sensation. Maybe she needed a belt of good Mexican hooch to loosen up—and if she did, more power to her. But him? He was already drunk on the vision of Callie climbing over his lap, her soft, warm sex brushing across his hardness, the cool silk of the negligee he distinctly remembered buying her on their honeymoon ratcheting up the tension.

She filled a shot glass, then leaned seductively backward to place the tequila close at hand. Arching her back to complete the move, her breasts taunted him, her dark, hard nipples poking through the lacy slits on the bodice. Before he could maneuver the taut flesh into his mouth, she turned and licked his shoulder—a long, moist swipe that sent sensations skittering through his bloodstream and scrambled his brain. When she dangled the salt shaker over the wet spot, he wasn't entirely sure what she had in mind.

"You're not—" he said, guessing.

"I love tequila shots, don't you?"

"Haven't had them in years," he said, groaning when she shifted so that he was nestled between her thighs in a way that begged for him to delve into her. Deeply. Fully. But it was too soon. Too soon.

"Since our honeymoon, maybe?" she asked.

He gave his head a little shake, hoping to clear a measure of the fog from his brain. Honeymoon. Mexico. Zihuatanejo Playa La

Ropa. A condo on the mountainside, overlooking the Mexican Riviera. An infinity pool on the ledge of the deck that reflected the turquoise blue of the waters below. Callie dressed in nothing but a tan, sipping tequila from the handblown shot glasses they'd bought in town, licking salt off the sensitive spot just below her thumb.

She sprinkled the white granules on his shoulder.

Who was this woman? What had she done with his once unsure and anxious Callie? She'd always amazed him. From the first moment they'd met. She'd been around. She'd worked in diners and honky-tonks and dive bars from the age of fifteen, yet she'd blushed hot pink the first time he'd parted her blouse and feasted on the perfection hidden beneath her lacy bra. She hadn't been a virgin, but she'd taken lovemaking seriously. Sure, they'd toyed and played and eventually developed a deep trust. But never like this. Never with such bold wickedness.

Maybe it was because they weren't married anymore. Maybe it was because in the morning, Donovan knew he'd have no choice but to walk away.

But for tonight, he'd take what she offered.

"What are you going to do with the lime?" he asked, not entirely sure he wanted to know.

She squeezed the quartered fruit beside his lips, on the side opposite of the glass shard cuts, and let the sticky tart juice burst in his mouth and dribble down his chin and chest. She tossed the rind behind her, grabbed the filled shot glass, threw back the liquor, then swiped her tongue over the salt and then kissed away the lime. Good Lord. Why hadn't they thought of this back in Zihuatenajo?

She repeated the drinking game again, this time squeezing the lime over his nipples and the salt was applied near his belly button. Little by little, she lowered her one-woman drinking game until she'd dropped to the floor in front of him. He closed his eyes, expecting to experience an intimate sting as the combination of salt and lime tortured his sex, but she tossed the fruit and shaker aside, swallowed the tequila with one toss of her head, and then took him into her mouth.

Sensations burst through Donovan's body, electrifying every

nerve ending, firing every inch of flesh until he thought he might burn alive. But her tongue on his skin, the measured suction of her mouth, the gentle scrape of her teeth drove him into a new state of awareness. He dragged his fingers into her hair, entangling himself in the softness, surrendering to the pleasure Callie offered with bold and brazen need.

He teetered on the brink. With eyes closed tight, he watched a kaleidoscope of color burst in his eyelids. He stiffened, ready to burst. Could he hold back? He had to. Had to.

He pushed her away and when he finally managed to open his eyes, he caught sight of a flicker of triumph in her eyes.

"You're driving me crazy," he said.

"That's the idea." She climbed back onto his lap, wavered, but managed to balance nearer his knees so that she could unsheathe a condom and cover him with slow, tight skill.

"You don't think that's a little premature?" he asked, wondering just how tipsy his ex-wife was.

She licked her lips. "Just because you're wearing it doesn't mean you have to use it right away. I just thought it best not to interrupt any crucial moments."

With a torturous wiggle, she eased forward.

Donovan took a moment to inhale deeply, to push the thoughts of lifting her on top of him further back into his brain, as far back as an aroused man could manage. More than anything in the world, more than undoing the damage the day had wrought on his reputation, his sense of time and place, and his future, Donovan wanted to escape into the place Callie offered him— an enhanced taste of the past, flavored with the nuance only his former wife could bring to the mix.

Not that he didn't have something to offer himself.

He grabbed her at the waist and pulled her close, lifting her so that her breasts were at eye level. Before she could protest, he slid his tongue into the slit on her bodice, instantly finding the nipple within. She cooed, adjusting her position so he didn't have to hold her up, allowing him to put his hands to better use.

Held together with tiny dots of Velcro, the slits broke apart at the slightest urging from his fingers. He wrapped the lacy material around her breasts. He couldn't help but lean back, if only for a few moments, to feast on the sight of her nipples, dark and hard, and the plump flesh surrounding them.

"You have the most perfect breasts," he said, awestruck.

"I thought you were just crazy for my ass."

He rounded his hands beneath her bottom. The curves fit his hand with the perfect combination of weight and luscious ripeness. He wanted to flip her over and ply his tongue in the sweet crevice, feel her cheeks press tight against him.

His condom was stretched taut. "I'm crazy about all of you."

She scooted forward so her lacy panties, nothing more than a ribbon of material, scraped against him. Despite the barrier of latex, moistness kissed him. She was ready for him. Hot and wet and ready. "Every inch of me?"

"Every…"

He couldn't continue speaking while his mouth watered to taste her. With as much ease as his lust would allow, he lay her back on the cushions, pressed one leg off the couch and hooked the other over the top. The position was brazen and on any other woman, vulgar. But with Callie, she was simply opening herself to the ravishing she deserved.

And he didn't deny her—or himself. He ripped the panties away and lovingly devoured her with his mouth, laving the sweet pink folds of flesh until she was thrashing for more. He dipped a finger inside and found her clit while he sucked her pleasured juices and swirled her to insanity. She clutched at his arms and shoulders. Pain from his injury battled against the need to bring her over the edge and lost. And when she fell, he pressed his hand tight against her, his finger still inside, and milked every last quiver of release from her body.

But he wasn't done.

In her lax state, he surrendered to his fantasy and flipped her over. She didn't protest. One by one, he undid the tiny snaps that held the negligee in place. He parted the material with reverent slowness and he heard her sigh as she wrapped her arms around a pillow and scooted until her body molded into the soft leather couch.

He ran his hands down her spine. "You're so relaxed."

She didn't reply except to hum in agreement.

Was this really happening? Usually after an orgasm, Callie wrapped herself up in the shyness he found so alluring, but tonight, she hadn't pulled away. She pressed her cheek softly against the pillow beneath her and while her eyes were closed, he spied a satisfied smile curving her lips.

"I think a massage would be wasted," he said, even as his hands pressed against her flesh.

Her little whimper told him otherwise.

He obliged, pressing his fingers into the sweet curves of her muscles, adoring her flesh with his palms. He dotted her skin with kisses as he dipped lower and lower, until he could pay reverence to her backside with his hands and mouth, then indulged his need to stretch his sex against the length of the opening between her cheeks.

She shifted upward, pulling her knees beneath her.

He groaned.

She glanced over her shoulder.

"You always wanted to do it this way, didn't you?"

She wiggled her ass and for a moment, he couldn't speak.

Lifting her arms beneath her, she tilted her body so he could see how her sex pulsed, ready and willing.

"Come on, baby," she urged. "You know you want to do it like this. From behind. I never wanted to try until tonight. Do me right."

She didn't have to ask twice. Freed from the inhibitions that had once stood between them, he eased the tip of his sex into her. The channel was hot and smooth, enveloping him instantly. He stopped, but she whimpered, then scooted back so they were joined completely. Her bottom pressed against his groin, her thighs leveraged against his, she lifted herself higher, then lower, establishing a rhythm that took him a few shocked moments to mimic.

"Oh, God. Callie. What are you…?"

Pleasure surrounded him, penetrated him, drove him. He could hear nothing but her soft squeals of delight, see nothing but the curves of her body against his. He reached beneath her and toyed with her breasts until he knew from her panted breaths that her orgasm was seconds away, just behind his.

He couldn't wait any longer. He pumped until his body burst within hers. He cried out in a mixture of surrender and victory he'd never experienced before. He pressed his sex hard and tight inside her body as he climaxed, then realized she hadn't quite joined him. She was still writhing, still reaching, so he bent fully over her, found her center and flicked his fingers until she cried out in uninhibited release.

She collapsed against the couch, then rolled over so he could join her. Now lax, his sex slipped from between her thighs and his heart lightened at her tiny groan of disappointment.

He reached up and found the comforter that had been artfully tossed over the top of the couch. He wrapped them in a cotton cocoon and snuggled against her, his mind battling a thousand different thoughts, none of which he had the energy to make sense of.

And then, he slept.

8

THE MORNING DAWNED, as usual, but even without opening her eyes, Callie knew today would be nothing close to ordinary. She rolled over, away from the warm, gently snoring body of her ex-husband, slightly aware that sometime during they night, they'd moved from the couch to the bedroom. She scooted away on her king-sized bed, not wanting to look at him. Donovan was handsome when he was showered, shaved and dressed in his designer best, but in the morning, when the shadows of facial hair darkened his square chin with intrigue and his eyes still possessed the weight of sleepiness, he was downright devastating. She'd never be able to resist him—not that she wanted to resist him. She certainly hadn't last night.

But she'd promised herself only one night—one glorious night, which she'd gotten in spades. Anything more would destroy her once he left. Even now, her body thrummed from within. Just allowing a flash of erotic memories to skitter across her mind renewed the intimate throbbing that fell in time with her instantly accelerated heartbeat. Their lovemaking had been everything she'd fantasized about—and more.

They'd never had trouble pleasuring each other, but flying on the spirit of Janie's suggestion, Callie had thrown caution to the wind and kicked her inhibitions to the curb. Starting with her suggestion that they do it "doggie style," which Callie still blushed over, they'd admitted several other sexual fantasies to each other—and then made all but one come true. They'd simply run out of energy.

But now, Donovan stirred. She heard that deep, masculine grumble that announced he was about to wake up, albeit grudgingly. The day would truly begin and for all intents and purposes, their affair would be over.

Because, if for no other reason, the team was leaving. Not that she really gave a damn about that. But if the team went, so would Donovan. And with all of Louisville hating his guts, she couldn't imagine he'd ever return.

At least, not to stay.

"Hey, you," he said, his voice throaty, deep and mesmerizing.

Callie turned over, rubbed the sleep from her eyes and yawned. "Morning."

He leaned forward to kiss her, mindless of morning breath or bed head or any of the other afflictions that usually sent Callie scrambling to the bathroom in the pre-dawn hours before her lovers woke up. The instinct to bail this morning hadn't even occurred to her. She'd been more than content to remain, if not in Donovan's arms then in his bed. Or, technically, her bed—with him enjoying a not-so-hostile occupation.

"Want coffee?" she asked, lifting the sheet and reminding herself that she was, indeed, still naked.

"Not quite yet."

He slipped his arm beneath her and tugged her closer.

"I haven't even brushed my teeth yet, Donovan."

"Since when did I ever care about that?"

"Never, but we're not married anymore. You don't have to put up with stale tequila breath."

"I don't mind."

"Of course you don't, but I do."

"I think you just want to escape."

"There is that."

His expression darkened. "You never have to run from me, Callie."

A burst of laughter shot out of her. "Wrong."

The combination of hurt and concern in his dark blue eyes caused a twinge of regret. Still, Callie knew this affair couldn't last. No way, no how. For reasons that would probably take her until nightfall to list entirely—and that was if she started now— she and Donovan would go back to their mildly antagonistic existence and last night would become just another bittersweet memory to add to the collection. That was, if he stuck around. Which she doubted he would.

"I've done a lot of things wrong with you, Callie, but I've never intentionally hurt you."

With the sheet pulled ridiculously tight just over her breasts, Callie twisted around and lifted her pillow against the headboard. Leaning back, she glanced at Donovan through chastised eyes. "I know. But come on, Donovan. This situation is ripe for one or both of us to get burned."

He leaned sexily on one elbow. "Not if we don't let it."

"We won't have a chance."

He frowned. "Because last night was it for us?"

"That was the deal," she said.

"That was *your* deal."

"You agreed."

"I didn't have much of a choice."

"I didn't hold a gun to your head!"

"No, you held something much more dangerous."

She expected him to glance down at his crotch, making a crude but honest reference to how she'd been the seductress. He didn't. What, then, had he meant?

"Why the perplexed look?" he asked.

She shook her head. "I'm just wondering how I can get out of bed without you whistling at me on the way to the bathroom."

His smile spoke volumes. And, of course, the minute she threw back the covers and padded to the bathroom, a deep, seductive whistle rent the air. And because her back was turned, she allowed herself a smile.

She took a quick shower, pulled her hair into a damp ponytail and dressed in the clean sweats and cropped T-shirt she kept on the peg behind the door. When she emerged, she heard the shower running in the guest room, which gave her enough time to head to the kitchen and brew up a pot of Cuban roast. She'd just warmed the milk when Donovan sauntered in wearing the pants he worn the night before—and no shirt.

"Make yourself at home," she said, averting her eyes quickly, trying not to openly gape at the muscled chest that had driven her wild in the darkness. In the bright sunlight pouring into her kitchen, she might not be able to contain her drooling.

"Sorry, babe. My wardrobe choices are limited."

She nodded as she dug into her cupboard for a mug that didn't have some pithy feminist saying or man-hating quip. She had a lot of those. Too many. When had that happened? She figured most people didn't know what to get the divorced woman who had everything, so they went for the funny. And they usually were, but Donovan still had a bit of that kicked puppy droop in his shoulders and she wasn't one to dig at someone when they were down.

Finally, she found a pair of pale green mugs from the restaurant. She filled them with steaming milk, mixed in strong coffee and then added the single teaspoon of sugar she somehow remembered that Donovan liked.

She delivered the drink and when he grinned like a Cheshire cat, she stuck her tongue out at him.

"Very mature," he quipped.

"You bring out the juvenile in me."

"I wouldn't use the word juvenile to describe last night, babe."

"I don't want to talk about last night."

"I'm sure you don't."

She spun and skewered him with her best imitation of being incredulous. "What's that supposed to mean?"

"It's supposed to mean that you thought you'd have your little fantasy and then this morning, I'd disappear back into the hell I created for myself."

She knocked her fists onto her hips. "Isn't that what you're going to do?"

He sighed and took a long sip of coffee, humming in appreciation. Needing her own strong jolt, Callie grabbed her mug, added three heaping teaspoonfuls of sugar to her *café con leche* and joined him at the table.

"I suppose I don't have a choice."

"You can stay here as long as you want, Donovan. I mean,"

she said, stumbling over her words, "I'm not going to throw you out and watch those media wolves tear you apart."

"It's not just the media."

She thought back to the sight of him sitting on the hood of his crunched car, blood seeping from a cut on his face, which now seemed to have scabbed nicely.

"Why did you do it, Donovan?"

"You really want to know?"

She closed her eyes. God, but yes, she did. As much as she didn't want to have her idealistic images of Donovan burst into as many broken pieces as his car windshield, she had to understand.

"You're not a greedy man. You're ambitious and you want to succeed and, God knows, you like money as much as anyone else, but how could you sell out the team?"

Donovan took a deep breath. "I shouldn't tell you, Callie, but I need you to know the truth. You, of all people. I can't have you think I've changed so much that I'm not the same guy you married. Though I'd like to think I'm wiser now."

She shook her head. "Wise enough to risk your dream?"

"Promise that what I tell you won't leave this room."

"Of course! Donovan, what do you think I'll do? Sell your story?"

"No, Callie. But as much as we like to tease each other about being bitter ex-spouses, I care about you. And as much as you'll deny it, I know you care about me."

Her gaze dropped into her lap. She supposed she had been pretty hard on Donovan since their divorce. Not in a harpy, snotty way, but with snippy comments and sarcastic quips that criticized everything from his choice of dates to his extravagant lifestyle—a lifestyle that had not only provided her seed money for her restaurant, but that kept her more than comfortably in the black during both the on- and off-season.

"I don't deny it, Donovan. Not today. Not after last night."

He pressed his lips together, his eyes serious and his shoulders tense. "When the news first broke, I knew the better part of Louisville was going to think I was a real asshole. I can live with that, Cal. But not when it came to you. I wanted to explain."

"So explain."

"You're sure you can keep this quiet?"

"God, Donovan. You're killing me. Of course, I can. Spill. How could you have made a deal with a creep like Baxter?"

"You never liked him."

"I met him once and no, I didn't like him. He's a Vegas sleazeball."

"He used to be a Louisville sleazeball."

"I remember. You guys knew each other in school."

"Yeah. He wasn't from money like I was, but we hung out. He looked me up after he made it big in Vegas. If there was one thing I knew about him, it was that he had the ears of men with more important secrets than mine."

"I don't understand. Why would you have any secrets at all? You're a legitimate businessman."

"Even legitimate businessmen get in trouble sometimes."

Callie sat back in her chair, winded by the implication. "Financial trouble?"

"Of the worst kind. Do you remember Wallace Meeks?"

Callie reached deep into her memory. The name sounded familiar, but not from Donovan. From Peggy, Donovan's mother.

"He worked for your father. He retired, didn't he?"

"Actually Dad let him go about two years ago."

Callie gaped. Even though she couldn't place the man, she couldn't imagine Louis Ross dismissing someone she had a feeling was part of his inner circle.

"Wait. Wasn't he CFO?"

Donovan nodded. "For twenty years."

"What happened?"

"Wally Meeks was the best kind of guy, don't get me wrong. He moved with the times, really worked hard to try and take Ross Industries into the twenty-first century. But he was getting up there in age and wasn't as sharp as he used to be. He made some unwise choices."

Callie leaned forward. If there had been financial trouble at

Ross Industries, she hadn't heard about it—and since Ross Industries employed thousands of Kentucky residents in countless subsidiaries, she couldn't imagine something that big getting past her.

"What kind of unwise choices?"

"Remember the Ralston Ross Pension Fund?"

Callie nodded. Ralston Ross had been Donovan's great-grandfather. When he'd founded the company, he'd set up a discretionary fund out of his own pocket, specifically to pay an extra pension to retirees in need. Over the years, the Ralston Fund had become a major selling point of Ross Industries—the reason why Kentucky's best and brightest came home to Louisville to work rather than taking off for bigger cities and bigger corporations in Seattle or New York City or the Silicon Valley. The pension cost the employees nothing and the longer they worked, the better their retirement future became. Between the fund and company's modern 401(k), Ross employees usually retired with a comfortable future ahead of them.

"Something happened to the fund?"

Donovan's mouth curved grimly. "Meeks decided it would be a good idea to invest part of the fund. Unfortunately, he didn't do a very good job."

"Don't tell me he lost it all at Baxter's casino?"

Donovan's eyes widened. "God, no. Nothing like that. But he did lose it."

"All of it?"

"The first investment tanked so royally, he tried to make it up. By the time he finally came to my father, there wasn't much left."

"How come no one knows all this?"

"Do you know what would have happened if this would have gotten out? All our top executives might have left. Tons of employees might have sued. The press would have raked the company through the mud until there was nothing left. And Meeks would have been destroyed."

Pushing her coffee away, Callie pressed her hand to her stomach. God, how could the Ross family have gone through this without telling anyone?

"What did your father do?"

"He asked Meeks to retire and immediately replaced him with someone he could trust."

"Your brother!" Callie said, finally making sense of a decision that had perplexed her for years. "I remember thinking that was an odd choice. Jack was so young."

"But he takes orders from Dad without question and he would never do anything to hurt the company. And he does have a business degree."

"What about the money? Is that where Baxter came in?"

Donovan took a long sip of his coffee. "No way. My dad hates Baxter."

"Most people do."

"And wisely so. No, Dad protected the fund by putting in his own money. He had to be careful. Donovan Industries is a privately held corporation, but if word leaked out, if someone requested an audit, things could get ugly. He tried to liquidate as much as he could and cut his personal expenses without doing anything too noticeable. But it wasn't working. The fund was starting to pay out more than it had, so my brother asked me to intervene."

"By putting up the team as collateral for a loan?"

"Not exactly," Donovan grabbed his mug and returned to the stove for a refill. "You know that most of my capital is in real estate."

"Moving enough property to pay what was lost into the fund could have taken years," Callie assessed, knowing that selling large parcels of land in most industrial areas for millions of dollars didn't happen overnight, "especially if you weren't trying to draw attention to yourself."

"Exactly. So I went to my old pal Douglas and called him on the 'what happens in Vegas stays in Vegas' thing."

"Clearly, he missed that commercial," Callie snipped.

Donovan responded with a choice four-letter curse. "No. He clearly only keeps secrets when it's to his advantage. I promised that if he fronted me the money, I'd use my clout with the other owners to see that the next expansion team went to Vegas."

"But that didn't satisfy him."

Donovan looked into his mug, then threw the coffee into the sink. "He wanted a guarantee, so I promised him majority ownership of the team if I didn't repay the loan within two years."

"And you didn't pay it off?"

"No, not all of it. But, damn it, I was *this* close." His mug thunked as he slammed it onto the counter, causing Callie to jump. "This isn't chump change we're talking about and I had to keep the franchise going. If I made too many changes, reporters looking for scandal would have started to poke around even more than they already do. I would have made the next payment by mid-season, if ticket sales stayed strong, along with licensing fees."

Finally, all the business talk and maneuvering made sense. Luckily for Callie, she understood how businesses ran. Donovan had been siphoning money from several ventures, mainly the Slammers, to make sure his secret loan from Baxter was paid off before the screwups at Ross Industries were revealed. And just as he got close to paying Baxter what he owed him, the news of the deal was leaked to the press. The city of Louisville was up in arms. People were already lined up outside the stadium to get refunds on their season tickets. Corporate sponsorships would bail next. Donovan's income would plummet, making it impossible for him to finish paying back the loan—forcing the team into Douglas Baxter's greedy, slimy hands.

"You need to let people know what happened," she insisted.

"I can't do that."

"Why not?"

"My father and Wallace Meeks have their reputations. If I lose mine, so be it. But I can't let my father lose all he's worked for all his life."

"That's not your decision to make, Donovan," Callie reminded him. "You've got a big heart, but you've always been one to try and fix everyone else's problems. Look at how you started me up in my restaurant and made sure I always had a steady stream of customers."

He arched a brow. "Are you complaining?"

"Not in the least! I appreciate everything you've done for me and I know I couldn't have made it so far so fast without you.

But your father comes from a long line of self-made men. He wouldn't want you risking everything to save his reputation. Besides, the company is in the clear now, right? The money from the fund has been replaced."

Donovan shook his head furiously. "That's not a can of worms I can open, Callie. There's too much at stake."

He wanted to be the hero. And, clearly, the martyr. Could she stop him from ruining his life? And hers? Because when the team left, he'd leave. And damn it, she'd miss him.

"So you're just going to let the team go?" she spat.

"I don't have a choice."

She jumped to her feet. "You always have a choice! What's wrong with you, Donovan? The man I knew was always such a fighter. You saw what you wanted and you moved heaven and earth to get it. You want your team to stay in Louisville, don't you?"

"Of course."

"Then fight. Fight dirty, if you have to, but don't let a slimebucket like Douglas Baxter beat you just because you don't want your father to pay the price for not supervising his management team."

The minute the words spilled from her lips, Callie desperately wanted them back. She loved Donovan's father. She respected him more than she could express, mostly because he'd welcomed her into his family instead of pegging her as some gold digger only after her son's inheritance. But one of his employees had made an honest mistake under his watch. Donovan shouldn't have to pay the price.

Slowly, with a loud scrape of his chair, Donovan rose to his feet. His eyes blazed with fury and Callie realized she might just have crossed a very dangerous line. She'd insulted Louis Ross, his father—a man both of them loved dearly.

"Donovan, I didn't mean—"

He cut her off. "Yes, you did. You always say what you mean, Callie, or you don't say anything at all."

He had her there. But one of the differences between them was that before her brief marriage into the Ross clan, Callie had never really understood the dynamic of a family. From the moment she was born, she'd had only her mom, and in all honesty, Callie was nothing more than an afterthought to the woman most of the time. But in the Ross house, family came before everything else.

"Please, let me—"

"I know what you're going to say, Callie."

"That I'm sorry?"

He shook his hand at her, dismissing her apology. "Doesn't matter. I thought you'd understand. Of all people."

She rushed forward to grab his arm, but a wall of ice shot up between them. As determined as Callie could be sometimes, she knew there were some lines she simply should not cross.

"You're protecting your father, I understand. You're sacrificing your dream to save what will be your legacy. The reputation of Ross Industries clearly means more to you than the Slammers and, in all honestly, that's commendable."

His eyes met hers. The ice melted. "It's just a baseball team."

Callie pressed her lips tightly together as a sudden wash of wet heat stung her eyes. Suddenly, he sounded just like her—and she didn't like it one bit.

"It's not just a team. It's your dream."

"And it was great while it lasted."

"But everyone hates you."

He shrugged. "I can't help that."

Frustration filled her. She circled around and might have slammed him in the chest if not for the broken look in his eyes. This was killing him. Now she knew why he'd come to her last night.

He'd been alone and even after six years, when he needed to find someone who understood, he'd turned to her. And what had she done? Turned the whole night into an explosive exploration of hot sex.

Not that this was a bad thing.

"If you don't intend to fight, I understand why," she said.

He narrowed his gaze. "You do?"

She scrunched up her nose, trying to form the lie again, but she couldn't quite manage. "No, I really can't. Look, I just want you to consider something. Baxter didn't play fair, right? You think he's the one who leaked the deal to the press."

"Who else?"

"Then why do you have to play fair?"

"Because I have to protect my father and the company he's worked his whole life to keep solvent and strong. I can't betray him."

Callie tugged at his arm, twice, before he finally followed her back to the table. They sat and this time, she eased her chair closer to his.

"Does Baxter know why you needed the money?"

"You mean does he know I funneled the money back into Ross Industries? No. He never asked why I needed the cash, and I wouldn't have told him, anyway."

Callie grinned. She knew Donovan was too good of a businessman to lay all his cards on the table, even in Vegas. "Then why don't we put our heads together on this one. I can help you, I know I can. We can find a way to outsmart him. Maybe even keep the team."

"We?"

His arched brow told Callie that Donovan expected more out of that simple collective pronoun than she'd intended. But when she stepped back and looked at the way their conversation had gone, she realized that they'd come a hell of a long way since saying, "I do," followed soon after by, "I don't."

"Yeah, *we*," she conceded. "For now. Until we fix this."

But by the slash of a grin Donovan tried to hide, she knew he wasn't so convinced.

9

April 2, 2006
Slammers' Opening Day

As THE SOLOIST reached deep into her diaphragm to pull out the last notes of the national anthem, Callie held her breath. The audience below—the heartiest of baseball fans who'd braved the bad press and picket lines to attend the Slammers home opener—roared. Callie pressed her hands against the glass in the luxury box, watching with trepidation as the flag corps left the field and—with no entourage, no assistant, not a single person beside him—Donovan marched across the field to the microphone set up just in front of the pitcher's mound. She whispered a silent prayer to the heavens, nearly jumping out of her skin when Peggy Ross, her former mother-in-law, laid her hand on her shoulder.

"Nervous, dear?"

Callie tried to laugh away the anxiety, but didn't succeed. Boos and hisses echoed and bounced off the walls, every jeer and jibe audible thanks to the television monitors in the room. Below her, Donovan tapped on the microphone, but the crowd didn't settle. Not that it was much of a crowd. Not compared to a normal home opener.

"They won't listen to him," Callie lamented. God! She'd worked for two weeks on her ex, plying him with wine and sex and everything else she could think of to convince him that he had to use the one weapon he had at his disposal that Douglas Baxter couldn't fight—the truth.

"Give him a minute," Peggy said reassuringly. "He's a charming man, my son. They won't be able to resist him."

Callie grunted. "Tell me about it."

Peggy smoothed a delicate palm over her stylishly cut, frosted blond hair. "I'd ask *you* to tell *me* about it, but there are some things a mother should not know about her son and his wife."

Naughty innuendo danced on each and every syllable Peggy spoke, causing Callie to blush deep red.

The older woman giggled.

"Ex-wife," Callie reminded her former mother-in-law.

"Yes, right. I forgot," she replied, not the least bit repentant. "It's easy to let something like that slip my mind since you haven't been acting much like his ex for the past few weeks."

Callie cleared her throat. The truth of that statement reached into the most intimate parts of her life and as much as she loved Peggy, Callie wasn't admitting a damned thing. How could she? For all she knew, once Donovan had settled his problems with the team and no longer needed her, their intense affair would be as much a thing of the past as their marriage.

Below, the Slammers, lined up on the first baseline, shuffled under the crowd's increasing ire. A few cups landed unceremoniously on the field, followed by boxes of Cracker Jack and unopened bags of peanuts. The rain of refuse didn't reach anywhere near Donovan, but Callie couldn't help but look at the television for a closer angle. Donovan's expression remained frozen in a friendly smile, despite the derision assaulting him from above, below and all sides of the stadium.

Callie forced herself to breathe steadily. Peggy tightened her grip on her shoulder when the crowd suddenly went silent. Both their eyes darted to the home team dugout. Louis Ross climbed out from between the coaches and batboys and started across the infield, as sure of his step as his elder son. As soon as the crowd recognized who was coming to the rescue of their beleaguered team owner, they clapped politely.

Callie guessed that everyone in the audience was either employed by Louis Ross or knew someone who was—someone close, such as a parent, a sibling or a child. She was heartened to realize that the older man's influence in Louisville, the town he'd been named for, had not diminished in light of his son's blackened reputation.

"I can't believe you talked him into this," Peggy said, an amused smile in her voice.

Suddenly, the polite clapping turned into raucous applause. Below, Louis Ross met his son at the microphone and enveloped him in a bear hug, complete with the traditional male slapping on the back. Callie inhaled deeply, trying to ward off the tears.

"Donovan would never have budged if you and Louis hadn't called him from Paris." She turned to look at her mother-in-law. Former mother-in-law, she reminded herself. "I'm so glad you figured out what your son had done—and why."

Peggy sneered, as if she'd suddenly thought of something unpleasant. "I never approved of his so-called friendship with Douglas Baxter. Even as a young man, he struck me as a sleazy con. I should have put my foot down and nipped that relationship in the bud."

"You can't blame yourself. Donovan's a man now, not a boy. But that doesn't mean he doesn't need his family. And now that I think about it, I guess the Ross men in particular do need to find women who've been around the block a few times," Callie said.

"Yes, they do need street-smart women. And not just for a year's worth of marriage, or two weeks' worth of sex."

Callie opened her mouth, first in shock, and then to refute Peggy's assessment of her last fourteen days with Donovan, when Louis's voice boomed over the sound system. In a strong, forthright tone, Louis asked the crowd to listen while he told them a story about bad business choices and a son who would rather give up his dream than betray his father and the company so many of them loved.

Donovan stared down at the ground, his hands in the pockets of his tailored slacks. Callie knew he was paying a heavy price for allowing his father to "out" himself, but Louis had laid down the law once he'd realized precisely how his son had drummed up the capital to ensure his father's stellar reputation. Louis recounted the tale to the shocked crowd, coyly leaving out the name of his former CFO and taking full responsibility himself. Only thirty seconds into the explanation, Callie figured she could have dropped a pin out the luxury box window and heard the ping ten stories below.

"This isn't easy for either one of them," Peggy said, her voice a hoarse whisper that reflected all the pain and regret coursing through Callie for suggesting they take this course. She knew it was the right thing to do—for Donovan, for Louis, for the Slammers and for the city—but Callie had learned a long time ago that what was right often hurt the most. Such as when she'd asked Donovan for a divorce.

Over the past two weeks, the ache from that moment had been like a festering wound. Even if Louis's confession meant the team might manage to stay in Kentucky, she and Donovan had no reason to stay together beyond tonight. He still had the same lifestyle that had driven a wedge between them before. She still had the same needs and ambitions. The fact that they'd rediscovered each other and renewed the passion that constantly simmered between them changed nothing.

Louis went on. He spoke of his pride in his son and the team he'd brought to Louisville, a city that had been synonymous with baseball for more than a century. Donovan stood straighter, removed his hands from his pockets and grinned at the crowd, which wasn't quite so antagonistic anymore. Now, if word of Donovan's circumstances for his deal with Baxter—and the Vegas shyster's subsequent betrayal by leaking their personal, secret deal—made the airwaves *and* the team put together a strong, winning season, the Slammers might just lure back all the season ticket holders and corporate sponsors. If revenue peaked, Donovan would have the cash to pay back the last of what he owed Baxter and the team would stay.

Callie knew he could make it work. Except for a few members, the team had rallied behind him. The coaches who hadn't already quit rededicated themselves to the game. Even Janie and Babe didn't hate Donovan so much now that they understood the whole story. Callie watched the monitors, willing the camera to pan to the crowd so she could gauge reactions.

When Louis finished his talk, every man, woman and child rose to their feet in applause.

"I think it worked!" Callie exclaimed.

Peggy smiled knowingly, gathering her purse from the table by the door. "The truth usually works that way. You should try it yourself one day."

Callie drew her hand to her heart. Had her former mother-in-law just accused her of lying?

"Excuse me?"

"Don't look all offended at me, Ms. Callie Andrews Ross. The lies you tell are to yourself. But to be honest, since that's the theme of the day, your inability to admit the truth about your feelings is hurting my son. So cut it out."

She softened her chastisement with a wink and a smile before she left the luxury box, probably to meet her husband in the Ross corporate suite two floors below.

Thirty minutes later, Callie was still mulling over Peggy's reprimand when Donovan entered the suite. She could hear a cacophony of voices on the other side of the door, but he begged them off. His entourage had been dismissed so soon after they'd finally accepted him again as their leader?

"I can't believe you sent them away," Callie confessed.

Donovan's dark blue eyes honed in on her, as if a dozen people weren't standing outside the door on the opposite end of the luxury box and thousands of fans weren't watching the game below. In that instant, he had eyes only for her. Callie forced herself to swallow hard. She had to say what so desperately needed to be said.

"Donovan, I'm proud of you."

His half grin brought that dimple of a scar into view, sapping her breath. They'd made love so many times over the past two weeks, but no matter how much pleasure they exchanged, she'd never seen his eyes twinkle with as much sparkle as right this minute.

"I'm not sure I did the right thing for my ego," he admitted, "but I certainly did the right thing for the team."

"And for your father," Callie added. "He wouldn't have been

able to live with himself if he'd known his mistake had cost you your dream."

"That's what he keeps telling me."

"You're both cut from the same cloth."

Donovan smiled shyly and she knew she'd just offered him the ultimate compliment. She wasn't entirely surprised when he slipped his hands around her waist, pulled her close and kissed her until his father was the last thing on either of their minds.

She started pulling away, but he spoke before she could.

"Thank you, Callie."

Her entire body shivered. She felt so good in his arms. So natural. So relaxed. But it couldn't last. It wouldn't.

"You just needed a little push in the right direction," she said. "You did the hard stuff."

"Not many people have the guts to push me in any direction."

"You're a powerful man."

"I was, and then I wasn't and maybe now I will be again. But the only constant in all of this has been you."

Uncomfortable with the deep, duskily emotional tone in Donovan's voice, Callie gently twisted out of his arms. Fantasies were one thing—she'd never regret accepting Janie's challenge and taking what she wanted for the time being—but now things had changed. Even if Donovan succeeded in keeping the team in Louisville, which she had no doubt he would, he was still a baseball team owner with obligations around the country and she was still a respected restaurateur who wanted a rooted life. They'd proved once they couldn't make a relationship work. Nothing had changed.

And yet, everything had changed.

"Constant is what I've wanted to be all my life, Donovan," she pointed out. "You know about my past, and better than anyone else, you know what I dreamed of for my future. Now that you're back on track and I've indulged my most secret fantasy, I think it's time we go back to the way things were."

The light dimmed from his eyes, but only seconds later, his blue irises flamed with anger. "What?"

She took a step back. Donovan was a man of extremes and

while she knew this argument wouldn't get physical, her eardrums really didn't need a workout today.

"I think it's better if we go back to being just…friends."

"You think we've been friends since the divorce?"

"We interact well. You're in the restaurant nearly as much as I am, and despite a few verbal barbs now and again, we've managed to coexist."

"That's not coexisting," he snapped. "That's passive-aggressive behavior. And it's going to stop right now."

10

DONOVAN TOOK a deep breath, then released his anger in one long, cleansing exhalation. Just a half hour ago, he'd thought the hardest moment of truth in his life had happened on the ball field. Wrong. It was happening now, here, with Callie.

"I'm sorry," he said.

She arched a brow. "Wow. That's twice in a month's time."

He forced a grin. "What can I say? I'm a slow learner."

Callie shifted on uneasy feet, her gaze darting first to her purse and then to the door. She wanted to escape, but he couldn't let her. Not now. Not ever.

He held out his hand.

"What?" she asked.

"Don't go."

She pressed her eyelids closed tightly. When she opened them, her hazel eyes glittered with moisture. Not tears, just deep emotion—the kind that a woman like Callie would fight to the death. That meant something, right?

"Donovan, we've had a great couple of weeks. Let's not ruin it with expectations neither one of us can fulfill."

"Speak for yourself," he ordered, confidence lilting his voice. "My expectations aren't that hard to meet."

"You want arm candy."

"Give me a little credit, Callie. Do I want a wife I can show off? Sure. Every man wants that. And honestly, what woman in the world is more perfect than you?"

"I have a job," she insisted.

"You have a career you love and one that, luckily, I have no trouble supporting."

She couldn't argue. He'd been one hundred percent behind her opening the restaurant since the idea first occurred to her.

"You travel all the time," she threw out, but he could see the desperation in her eyes. The same old arguments against their marriage now had new answers. They weren't stupid young kids anymore who thought they had to be together 24/7 in order to make a marriage work. And he wasn't a rookie team owner who had something to prove by following his team every time they left Louisville.

"I don't have anything keeping me here in Louisville right now. But that could change—it's up to you."

Callie wavered, and Donovan couldn't resist taking her elbow to steady her. She was shaking her head and her entire body seemed to vibrate with a refusal to believe they'd changed so much in so short a time, but Donovan knew she couldn't win the argument she was waging in her head—not if he engaged her heart. Because, honestly, the changes had been in the works for a long time, and his deal with Baxter and the threat of losing the team had only brought their emotions to the surface.

He held her close, inhaling the sweet lavender scent of her perfume, absorbing the warmth of her body, knowing he needed her more than money and the team and even, possibly, more than air to breathe. How he'd existed this long without her as a permanent fixture in his life was beyond him—but he wasn't about to tempt fate again.

"Callie, I need you."

Her voice shook. "You don't need me. You just want me. We've had a lot of wild sex these past two weeks, but the lust will wear off eventually. We learned that before."

He threaded his fingers into her hair and forced her gaze to battle with his. "The lust never wore off and you know it. We just couldn't find a way to coexist. Now we can. We've learned that we can't live without each other. Don't tell me you don't look forward to seeing me when I come into the restaurant. Don't try to convince me that during the off-season, you don't miss me a little."

"I don't," she said, her lips pouted.

He laughed. "You're a horrible liar. But I'm going to admit to you now that I think about you all the time, Callie. I have since you left. I've tried to deny it. I've tried to fill my life with other interests and other women, but they never measure up to you. I settled for five minutes of banter before you sat me at my regular table rather than marry someone else and never have you look at me again."

Donovan allowed silence to reign, because he couldn't believe the depth of what he'd admitted. He saw the shock in her eyes, then the glimmer of hope. God, he hoped that's what he saw. Because he was going for broke.

"Yes, I want you," he continued. "I want the hot sex and the wild nights—but with you. Only you. You balance me. You support me. You love me. Deny it. Go ahead. I dare you."

She bit her lip, shook her head, but the denial didn't reach her liquid hazel gaze. "Doesn't matter if I love you or not, Donovan. We can't make it work. We proved it. I don't want another broken heart."

"I love you, Callie. I've always loved you. Seven years ago, I didn't realize that loving someone meant sacrificing for them. I thought if I offered you a dream life, you'd come along willingly and we'd both be gloriously happy forever. I was wrong. The dream life I offered you was *my* dream. Now, we have a chance to build *our* dream. Together."

He led her to the bank of floor-to-ceiling windows that gave them an awesome view of the stadium below. He pressed her close and together, they watched Riley Kelleher throw a perfect fastball across the plate. The umpire called the strike, the third for that batter. The side was retired and the crowd went wild. The antique pipe organ he'd spent over a million dollars to install rent the air with its high-pitched version of "Take Me Out to the Ballgame." Vendors in bright blue-and-green shirts walked up and down the aisles, hawking peanuts, popcorn and beer. Children waved great big pink fluffs of cotton candy in the air and danced when the team's mascot, a creature of undetermined species, jumped on top of the dugout and cued the latest hip-hop tune over the speaker system.

"Looks like the Louisville fans have given me a second chance, Callie. Can't you?"

He was almost afraid to look at her again, terrified that her answer would end what had become the most crucial relationship in his life. But just as he'd finally drummed up the nerve to see if he'd changed her mind, she leaned her head against his shoulder and sighed.

"You're right. I do love you, Donovan. And since you're forcing me to be honest with you—and with myself—I want a second chance, too."

"Then you'll marry me? Again?"

She rolled her eyes, as if the answer should have been obvious. "Yes!"

He swept her into his arms and twirled her around until she squealed in protest. Guiltily, he put her down, but she laughed, threw her arms around his neck and pressed her sweet, curvaceous body hard against his. "We're crazy, you know that?"

"Insane," he replied, then leaned back to flick a switch beside the windows. If there was one feature he'd spent too much money on in his luxury box, it was the special coating and lighting on the windows that, when activated, blocked out any view from the outside.

"What was that?"

"I never wanted curtains on these windows, but since I live here, I couldn't have the grounds crew watching me prance around in my tightie whities on off nights."

She pursed her lips, igniting a simmering fire that the added privacy only fueled. "Or see you screwing around with your latest squeeze?"

"That's the past, Callie," he admonished. "But you know as well as anyone that this luxury box is usually full of people during every home game. I can honestly say that I've never made love to a woman during a game. Yet."

At the suggestion, her eyes darkened and her tongue darted out to lick her lips.

"Must have taken a lot of finessing to convince your management team and various hangers-on that the Ross Industries suite was the place to be tonight instead of here."

He dropped his hands around her warm, curved backside.

"I'm a very determined man. You see, I have this fantasy about making love to you up against the glass."

"Ooh, against the glass?"

She pressed closer, so that her hardened nipples, clearly free of any binding undergarment beneath her draped, silk blouse, raked against his chest. His sex stiffened and for an instant, he experienced a wave of light-headedness only Callie could inspire.

She rose on tiptoe and swiped her tongue boldly across his mouth.

"Tell me more about this fantasy," she invited.

"How about if I show you instead?"

He flicked open her blouse, tore away the material and feasted on her breasts until she was nearly weak with pleasure. In a flash, they were both undressed. She leaned coyly against the glass, glancing over her shoulder, clearly wanting to be certain that the city of Louisville wasn't getting a shot of her bare bottom.

Donovan took her hands, swung her around and pressed his own back to the glass. "No one can see anything, believe me, but if I'm wrong, it'll be my bare butt on the evening news, not yours."

She laughed as she slid her palms up his thighs, then stroked him until he was hard and long and blind with passion.

"I'm not ashamed of loving you, Donovan, but I'd prefer you were the only man in Louisville to appreciate my naked bum."

He held his breath while she slipped a condom on him, then crouched down and buoyed her bottom, as she climbed onto his lap.

"Callie, you're amazing," he said.

She quirked a half grin before shifting so that her body accepted his fully and completely. "Yes, I am. And don't think I'm ever going to let you forget it."

Dear Reader,

It's that time of year down here in Texas when the bluebonnets are wilting and the pavement is cooking. But this isn't the only place the temperature is heating up.

When Babe Bannister, baseball fan and owner of the gourmet ice cream shop The Sweet Spot, hears that her beloved Louisville Slammers might be leaving town, she decides that she's through fantasizing about her favorite player. She realizes that this may be her last chance, so she decides to live out her most erotic thoughts by propositioning Mr. Fantasy.

Babe's best bud, coach Brodie Jessup, isn't all that eager to see her step up to bat, however. Brodie's been doing a little fantasizing of his own, with Babe as his top pick, and he wants her all for himself.

What's a guy to do when the woman of his dreams lusts after another man? Offer to coach her in the art of seduction, of course. A few lessons and Brodie is sure that Babe will recognize the chemistry between them.

Brodie is right, of course, and the result is my latest blazing-hot story of love and lust and baseball. So pour yourself a nice cool drink, crank up the air-conditioning and get ready for some hot summer reading!

All my best,

Kimberly Raye

P.S. I love to hear from readers! You can visit me online at www.kimberlyraye.com.

THE SWEET SPOT
Kimberly Raye

This story is dedicated to my father,
James Harlin Adams,
a wonderful man and the biggest sports fanatic
I've ever known.
Thanks for encouraging me, loving me
and giving me the confidence
to follow my dreams.
I'm going to miss you.

1

Three weeks after the opening game

"I WANT TO LICK YOU all over." Babe Bannister stood in the back storage room of The Sweet Spot and stared at her reflection in the stainless steel napkin holder. She narrowed her gaze just so to give herself a sexier, more dreamy-eyed look. Sexy and dreamy were must-haves if one intended to proposition a man. "*I* want to lick *you* all over," she murmured, imagining herself having the nerve to actually say the words to a man. One certain man. "From your head to the tips of your toes. Or from the tips of your toes to your head. Your choice."

Can we be a little original?

She pouted for effect and tried the pickup line again. "I want to lick you all over like a double-scoop sugar cone." She licked her full lips—with an extra twenty pounds on her five-foot, three-inch frame, everything about Babe qualified as *full*. The image of a certain handsome shortstop danced in her mind. "A sugar cone dipped in dark, sinful chocolate. With crushed pecans and almonds."

As soon as the words left her mouth, his image started to blur and he quickly morphed into the cold confection she was currently cooking up in The Sweet Spot's kitchen. Babe forgot all about perfecting her pickup line to wow said man and, instead, found herself thinking about her new dessert as an idea struck.

"Crushed pecans and almonds," she repeated as her imagination raced and the creamy creation took shape. "Topped with a strawberry swirl glaze."

That was it! What she'd been missing in the taste combination for the latest flavor she'd been developing. *Strawberries*. It was so simple. Yet she'd been racking her brain and trying everything from caramel to pineapple for the past six months.

She smiled. While she wasn't any closer to perfecting a pickup line, she *had* nailed down her next masterpiece.

One down, one to go.

She finished refilling the holder. Adding it to the dozen others on the tray, she turned and tossed the napkin wrappers into a nearby trash.

She'd just hefted the tray into her arms and taken two steps when she heard the bell on the front door of the shop chime.

Her heart slammed into her ribs and started a frantic beat that outraced the furious *bam bam* of the classic ZZ Top song drifting from the storage-room radio. She swiveled a gaze to the clock on the wall and managed to catch her breath.

She still had five minutes until the big C.

Closing time, to everyone in the sports complex.

Cody time for Babe Bannister, owner of Louisville's hottest gourmet ice-cream shop and creator of the seventy-six ice-cream flavors that had earned her a spot as one of the Food Network's Top-Ten Dairy Divas.

Okay, it wasn't Miss Hawaiian Tropic, but Babe wasn't going to quibble. She never quibbled. She settled. She'd been doing so her entire twenty-eight years.

Until now, she reminded herself.

For the first time in her life, she was going for the gusto. Shooting straight for her dream. Pursuing her most erotic fantasy.

Babe Bannister was going to proposition Cody Cameron.

In exactly three minutes and twenty-eight seconds.

Every Thursday night, the star shortstop for the Louisville Slammers baseball team dropped into The Sweet Spot after practice for a scoop of his favorite ice cream—the Cody Cameron Explosion.

Babe's nostrils flared. She could practically smell the enticing aroma of fresh soap and hot, handsome male. The scent was enough to distract her from the temptation that surrounded her as she adjusted her grip on the heavy tray and made it the rest of the way through the kitchen.

Large plastic containers with everything from M&M's to Reese's peanut butter cups lined the wall to her left and called her name. To her right, gallon-sized cans of fudge and caramel sauces stood sweet and tempting. Homemade waffle bowls baked inside the monstrous stainless steel commercial oven in the far corner. The aroma curled across the space in an unmistakable "come here, baby," gesture.

Not tonight.

She wasn't going to risk gaining even one more pound until she'd done the deed with Cody. He had a reputation for liking beautiful, thin, svelte women and she didn't want to stack the odds against herself any higher. Next week, she told herself. She would proposition him tonight and set the rendezvous for next weekend—she didn't want to appear *too* eager. Which meant she only had to resist temptation for seven days.

Unless he wants to dispense with formality, rip off your clothes and take you right here and now.

She should be so lucky.

But Babe had never—repeat NEVER—been lucky. Rather, she'd been born with three strikes against her, which had pretty much set the stage for her crappy love life.

Number one? She'd been born to parents who'd always dreamed of having a son play in the majors. Parents so obsessed that they'd named each of their three children—all girls, by the way—after a baseball great.

Strike two? Babe's two sisters were now and had always been more athletic, more outgoing and more athletic. The oldest, Mickey, had been the bubbly, drop-dead gorgeous cheerleader who'd fallen in love with the captain of the football team, married him right after college graduation and was now the bubbly, drop-dead gorgeous mom of four boys with a successful sports agent husband. Sandy, aka Miss Jock, the youngest, had played EVERY sport, served as captain of every team and gone to college on a softball scholarship. She now owned a fitness and aerobics center, was president of the Louisville Young Female Athletes' Association and was dating a personal trainer who once played for the Red Sox. Meanwhile, Babe was the middle daughter who'd never really been *that* into sports. Sure, she loved baseball and could recite the final scores for every World Series game, but she simply wasn't very athletic. She never had been.

Hence, strike number three... Babe didn't exactly live up to her name (i.e. total babe, hot babe, what a babe, etc.) when it came to appearance. She was a size six trapped in a size ten body. Okay, *okay*. So she was actually a size eight trapped in a size twelve body (on a good day when she wasn't retaining too much water, that is). She'd tried diet and exercise and even one of those positive thinking yoga mantras that she'd kept taped to her refrigerator, but so far, nothing had worked. How could it when Babe was a stickler for quality? Integrity required that she personally sample each and every batch of ice cream before it left the production room. Which pretty much shot any and every weight-loss regime to hell and back.

You're outttt!

Not that the weight bothered her, mind you. Well, maybe when she'd been a kid. She'd wanted to be as thin as her sisters. As athletic. As perfect. But over the years, she'd come to the realization that it wasn't going to happen. And that was okay. While she wasn't a lean, mean beauty queen, she certainly wasn't ugly, either. She had nice blue eyes and long blond hair, and she was smart. Even her parents, who'd retired to Florida five years ago, had admitted as much.

Her so-so looks and impressive smarts had landed her a handful of boyfriends and her share of sexual encounters. Unfortunately, none of them—neither the men, nor the sex—had been memorable. The guys had all been ordinary, from their looks to their jobs. There had been Mark the accountant. Wilson the head of statistics for a local research firm. Jack the plumber. The only one who'd been remotely exciting had been Mitchell, who'd supervised food preparation for a local school district. While they'd had a common interest—baking—there was only so much that could be said for making a stiff meringue or a crispy pie crust.

And the sex? Just as boring, as bland, as *ordinary* as the men. Babe wanted more.

She'd admitted as much to herself several weeks ago when she and her two best friends, Callie Andrews and Janie Nolan, had first heard the news that the Slammers might be leaving Louisville at the end of the season. Callie owned Diamond, an upper-crust restaurant located in the same complex that housed The Sweet Spot, while Janie ran a memorabilia store next door. The three of them had sat in the storeroom of Janie's shop, Round The Bases, sipped wine and talked about the business they stood to lose should the team actually move. They'd also talked about what they stood to gain—a fantasy come true—should they throw caution to the wind, act on their impulses and proposition their player of choice.

Babe wanted a sexy, good-looking, exciting man who could give her one wild night that she would never, ever forget. The kind she would reminisce about with her cat when she was an old, lonely ninety-year-old living in the local nursing home.

Just once, Babe wanted to make a bona fide memory, and Cody Cameron, the Slammers shortstop and star of her most erotic dreams, was just the man to give it to her.

She pushed through the swinging double doors into the front of the ice-cream shop and came to a dead stop.

Her heart jumped into her throat and she stopped breathing as she found herself staring into the most vivid pair of lavender eyes.

"You're early," she blurted. Okay, so it was only by a minute and a half, but he was never early.

"Coach let us out of practice with a few minutes to spare. He had to take an important phone call." The coach in question—actually, the manager—was Brodie Jessup. Brodie had once played for the Slammers before an accident had ended his playing days. Now he managed the team. He was dedicated and focused and drop-dead gorgeous. If a girl happened to like the dedicated and focused type.

Babe, however, had set her sights on wild and reckless and temporary. The stuff of fantasies, not 'til death do us part. She smiled at Cody. At least, she tried for a smile, but with her heart pounding so fast, it was all she could do to breathe.

"You okay?" Cody asked.

"Sure." She cleared her throat. "Fine." She nodded vehemently and almost gave herself whiplash. "Never better."

"That's good." He glanced at his watch and then winked at her. "So what's up?"

This is it. This is your chance. Just tell him what you want.

"I'm, um, really glad that you asked that. You see, I was, um, wondering…" She licked her lips and groped for her courage. "That is, I wanted to, um, ask you something really important—"

The shrill ring of his cell phone cut off the rest of her sentence. "Just a sec." He pulled the slim silver piece from his pocket, flipped it open and pressed it to his ear. "Hey," he said.

Babe retrieved her ice-cream scooper, flipped open the lid on the freezer and busied herself filling a waffle bowl.

"Oh, yeah?" he said into the phone, followed by a laugh. "No way." Another laugh.

The sound shook her already fragile nerves and she tried for a deep breath. *It's good that he's distracted. This gives you a chance to get it together and figure out what you're going to say.*

That's what she told herself, but a few seconds later when he slid the phone back into his pocket, eyed the cup overflowing with several scoops of his favorite ice cream and said, "That looks great," she found herself momentarily speechless.

"Can I have it?" he finally asked after she simply stood there, bowl in hand, for several moments.

"Uh, sure." She slid a white plastic spoon into the ice cream and handed over the treat.

Do it, she told herself as he spooned a huge bite and slid it into his mouth. Don't just watch him. Although watching was good. Cody had a really great mouth and nice, firm lips. At least they looked firm most of the time. Right now, they looked sweet, slicked with the decadent ice cream—

"Did you need to ask me something?" He plucked a napkin from the holder that sat on the counter. "Because I've really got to go. I've got people waiting."

"Oh, it's nothing important." She waved him off before her determination stepped in and gave her a good mental kick in the pants. "Actually, it really *is* important and it'll only take a minute."

"Oh, yeah?" He arched an eyebrow and his grin faded into an expectant expression. "Shoot."

This is it. You go, girl. You get your man.

"I want…" She cleared her throat. "That is, I want to know if you…" She licked her lips. "I want to know if you would like to…"

"Yeah?" he prompted, chancing another glance at his watch before eyeing her. Impatience swam in the deep lavender pools.

"Nuts," she blurted. "I mean, I know you don't usually have nuts on your ice cream, but I thought you might want to try some. They're really good nuts. Crushed almonds."

"I'm allergic to almonds."

"Oh. Then I guess almonds are a bad idea." *Way to go, Slick. I seriously doubt he'll want to have sex with you if you send him into allergic shock.* "What about a cherry?" She reached toward the container that sat nearby and plucked a fat, juicy red one from inside. "I've got cherries."

"Sure. A cherry's fine." He held out his cup and she plopped the piece of fruit on top. "Thanks." He balanced the bowl with one hand and reached into his pocket with the other.

"Forget it," she said when he tried to hand her a ten. "It's on the house."

"Great." He slipped the bill back into his wallet and slid the expensive leather back into the tight pocket of his jeans—how, she had no clue, since they seemed to be painted on. She seriously wondered how he had blood flow, much less pocket space.

He grinned, winked again, and then her one chance at sexual nirvana turned and walked away.

So much for not wasting any more precious time. Sure, it wasn't even the end of April—only three weeks into the season—but with each day that passed, time was running out.

It had already been a full month since she'd sat in the storeroom of Round The Bases—the sports memorabilia shop next door—with Janie and Callie, and made up her mind to turn her fantasy into reality.

An entire month.

And the clock was ticking.

Thanks to the team's owner, Donovan Ross, who'd made some bad financial decisions, the Slammers would most likely be leaving at the end of the season. Cody would head to Las Vegas with the rest of his teammates and Babe would be stuck here with nothing but a very erotic dream to spice up her nights.

Dread rushed through her. How could she have blown it?

Again?

Before she knew what was happening, her hand had closed around a bottle of whipped cream.

Okay, so it wasn't *exactly* on her diet, but it wasn't nearly as fattening as the rest of the stuff in her shop and she was desperate. She tilted her head back, squeezed the nozzle and gave herself a mouthful of sweet cream.

"It can't be that bad." The deep, masculine voice slid into her ears, and her head snapped up. A drop of whipped cream hit her on the nose as her gaze collided with a familiar pair of green eyes so bright they were almost iridescent. "Otherwise you would have gone straight for the ice cream."

She swallowed. "I'm substituting." Her heart, which had stalled, revealed its normal tempo as she eyed Slammers' coach Brodie Jessup.

Brodie was several years older, but he'd lived in the house next to hers when he was a kid and so they'd grown up together. She could still remember sitting on the fence every afternoon, watching him practice pitching in his backyard.

Her older sister, Mickey, had sat with her sometimes, but Mickey hadn't been the least bit interested in Brodie's right arm. Rather, she'd been hot for the entire package. Evident by the fact that she'd always worn her slinkiest halter whenever she'd joined Babe.

Brodie, unlike the other boys at Jamison High School, had never paid Mickey any attention. He'd been too busy perfecting his throws to see anything beyond the ball's target. Too focused.

A trait that had taken him all the way to the majors, and then into coaching when his ball career had been cut short thanks to a motorcycle accident.

He was still as focused as ever—only now he helped his players perfect their technique rather than working on his own—and just as good-looking. Not that she really noticed what he looked like since he was her friend and she'd learned a long time ago not to get any romantic notions about him. He was a work-aholic, plain and simple. Gorgeous, but boring.

He came into the ice-cream shop a couple of nights a week after practice to eat a scoop of his favorite no-frills vanilla and talk shop with Babe, who knew as much about baseball as he did.

That, too, would end once the season drew to a close and the team headed to Vegas.

She felt an unexpected swell of disappointment.

Because she wouldn't be seeing Brodie? Hardly.

Okay, so maybe a little. He *was* like an older brother and she did enjoy talking game stats and having someone to rant to when things didn't go well at the shop. But the real source of the tight-ening in her chest was the fact that she'd just blown yet another chance with Cody. To top *that* off, she'd blown her diet, as well.

Talk about bummed.

"Aren't you supposed to put that on top of something?" He eyed the can of whipped cream she still held. He grinned and humor danced in his light green eyes.

"Usually." She set the can aside and reached for a napkin. "But this was an emergency." She wiped her lips, tossed the napkin and reached for a small cup, with The Sweet Spot printed on the outside in bright pink letters.

Her hand trembled and she sniffled as she scooped the smooth, creamy vanilla into a sizeable ball.

Brodie slid onto a stool, set his keys and cell phone on the counter and eyed her. His grin faded into a concerned expression. "What's wrong?"

"Nothing. I mean, there is, but you don't have to look so worried. My heart's not about to conk out or anything." She sighed. "I wish I could say the same for my hormones."

A strange light glimmered in his eyes. "I don't think I'm fol-lowing you."

"Have you ever wanted something—or someone—really,

really bad? And you just couldn't seem to make yourself take that first step?"

He shook his head. "What? You want to ask someone out?"

"Actually," she grinned, "what I have in mind involves staying in."

Realization seemed to strike after a long moment and where she expected him to smile, he frowned. "Who's the guy?"

She shook her head. "It's no big deal. So how are the guys shaping up? They looked pretty good this last game, but the outfield can stand a little work—"

"Not so fast. You brought this up, so finish it. Who?"

"Well, he's a really great guy." Her gaze drifted toward the door as if she expected to catch a glimpse of Mr. Great Guy. But he was long gone.

"*Who?*" he asked again before swiveling to stare in the direction she'd looked. The truth hit and his frown turned to a look of pure disbelief. "Cody Cameron?"

"I know it seems far-fetched and he's way out of my league. But I really like him."

"*Cody Cameron?*"

"What's wrong with Cody?"

"He's a total loser."

"He is not. He's this close to breaking the standing record for outs in a single season, and we're only halfway through. The guy's great."

"Professionally." He gave her a stern look, his dark brows drawing together. "Personally, he's a jackass and the last person you'd want to get involved with."

"I don't want a relationship with him. I just want one night."

"You want to have *sex* with him?" he asked, as if still trying to digest the information.

"I haven't spent every night dreaming about the two of us playing Scrabble." She stiffened and stared into his skeptical eyes. "Haven't you ever dreamed about anyone, Brodie?" Her voice softened and quivered with the sudden need that gripped her. "About being with them?"

"Having sex with them?"

"Living out a fantasy. A red-hot, bone-melting fantasy." She sighed. "The team has a lot of players that have *fantasy* written all over them, but I've been lusting after Cody since we were kids."

Silence settled between them for a long moment before he finally asked, "So why haven't you done anything about it?"

"We're talking about *Cody Cameron.*"

"He's not God. He's just a shortstop."

"A really good shortstop."

He nodded. "But he's still human."

"I tell myself that every time he comes in here, but it's so hard to remember when I'm actually staring him in the face. But I will remember. The very next time he comes in." She pulled her shoulders back and gathered her determination. "I'm going to proposition him. *I am.*"

"I really don't think that's such a good idea."

"You think it's hopeless, don't you? Because I'm not his type?"

"Are you kidding? He loves blondes."

"True, but he likes tall, leggy blondes, which I'm not. I'm short and blonde."

"You forgot voluptuous."

"If only I could." She shook her head. "And he doesn't like round girls. He likes them thin."

"You're thin."

"Maybe if you're comparing me to the average six-foot-plus pro ballplayer, but according to the guidelines established by the Presidential Fitness Program for all females between the ages of twenty and thirty," she recited, the stats having been drilled into her, back in the sixth grade by her father who'd wanted to see her excel in sports, "I've bypassed my age group by a good dozen pounds. Give or take another four or five."

"That's crazy. You look fine. Healthy."

"Healthy is just another word for plump. Look, can we talk about something else?" Otherwise, she might be inclined to think that size really didn't matter to Brodie Jessup.

But she'd yet to meet a man, particularly a good-looking, sexy-to-other-women-who-weren't-practically-a-sister-to-him man who didn't care about an overly abundant figure.

Brodie was her buddy and he was just being nice.

He ignored her question and said, "Healthy is the word for *healthy*. As in fit. You're just right. Round in all the right places."

She gave him a you're-not-making-me-feel-any-better look.

"And thin in all the right places," he added. "And this infatuation with Cody is the only thing unhealthy about you. Trust me, Babe. He's not the guy for you."

"How do you know?"

"Because I know him. I'm his coach—his momma and his daddy and his babysitter all rolled into one. That's my job."

One that Brodie took very seriously. His players were his livelihood and he made it his business to know anything and everything that affected their lives, both on and off the field. In Cody Cameron's case, Brodie knew a helluva lot more about the guy than he cared to.

Babe was right. She wasn't Cody's type, but the fact had nothing to do with her physical appearance. She was much too good for him, be it for a relationship or a one-night stand. Unfortunately, she didn't look any more convinced of the fact than she had when he'd walked in.

"There's really no use in beating myself up over this. So what if I didn't do it this time? No biggie. Time's not up yet. I'll just do it next time. This coming week. He'll walk in on Thursday night and I'll just lay it all out and ask him."

"I really don't think that's a good idea."

She seemed to consider his words. Finally. "You know, maybe you're right."

"Damn straight I am."

"I'm not his type, which means a straightforward proposition might just mean setting myself up for failure. Maybe I should try something more subtle." She smiled as an idea seemed to strike. "Something more, shall we say, *seductive*."

Her bright blue gaze collided with his and awareness bolted through him.

A familiar feeling that drew him back to his childhood. He could still see her sitting on the fence that separated their backyards. She had climbed up every day to watch him and to offer suggestions.

The watching he'd liked.

Especially since Babe had been the only one truly interested in what he'd been doing. His mother had been too wrapped up in her latest boyfriend and his grandfather had been too sick with emphysema to toss around the ball or take any sort of active interest in his only grandson's passion. The old man had spent most of his time hooked up to an oxygen tank, doing crossword puzzles and watching soap operas.

And Brodie's dad?

The man hadn't even known Brodie existed until a few years ago when Brodie's mother had passed away. The tall, gray-haired man had shown up at the funeral and given Brodie his first up-close look at the infamous Grady Merritt, the most aggressive pitcher to ever play for the Red Sox.

Brodie had known about him since he'd been a kid. But like most everyone in Jamison—a small suburb outside of Louisville—he'd wondered if there were any truth to the story. His mother hadn't been the most honest person, or the most faithful when it came to men. And so the story of how the famous Red Sox pitcher had fallen hook, line and sinker for her had been hard for most people to swallow. Especially Brodie.

But he'd wanted to.

He'd wanted to buy the whole tale of how his mother had been desperately in love with his father. How she'd left the relationship and kept her pregnancy a secret because she hadn't wanted to break up his marriage.

He'd wanted to think that he wasn't just Anna Jessup's bastard son, but a chip off the old block. The son of a man who would have wanted him if he'd only known.

Brodie had wanted so much to believe that he'd taken up the sport and pushed himself to prove to everyone and, most of all, to himself that it was, indeed, true.

He'd pushed himself right into the majors, and then he'd pushed himself into coaching when a motorcycle accident had shattered his shoulder.

He'd been pushing ever since, but it hadn't been because he'd had to prove he was Grady's son. He'd kept his nose to the grindstone because he'd been the youngest coach in the majors and he'd had to show the entire league that he had every right to be there. That he deserved to be there, even if he hadn't put in the playing time most of the other coaches had. Baseball had become his life. It was all he knew. All he was really good at. And so the meeting with his father hadn't eased the burden of proof in any way.

He'd been so busy with the team, in fact, that he hadn't had the chance to get to know the man behind the story his mother had told him all those years ago.

But that was about to change.

Donovan, his boss and the owner of the Slammers, had made some bad choices and it looked as if the team would be headed to Las Vegas at the end of the season. Grady had left the majors several years back and now headed the baseball program at the University of Nevada, which would put him close enough to Brodie for them to actually get to know one another.

Which made Brodie the one and only person in Louisville who wasn't royally pissed about possibly leaving town. No, he was looking forward to it. He was tired of laying awake on the nights he didn't stop off at The Sweet Spot—vanilla ice cream had a soothing effect and he always went home and slept like a baby—and wondering why he wasn't half as happy as he should have been. Inevitably, he would find himself wondering about his old man and how life might have been different if Grady had known of Brodie's existence.

Brodie wasn't foolish enough to think the man would have wanted him back then. Grady wasn't the picture of father perfection that Brodie had dreamed of. He'd not only been divorced several times over the years, but he'd been rumored to have a penchant for extramarital flings.

At the same time, Brodie was tired of feeling restless when it came to his personal life, as if there was something missing.

A relationship with his father?

Maybe. Not that Brodie had any notions about them becoming

best buds. But maybe if they had the occasional dinner and got to know each other a little, Brodie wouldn't feel so unsettled.

Maybe…

Maybe not.

He didn't know. He only knew that moving to Vegas would at least give him the chance to get to know the man and, possibly, ease the unsettled feeling deep in his gut.

In the meantime…

His gaze caught and held Babe's. Yep, he'd liked her watching him pitch, all right. He'd liked seeing her perched on the fence, her blond ponytail bouncing every time she turned her head to follow his throw. He'd liked feeling her blue eyes on him while he warmed up. And he'd really liked the way her nose crinkled every time she smiled.

He'd liked *her.*

Not that he'd acted on the feeling. He'd been too busy working his ass off to get a scholarship. He hadn't had time for girls.

Even so, the feeling had been there. He'd liked her, all right.

As for her suggestions… Well, he hadn't much cared for those, but they *had* helped improve his pitching arm. Babe was the daughter of a pair of serious baseball fans, after all. A couple so in love with the sport that they'd named their three daughters after their favorite players. She'd been reciting stats before she could walk, and so she knew the game. Her comments way back when had been right on the money.

For that, he owed her. Not to mention, she was the only person who'd never doubted his past. Rather, she'd been excited for him. And hopeful. And not the least bit surprised when Grady Merritt had shown up at Anna Jessup's funeral.

Brodie couldn't very well let her get mixed up with the likes of Cody Cameron.

"He's not likely to say yes if I just come out and ask," she continued, her mind obviously racing, "not when the only thing on his brain when he waltzes in here is ice cream. I mean, what was I thinking? The man needs to be in the right mind-set. To be so turned on that he can't see straight. Then there's no way he'll turn me down."

"True, but the real challenge will be getting him to that point. I doubt reciting stats will have him eating out of your hand."

"You're right. I mean, I can't set a seductive mood if I don't know anything about his personal likes and dislikes. I need to know his favorite food. His favorite song. His favorite color. His favorite position." Determination lit her eyes. "I'll just have to go the distance and find out."

He had a vision of her skulking in the bushes outside Cody's house, watching the shortstop with the same intense blue gaze she'd once reserved for Brodie himself. Something sharp knifed through his gut and he heard himself blurt, "You won't have far to go."

She stared at him. "What's that supposed to mean?"

He reached out and swiped the spot of whipped cream from the corner of her mouth. He raised it to his own, tasted the sweet cream and grinned. "It means, you've got me."

2

"LET ME get this straight," Janie Nolan paused, one hand holding a stack of Slammers' pennants and the other deep in the crate in front of her. Her light brown hair, tied back in the usual ponytail, whipped to the side as she turned a deep brown gaze on Babe. "You not only decided to go through with our whole fantasy idea and proposition Cody Cameron, but you asked Brodie Jessup to help you?"

Babe pulled the last Cody bobble head from a cardboard box and set it on the shelf that ran the length of the wall. They stood in the back room of Round The Bases, the memorabilia shop next door to The Sweet Spot. The area was messy and filled with merchandise, but Babe felt as comfortable here with Janie as she did in her own kitchen.

Babe headed over to Janie's at least once a week after The Sweet Spot closed to help her friend unpack merchandise and to dish about the day's events.

Most of their recent conversations had centered on the Slammers' possible move and Janie's idea about hitting a few home runs of their own before the team relocated.

Tonight was no different, except that Babe had managed to find a bat and was now ready to step up to the plate and start swinging.

"First off, I'm going to seduce Cody—propositioning only works if the person you're proposing to wants to accept and I don't think Cody thinks of me like that." *Talk about an understatement.* "Which means I need to open his eyes and make him see me in a different light. A sexier one. And I didn't ask Brodie. He offered."

"Brodie offered what?" The question came from Callie Andrews who stood in the doorway that separated the front of Janie's shop from the storeroom.

"How did you get in?"

"The front door was unlocked."

"I thought I locked it." Janie left the pennants and started for the front until Callie waved her back to work.

"Don't worry about it. I threw the dead bolt, so no one's coming in."

"Why didn't you use the back door instead of walking all the way through the restaurant?" The back door sat near Callie's office, which made slipping away to see her friends convenient.

"Because I didn't go into the restaurant tonight."

Babe and Janie exchanged surprised looks before eyeing their friend. Callie shrugged. "I took the evening off."

"You never take off from work," Babe said.

"I do now that I have a perfectly competent assistant to handle things in my absence."

"You've always had a competent assistant," Babe reminded her.

"But she hasn't always had a hot man waiting in the wings to show her a good time." Janie grinned and Callie smiled.

"Donovan had a special getaway planned somewhere where I wouldn't be tempted to taste his steak for quality control or stress over the service at the next table."

"Where did he take you?" Janie's eyes gleamed with excitement. "That new restaurant downtown?"

"He's still public enemy number one as far as the good citizens of Louisville are concerned," Babe said. "He's not going to take her anyplace around here. They probably stole away to some quaint inn in a nearby town and had a candlelight dinner."

"We had fried chicken and apple pie on third base at the stadium," Callie told them. "It was very private. For the most part. But toward the end of dessert, one of the security guards had an issue with an angry fan and Donovan had to go to the main office to deal with it. So I walked over here to kill time with the two of you."

"Until Donovan finishes up and takes her home for some wild, frantic sex," Janie teased.

"You mean *more* wild, frantic sex." Callie shrugged. "What can I say? We picnicked while we *picnicked*."

"That explains the smile," Janie said. "Orgasms always do that to me."

But the satisfied look on Callie's face indicated more than just sexual gratification. Something about the restaurant owner had changed since she'd reconciled with her ex-husband. Sure, she was her usual stressed-out self when it came to Diamond, but even during reservation mix-ups or customer complaints, she seemed more at ease than before. Calm. Content.

In love.

Not that that's what Babe envied, mind you. It was the wild, frantic sex part her friend engaged in on a regular basis that stirred a pang of longing.

At least that's what Babe told herself.

Callie collapsed in a nearby chair and crossed her long legs. "So what did Brodie offer?"

"He's going to help Babe seduce Cody Cameron."

"A threesome?" Callie came up short in her chair. "No way."

"No way in hell, heaven or the in-between," Babe informed her friend. "I haven't managed to have a memorable night with one man. I'm certainly not ready to take on two. As if that would ever happen, anyway."

"I don't know. A threesome is one of the top-ten women's fantasies according to the latest *Cosmo* survey," Callie said.

"Oh, I read that, too," Janie added. "That was the one that listed bondage as number one." Callie nodded and Janie went on, "I don't really think about having sex with more than one man, but I wouldn't mind being tied up by the right man."

"Hear! Hear!" Callie grinned.

"Brodie's just going to help me get to know Cody," Babe told them. "So I'll be fully equipped to set up a first-rate seduction."

"Don't you think you're going to an awful lot of trouble?" Janie told her. "You're a sexy woman, Babe. He's a fool if he doesn't notice that right off the bat."

"Thanks," Babe said. "If only things were that easy." But they weren't because nothing had ever come easy to Babe. As a kid, she'd wanted to play softball in the worst way, but she'd totally sucked. While she knew what it took to make a good player, she just didn't have the skill and so she hadn't even bothered to try out for the team. Then she'd set her sights on being a cheerleader like her older sister, but she hadn't been nearly as coordinated. While she'd had the enthusiasm and the passion, she just hadn't had the moves. She'd dropped out during the first round of tryouts rather than risk getting cut.

Babe had always been more of a thinker than a doer. *The smart one.*

All that thinking—and re-thinking—had kept her from following through more times than she could count.

Not this time. She was *doing* this time, following through, regardless of the consequences. At the same time, she intended to do everything possible to make sure those consequences involved Cody, a bed and a toe-curling orgasm.

"Forget all the fuss and just tell him what you want," Callie offered.

"And have him turn me down?"

"He's a man," Janie added. "Men don't turn down free sex."

When Callie cleared her throat, Janie added, "That is, single, healthy, red-blooded, professional baseball-playing men don't turn down free sex. Faithful, committed, loving ex-husbands turn down sex with everyone. Except the person they've committed to, that is." Callie smiled and Janie added, "Besides, Donovan's the team's owner, not a player. In any sense of the word."

"I don't care about Cody's integrity," Babe said. "We're talking one night, not forever. He's hot and he's my fantasy and I fully intend to seduce him just as soon as I'm armed and ready."

Janie arched an eyebrow. "And when does the battle training with Sergeant Brodie commence?"

Babe smiled. "Tomorrow night."

"IF YOU'RE HUNGRY, I can make you something at The Sweet Spot. I've always got sandwich fixings on hand. It's the least I can do since you're helping me out."

"This isn't for me. This is for you." Brodie steered Babe through the doorway of Hot Buns, a new bar and grill in the heart of the sports district, just around the corner from her ice-cream shop. "You want to know what the real Cody Cameron is like? Well, this is it." He motioned to the busy interior. "This is Cody's favorite restaurant."

"I already know that." But she'd never had the chance to see firsthand. She glanced around and noted that most of the patrons were men. With the exception of the waitresses. A bevy of curvy, attractive women clad in Slammers' tank tops and short-shorts rushed here and there. Some carried trays laden with sizzling burgers and homemade hamburger buns. Some served up beers. All had the words HOT BUNS plastered across their shapely rear ends in hot pink lettering. "It's sort of like Hooters, but in reverse. So this is the place that he comes to twice a week."

"How do you know that?"

"I know a lot of things. General information. But I don't know the details." She smiled at Brodie. "That's what you're here for."

Brodie frowned. "He comes in every Friday night with a few of the other players."

Babe nodded and made a mental note as she followed Brodie to the table.

Seduction tip number one—wear revealing clothing. Make that revealing, self-explanatory clothing.

While it was obvious the women had nice buns, it obviously didn't hurt to point out the fact.

"It's not really a place for ladies." Brodie said, once they were seated.

"Actually, it's the opposite. I see plenty of ladies."

Brodie frowned and picked up his menu.

"So what's his poison?" Babe eyed him over her menu. "Is he a nacho man? Does he go for a salad? What?"

"Cody usually orders a double meat with chili and jalapeños."

"Which means he likes things spicy."

"What it means is, he has no consideration for his digestive system and has to pop a roll of Tums before every game. If he doesn't give a fig about himself, what makes you think he's going to be all that in bed?"

She met his intense green stare. "What makes you think he won't be?"

"I just don't want you to be disappointed." He eyed her. "Have you ever thought that maybe, just maybe, he isn't nearly as good as all the rumors floating around?"

Actually, she hadn't really thought about it.

What if he wasn't half as good as she'd built him up to be in her mind?

As soon as the question struck, she pushed it back out. While she knew people exaggerated, she experienced Cody's sex appeal firsthand every Thursday night. If he could tongue-tie her with one glance, she could only imagine what he could do if he actually touched her.

"The sex will be great."

"If you say so."

She frowned. "Can we just get on with this?"

"Be my guest. I'm an open book."

"What does he drink?"

"Beer." When she gave him a pointed stare, he added, "Corona."

"Appetizer?"

"Onion rings."

"Dessert?"

"Chocolate cake."

"Chocolate, huh? And you think we don't have anything in common?" Babe grinned and Brodie frowned.

She watched while he ordered a grilled chicken sandwich and a side salad with low-fat dressing. When the waitress turned a laser-whitened smile on her, as well as a perky pair of breasts, Babe fought down a wave of guilt and opted for a double meat burger.

Not that she intended to eat it all, mind you. But she needed to know what it was that stirred Cody's taste buds, didn't she?

She traded the onion rings for a salad, however, and ordered a diet soda rather than the beer. She'd had both and, to be honest, they gave her indigestion, as well.

The realization made her smile. While she might not be his type, they really did have a few things in common, after all.

"It doesn't bother you that Cody comes to a place like this? A place that blatantly objectifies women?"

"I told you. I want to have sex with him, not marry him."

"That sounds really shallow."

"This from a man who dates more than one woman at a time?" She reminded him of his past—namely, the rumors a few years back that had linked him to not one, but two local socialites and a well-known model.

"They all knew about each other. Besides, I wasn't serious with any of them. It was all about—"

"—sex," she finished for him.

"I was going to say that it was all about enjoying each other's company."

"In other words, sex."

"Actually, we had a lot in common."

"I'm sure Cody and I have some similar interests."

"Sure you do. If the sex fizzles, you can always share a piece of chocolate cake in lieu of an orgasm."

"Actually, I've had some of my best orgasms courtesy of a piece of chocolate cake. Not only are we talking tantalizing, but you get to avoid the whole awkward moment after which makes it that much better." She busied herself opening her notebook rather than staring into his eyes, which seemed to see straight through her to the all-important fact that while she had had some nice chocolate-induced orgasms, they'd been just as ho-hum as the ones she'd had with any man. "I thought you wanted to help me."

"I do. I think this is a crazy idea and I'm trying to change your mind."

"That's not going to happen." She lifted her gaze and met his. "I could really use your help on this. Please."

He stared at her a long moment, and she had the feeling he wanted to toss his napkin down and tell her to forget it.

Instead, he shrugged. "Okay. You can ask me questions and I'll fill you in. But don't expect me to keep my opinion to myself."

"Fair enough. Now what's his favorite music? I'll need to

have something playing in the background when I invite him over to my place."

"Your place? You're going to take him *home?*"

"I can't very well take him to a motel. He would definitely be suspicious and more likely to back out before I get him inside and shift into seduction mode."

"So the plan is to lure him to your house and then kick up the seduction?"

She nodded. "I'm working on this chocolate mousse/ice-cream cake that's to die for—or it will be once I'm done. I figure I'll serve him a sample of my latest creation. Then when he's overwhelmed with the rich, decadent taste, I'll lure him back to my place with the promise of more. That should get him there. From that point, I haven't quite worked out the details. That's what all this is for. So what type of music?"

"He likes rap."

"Any artist in particular?"

He leaned back, folded his arms and eyed her. "Take your pick. He likes them all."

"Could you be a little more specific?"

"Why? Because you can't name a rap artist to save your life?"

"That's not true. I've listened to MC Hammer." He grinned and she frowned. "Okay, so I'm not up on the latest rap music."

"Strike one."

"So what if we don't like the same music? That doesn't mean we'll strike out in bed. What about his favorite color?"

She went on with her questions throughout dinner and jotted down Brodie's answers, minus his opinions, of course.

Because Babe wasn't going to let herself get discouraged this time. She was following through…even if it killed her.

BRODIE WAS READY to call it quits long before they finished their burgers. At the same time, he couldn't seem to make himself leave.

That's what he should have done. Called it quits and left her to figure things out on her own. But he couldn't forget the desperation he'd seen glimmering in the depths of her eyes, and so he stayed.

But he wasn't happy about it.

Except when she smiled the way she was right now as the waitress took her dessert plate. Then it almost seemed worthwhile. For a few heart pounding seconds, that is.

"That was great," she declared. "So what's—"

The shrill ring of his cell killed the rest of her question.

Brodie stared at the Caller ID and panic welled inside him. He pushed to his feet, excused himself and walked toward the front lobby of the restaurant.

"Brodie Jessup," he said once he'd flipped open the phone.

"Hey, Coach. I got a problem."

"Cameron?"

"Yeah."

"What the hell are you doing calling from the hospital?"

"I was helping Lolly move a few things to my place and I dropped her hot rollers on my foot while I was walking up the stairs."

"And?"

"I sprained my big toe."

"Because of a set of hot rollers?"

"We're talking a big-ass set. There must have been fifty of them all attached to this giant tray. Let me tell you, it hurt like a son of a bitch." His voice grew muffled for a moment. "It's okay, baby. It wasn't your fault."

"So what does the doctor say?"

"That I'm going to have a lot of swelling, but if I pack it with ice and elevate it for the next twenty-four hours, I should be good to go for Tuesday's game. I won't make practice tomorrow morning, though. I can't even get my shoe on." His voice grew muffled for a moment. "It's okay, baby," he murmured again. "It really wasn't your fault."

"Who's Lolly."

"My girlfriend."

"You don't have a girlfriend."

"Sure, I do. We're just keeping a low profile. Lolly's got a lot of fans and I don't want her tips to suffer."

"Good thinking. We don't need to give the fans any more reason to hate us right now... Shit." *Lolly. Fans.* The words started to sink in. "You don't mean Lolly as in Lolly Popp? That stripper from The Funky Monkey bar?"

"Her real name's Clara Glump, but that doesn't have as catchy a ring to it, so she changed it. And she's not a stripper. She's a waitress."

"She gives table dances."

"But she doesn't take anything off."

"That's because she's not wearing anything in the first place."

"She is, too. She wears a uniform."

Brodie was about to remind Cameron that the Funky Monkey *uniform* was little more than a thong and a couple of pasties, when the shortstop added, "We've been seeing each other for a few months now." His voice grew serious. "She's really great." The almost reverent way he said the words made it clear he referred to more than just her sexual abilities. "I've never met anyone like her. *Ever.*"

Brodie's gut told him to warn the man off. But there was something almost hopeful in the shortstop's voice. Before Brodie could think better of it, he heard himself say, "Get home and get that foot on ice. We'll have Jack take a look at it in the morning." Jack Burke was the team's orthopedist and the only person Brodie trusted when it came to injuries. The orthopedist had been the one to put his shoulder back together following the accident. Brodie had lost the agility he'd once had when it came to pitching, but, for the most part, he'd regained full range of motion of his right arm. He owed Jack for that. He also owed the man for keeping his crucial players in tip-top shape. Cody included.

"Do you need a ride home?" Brodie asked.

"Lolly drove me over in my car. She'll get me home."

"Rest," Brodie told him. "And no more moving tonight." He folded his phone and slid it back into his pocket. He made his way back to the table to find Babe having a very detailed conversation with the waitress who'd just returned Babe's credit card, along with her receipt.

"So how short is too short?"

"Well, when you're going for a good fit, you want them at least two inches above the curve of your butt cheeks so the flesh plumps out just enough to draw attention, but not enough to make your ass look fat. See?" She hiked her shorts up another inch and sure enough, her bottom seemed to widen.

"Wow. You're right."

"I haven't been the Best Buns calendar centerfold three years running for nothing." She winked at Babe, frowned at Brodie and headed for the bar area.

"So when's our next lesson?" Babe asked as she slid her card into her purse and pushed to her feet. "I want to know *everything* about Cody."

As in, he has a girlfriend and is now completely off-limits.

That news would certainly put an end to her ridiculous plan. At least when it came to Cody. But Brodie couldn't forget her comment that night at The Sweet Spot.

The team has a lot of hot players that have fantasy *written all over them, but I've been lusting after Cody since we were kids....*

If she found out Cody had a girlfriend, there was the very real possibility that she would turn her attention to one of the other guys. Babe had her sights set on one night of hot, passionate lust, complete with a mind-blowing orgasm, and she felt certain his players could deliver.

Crazy.

The last thing she needed was an immature, egotistical man who slept with anything that came along—which described most of the single players on his team. Guys who ogled women at Hot Buns and visited Miss Marla's House of Massage and paid for table dances at The Funky Monkey.

No, if Babe wanted a one-night stand, she needed a knowledgeable lover who not only knew his way around the bedroom and could love her sixty ways 'til Sunday, but one who would consider her feelings, as well.

One piddly-ass orgasm? She called *that* a fantasy?

She needed a man who could give her not one, but a whole damned slew of them. A man considerate enough to make her scream all night and then serve her breakfast in bed the next morning.

A man like Brodie himself.

When the thought struck, he should have pushed it right back out. He would have if he'd been at the ice-cream shop, and she'd been safely across the counter from him and they'd been having one of their usual conversations about home runs or prospective rookies or the like.

Babe was his friend, his buddy, his *pal*.

At the same time, she was a luscious, desirable woman who made his heart pound and his blood rush and his cock as hard as granite, and tonight proved all three. While she wore the same jeans and T-shirt she often sported at the shop, she'd shed the apron and let her ponytail down and there was just something about the way she looked…. Her gaze was so bright and optimistic and hungry that it made him think more about licking her than any of the flavors she sold.

His gut tightened, his muscles bunched and he had the overwhelming urge to see if her lips tasted as sweet as the whipped cream she'd worn the night before.

Get real, guy. This is Babe. She's not just somebody you can sleep with and walk away from the next day.

The warning sounded in his head, reminding him of his no-strings-attached policy when it came to sex. He'd always had too many unresolved issues in his life to risk cluttering it up even more with a relationship. He'd promised himself never to be the type of man who played with a woman's emotions just to get her into bed. He'd heard his mother cry herself to sleep too many times to count, because she'd trusted some man who'd broken her heart. Brody wasn't about to hurt anyone, and he sure as hell didn't intend to get hurt. And so he'd always kept things easy and casual and temporary when it came to women.

Or he used to.

Over the past few years since his accident, he hadn't even done that. He'd kept his nose close to the grindstone, determined to get his coaching career off the ground. Shit, it had been *months* since he'd been with a woman. No wonder he was picturing all sorts of sexy scenarios.

Babe wearing nothing but a whipped cream bikini and a come-and-get-me smile.

Babe wearing nothing but the smile.

Babe...

But the Babe dancing in his head—the same one sitting across from him—wasn't interested in a relationship. She wanted a fantasy. A one-night stand. *Sex.* And so there really was no reason for him to hesitate.

They were a perfect match.

Or they would be once Babe came to the same realization.

"Hello?" Babe's soft voice drew him from his thoughts. She waved a hand in front of his face. "Earth to Brodie? When can we get together again?"

Brodie stared into her expectant gaze. "Tomorrow night after the game. I've got a few commitments right after, but I should be done around nine." He smiled, slow and easy, and watched her bottom lip quiver ever so slightly with awareness. "Then we'll see if we can line up a few Grade A orgasms."

HE DIDN'T mean it literally, of course.

Babe told herself that as she walked into her apartment later that night. Brodie's parting words played over and over in her head.

But it wasn't just the words that made her hands tremble as she pulled off her shirt. It was the way he'd looked at her when he'd said the words.

As if he intended to be the one delivering those orgasms when the time came.

She shook her head and busied herself sliding off her jeans. No way.

No, make that no way in hell.

Brodie didn't like her like that.

She'd seen him every day during her childhood, and at least a few times a week as an adult. Not once had he ever looked at her as if he wanted to nibble his way up and down her body and savor every bite.

Not once.

Not that he didn't enjoy nibbling. She knew his reputation as well as she knew that of each of his players. He might be their manager now, but he was still one of the team at heart. He'd been linked to dozens of women over the years. Beautiful and temporary. That's the way Brodie liked his women. And he liked them often.

Then again, she couldn't really recall any specific mentions of any romantic escapades in the local papers these past few years since he'd stepped up to be coach. Not that it meant he'd adopted a life of celibacy. He would have to keep a low profile now. He was the mother, father and babysitter, to quote him. He would have to set a good example.

She remembered the way several of the waitresses had stared him up and down. Despite the fact that the whole town was angry at the possible move, the women had still been interested in Brodie.

They'd wanted him.

And he'd spent the entire evening staring at Babe.

She turned that fact over in her head for a few, heart-pounding moments before tossing it out along with all the other not-in-this-lifetime-or-any-other thoughts she'd had over the years.

Why, she'd never even fantasized about him. Not once.

Okay, maybe once. But she'd been twelve and he'd been leaving for college and the entire scenario had involved him handing over his letter jacket and giving her a chaste kiss on the lips. The whole thing had fallen into the *Not!* category when it came to fantasies.

Babe's late night thoughts always seemed to fall into two categories. The *Not!* fantasies, which usually involved dating or falling in love or living happily ever after with completely unattainable men. Men too rich or famous or unreachable. Like the time she'd envisioned walking down the aisle with Brad Pitt. *Not!* And the time she'd imagined having babies with Jon Bon Jovi. *Not!* And the time she'd dreamed of dancing cheek to cheek at her senior prom with Brodie Jessup. *Not!*

On the opposite end of the spectrum were the *Why Not?* fantasies. The ones that involved sex only. Sure, they were very intense and a little out of this world, but they were doable if she set her mind to it.

Like now.

She'd never had a *Why Not?* fantasy involving Brodie Jessup. No deep kisses and intimate touches. No licking or sucking or moaning. Nothing. Nada. Zip.

She stared at her reflection in the mirror and remembered a picture she'd seen of Brodie with some hoity-toity socialite in one of the local papers. She'd been tall and thin and brunette. While she'd been educated, she hadn't known a thing about baseball, according to the article. She'd probably never sat in the stands and scarfed down a hot dog in sixty seconds flat. Or shoved her hand into a foam finger and chanted encouragement during a bad call. Or cried—yes, *cried*—when the team had lost a particularly important game.

Brodie liked his women separate from his job. And he liked them clueless. So he couldn't like Babe.

Not like that.

Disappointment spiraled through her.

Disappointment?

No way was she disappointed. She was deprived.

Major deprivation from lack of decent sex. That was the only reason she tossed and turned for the next few hours and replayed the last moments of their conversation. The more she remembered, the sexier his parting smile seemed. His gaze glittered with unspoken promises, and his voice took on a raw, desperate edge when he said the word *orgasms*.

Wishful, desperate, *dangerous* thinking. That's what it was. That's all it was. Which meant she needed to get her plan into motion as quickly as possible.

3

"Mmm... Touch me just like that." Babe clamped her eyes shut and caught her bottom lip against the exquisite sensation of fingertips playing up the inside of her thigh. Her legs fell open as the strong, purposeful touch moved higher.

Her heart pounded, her pulse raced and her breath caught as the touch halted just shy of ground zero. One callused fingertip made a lazy, teasing circle and she grew hotter, wetter, more desperate.

But that was the point. To prolong the pleasure until she ached and burned and begged for more.

He stroked and played around the sensitive folds and they swelled in anticipation.

And then he touched her.

One fingertip rasped from her clit down and back up again, tracing the slit and making her gasp. Pleasure drenched her senses. The fingertip parted her, paused and then pushed deep. So deliciously deep that she arched up off the bed, her body grasping at the intimate touch, eager for more.

He didn't oblige her. Not yet. Instead, he withdrew, so slowly that she felt every nerve-racking slide of his skin against hers, until he pulled completely free.

She opened her mouth to ask for more the way she always did when they were together, but before the breathless *please* could tremble from her lips, he slid back in.

Unlike the other times, he seemed to know what she wanted now and he gave it to her.

He touched her so deep until she quivered and gasped. Heat coiled in her stomach, winding tighter and tighter until her entire body went rigid. And then he pulled back.

"Wait," she murmured. "You're not supposed to stop. Not until we're finished."

"I'm not stopping," he replied, his deep, husky, familiar voice drawing her eyes open. "I'm slowing down and taking my time."

Babe stared up at the handsome, hunky man who leaned over her, his green gaze bright and hot and hungry. Her heart stalled, and then stopped altogether because it wasn't Cody Cameron who smiled down at her. It was...

Babe bolted to a sitting position, her heart pounding its way through her rib cage. She lay atop her favorite down comforter, her T-shirt hiked up above her waist, her panties lost in the tangle of sheets to her left. Her handy vibrator sat on the nightstand, ready for phase two of the fantasy.

Only she hadn't gotten that far this time because the scenario hadn't gone quite the way it usually did.

Brodie Jessup?

She drew a deep breath and threw her legs over the side of the bed. A few moments later, she stood in the bathroom and splashed cold water onto her face.

Brodie?

The name echoed through her head and denial rushed through her.

But she'd *never...* That is, she couldn't... Not *now... Not* when she had to see him tonight.

Forget deprived. She'd passed that days ago, along with irrational and needy.

Now she was just plain *desperate.*

She needed a phenomenal orgasm in the worst way. So badly, in fact, that she was starting to get ideas about Brodie, of all people.

Not that she *really* wanted him, mind you. Not really.

Babe told herself that over the next hour as she dressed,

guzzled black coffee and headed for the ice-cream shop for what would undoubtedly be a very busy Saturday.

It was game day, after all.

While the good folks of Louisville weren't exactly thrilled with the Slammers at the moment, the initial uproar following the announcement had died down. The anger had cooled to simmering resentment and a cynical curiosity that had most fans still flocking to the stadium for home games. It was as if the people of Louisville were looking for a reason to hate the Slammers that much more.

So far, the team had been on a winning streak, which made everyone that much more resentful.

At the same time, all good things had to come to an end.

She told herself that, but she'd yet to really feel the impact of the team's move. As the season drew to a close, however, the fans would lose heart completely and the resentment would surge again. Ticket sales would drop. Traffic at the sports complex would slow down. And the demand for her infamous Cody Cameron Explosion and the Brodie Jessup Jubilee would take a sharp turn south. The interest in any and all things Slammer would fall, as well, and Janie's place would surely take a hit. Likewise, Callie's restaurant would suffer. With the team gone, Diamond would lose the celebrity atmosphere it had become famous for.

They would each suffer.

But would they bite the big one? Hardly.

Callie's restaurant would survive—the food *was* spectacular, with or without a few players scarfing it down. And Babe had a line of desserts that she sold to area restaurants—Diamond included—that had nothing to do with the team and everything to do with an abundance of all natural, mouthwatering ingredients. She would make it, as well. With or without the team. She wasn't as sure about Janie's place. It was a memorabilia shop, after all.

Babe shook off the worry and unlocked the back door of The Sweet Spot. A half hour later, the kitchen was in full swing. She had her mixer going with the latest recipe she'd been perfecting for a cake that was a cross between a chilled mousse and a rich ice cream, a classic rock song drifted from the small stereo in the corner and sunshine streamed through the front windows of the outer shop and pushed through the small round windows set into the swinging doors that separated the kitchen from the ice-cream counter.

It was a typical Saturday morning.

If only it didn't feel more like Saturday night.

Her heart pounded and her hands trembled and she couldn't seem to push Brodie's image from her mind. Or the fantasy. Or the fact that she'd been *this* close to having an orgasm.

A spectacular orgasm. That's where she'd been heading.

A fantasy, she reminded herself. That's all last night had been. The reality wouldn't be nearly as good. Sure, Brodie was one heck of a gorgeous man, and he'd had his own reputation back in his playing days, but he'd reverted to his usual determined, focused, responsible, workaholic self since stepping in as coach for the team.

Workaholic men were *not* the stuff of fantasies.

Which meant she needed to lose the crazy, delusional notion that she'd felt something with Brodie those few moments when they'd said good-night at Hot Buns and get back to the business of building her arsenal of information. Then she could formulate a clear, concise plan to seduce Cody Cameron.

Cody.

He was her fantasy man. The numero uno of her explicit, carnal thoughts. The top dog in the hunky pound of her erotic musings. The—

"I have to use your laptop."

Babe dropped the spatula she'd been using to fold egg whites into her batter and whirled to see the young woman who'd just pushed through the double swinging doors separating the front of the shop from the kitchen. She wore the traditional Sweet Spot uniform—jeans and a crisp white T-shirt with the shop's name in bright pink lettering. A matching pink ball cap sat on the young woman's head.

Stacey Beech was one of a trio of local college kids who

worked for Babe on game days. They dished up ice cream, whipped shakes and built sundaes for the crowd of regulars who filled the sports complex before, during and after the big event. Stacey had the early shift today. A fact that had totally slipped Babe's mind, along with how many egg whites she'd just used in her new masterpiece.

"You scared the daylights out of me," she told Stacey as she fished the utensil out of the batter and reached for a hand towel. "Is it time to open up already?"

"Five minutes to go." Stacey set her purse in the small locker that sat off to the side of the kitchen next to several large shelves. "I need to hurry. So can I?"

"Can you what?" She set the towel aside.

"Use your computer?" She gave Babe an odd look. "Are you okay? You look sort of flushed?"

"I'm fine. Fine." *Not.* Babe tossed the batter-covered spatula into a large, commercial sink and retrieved another from her utensil drawer. "So why do you need my computer?"

"Lena Trumpet from KOOL, one of the country music stations, has a contest going right now to rename the Slammers." Stacey reached for the bright pink apron that hung on a nearby peg and hooked it over her head. "The winner gets free tickets to see Tim McGraw and I want to e-mail her my suggestion."

"Sounds like fun." But not half as much fun as Babe had been having last night during her fantasy.

She shook away the sudden thought, set her mixer on the low cycle and followed the young woman to the small room that sat just beyond the kitchen. It housed a desk and a computer and large file cabinet. Stacey settled herself in Babe's leather chair and double clicked the Internet icon.

"I know I'm going to win," Stacey declared as she logged on to the radio station's Web site. "I've got a feeling."

Stacey always had a feeling. She was a contest junkie who entered everything from the weekly Name That Vegetable down at the local Piggly Wiggly to Lubed For Life, the free oil change sweepstakes sponsored by the town's largest car care garage.

Other than having a special breed of new organic squash named after her cat, Juicy, she'd never actually won anything.

"Some of the suggestions are so lame," Stacey went on.

"Such as?"

"Las Vegas Losers. Nevada Nitwits." She shook her head. "That's too obvious. I think they should go for something more creative."

"Desert Dopes?" Babe offered her suggestion and ignored the niggle of guilt. She'd always been a loyal person and she'd been a baseball fan since she was five years old. While the Slammers, her home team, might be leaving at the end of the season, they hadn't packed their bags yet. "Desert Devils?" she added to soothe her conscience.

"I was thinking more like Desert Dumbasses."

So much for being supportive.

"It says Vegas," Stacey went on. "It says the Slammers are idiots for leaving Louisville. 'Nuff said." She typed in her suggestion and clicked Send. "Thanks again." She pushed to her feet, straightened her apron and reached for the radio. "Do you mind if we listen to the rest of her show in case she reads my suggestion?"

"Help yourself."

Stacey set the station and adjusted the volume to a modest level. A familiar female voice read the call numbers for KOOL before fading into an upbeat Gretchen Wilson song.

Stacey went to the front to turn on the open sign while Babe shifted her attention back to her work and tried to forget everything except the white chocolate mousse currently taking shape in her mixing bowl.

Tried, mind you. But she wasn't nearly as successful as she would have liked.

By the time she finished a sample of the new dessert and cut it into small wedges to hand out to the customers that had begun filtering into the shop on their way to the stadium, she was wound as tight as a starter who'd been benched over a poor call.

A state that didn't go unnoticed by her loyal employees.

"What's up with you?" Jake asked her just after noon when

he accidentally bumped her arm and she dropped an entire quart of M & M candies.

Jake had sandy blond hair and brown eyes, and drew in almost as much business as the Slammers themselves. He'd been captain of his high school baseball team and now pitched for the local junior college. He had a great arm, a lot of promise and a fan club of college girls who regularly flocked in to get a glimpse of him.

"You seem nervous," he went on.

"I'm fine."

"You look flushed." Stacey came up next to him. "Are you worried about today's game?"

"There's no reason to worry," Darla added. Darla was employee number three and reminded Babe the most of herself at that age. She attended Louisville's leading cooking school—Babe's alma mater—and had her sights set on a career as a pastry chef. While Stacey and Jake served customers, Darla whipped up cones and waffle bowls with Babe in the kitchen. She was smart, focused and totally invisible to the opposite sex, thanks to mousy brown hair and an overly abundant figure. "I heard on the way in that the Slammers are still the favorites to win. The Red Sox haven't beaten them in four seasons."

"I know. It's not that." Babe hadn't given the game a second thought. A fact that made her employees all the more suspicious because Babe *lived* for games. She always listened from start to finish.

Today, it had been Jake who'd tuned the radio in to the local sports channel a half hour ago when the broadcast had started.

"If it's not the game, then what is it?" Darla asked.

"Yeah," Stacey chimed in. "What?" She stared long and hard before an idea seemed to strike. "Oh, my gosh, you've got a date, don't you?"

Babe almost dropped the plastic container she'd been using to scoop up the candies. "A date?" she blustered. It wasn't like she had a *real* date with Brodie. They were meeting, of course, but it was strictly in the interest of a third party rather than any mutual attraction. Despite the fantasy. "Why would you say that?"

"Well," Stacy dropped to her knees and started to help Babe

scoop. "It *is* Saturday night. You're jumping out of your skin at every turn. That says hot date to me."

"A date?" Darla looked totally mystified and Jake just grinned his usual heart-stopping grin, causing the table full of girls in the far corner to start to giggle.

"I don't," Babe said firmly. "I mean, I do have a meeting with someone, but we're just friends." Her stomach fluttered. "Just two people who aren't the least bit attracted to one another, getting together to share information." The fluttering continued and Brodie's image lingered in her head.

Stacey grinned. "So you *do* have a date." She exchanged knowing looks with Jake.

Babe opened her mouth to argue the point, but it would only make her sound defensive. Which made her appear guilty. Which made her seem interested.

And she was *not* interested in Brodie Jessup.

At least that's what she was telling herself.

"I think we should all get back to work." She busied herself scooping up the last of the spilled candies and ignored the curious gazes of her employees. Soon they turned back to their duties and Babe breathed a sigh of relief.

Relief?

If only.

But over the next few hours, as the Slammers lost to the Boston Red Sox in a pathetic show, Babe's panic grew.

Not because of the loss.

Her time was running out. A *date*.

She did her best to remain cool, calm and as disinterested as any woman getting together with an old friend later that evening. But while her brain knew the truth, her body didn't seem to be catching on.

Her blood raced as she scooped flavor after flavor for the disgruntled fans who crowded into the shop to eat ice cream and talk trash about the team. Her hands trembled as she sprinkled nuts and dunked spoonfuls of chocolate sauce. Her stomach growled as she mixed scrumptious shakes and squirted dollops of whipped cream.

By the time she heard the last "Bye-bye, losers," served the final ice-cream cone, wiped down the counters and said goodnight to her employees, Babe felt like a woman on the verge of something desperate and dangerous.

She turned off the pink neon open sign that hummed in the window and straightened one forgotten chair as she walked through the small dining area toward the counter. She was this close to closing the glass top on the freezer display when her hand stalled.

The various flavors of ice cream called her name, promising satisfaction if she would just pick up a spoon. Likewise, the containers of candy toppings and mix-ins danced around her, teasing and tempting her with their bright colors and delicious scents. The row of sauces—everything from chocolate to butterscotch to rich, creamy caramel—begged her to dip a finger inside and take a taste. Or two. Or three.

Enough to sate the hunger consuming her, making her heart pound and her blood rush and her thoughts whirl.

She wouldn't… She couldn't…

Babe reached for the nearest spoon.

After a fifteen-minute tastefest that should have sated her sweet tooth for a full year, she didn't feel any more satisfied than when she'd started. Her nerves still buzzed and her tummy twisted this way and that. Anticipation coiled deep inside her.

Because she still wanted something more. Something basic and primitive and *carnal*.

Drawing a shaky breath, she headed for the small office located just beyond her kitchen. While she knew that what she was about to do wouldn't come anywhere close to satisfying her, it would be enough to take the edge off and keep her from doing something completely and totally stupid.

Like throwing herself into Brodie's arms, ripping off his clothes and begging him to finish what he'd started in last night's fantasy.

Not happening, she reminded herself as she shut her office door, sank into her desk chair and opened her bottom drawer.

She pulled out a small leather case and retrieved the vibrator she'd bought for herself last year during a naughty party she,

Callie and Janie had attended. She shimmied her jeans down, eased back in her chair and hit the on button.

BRODIE HAD NEVER been one to waste time when it came to something he wanted. Being aggressive was crucial in professional sports. But kissing Babe before they'd so much as said hello wasn't exactly what he had in mind when he walked into The Sweet Spot later that night.

He'd already come up with his strategy. He planned to tempt her throughout dinner and fan the flames that already blazed between them. Then, once the fire raged out of control, he would make his move. A kiss. A touch. Nothing extreme. Just enough to push her over the edge and get her to admit her attraction to him.

Then she would forget all about Cody, and she and Brodie would get busy turning her fantasy into a reality.

He didn't anticipate the soft, breathless sounds that came from behind her closed office door when he walked into her shop. Or the deep, throaty moan that slid into his ears as he stepped closer. The sound spiraled straight to his already hard dick and made him think that strategy was highly overrated.

And then she opened the door and convinced him even more.

With her hair mussed, her cheeks flushed, eyes glowing, bottom lip slick and full and trembling, she was the sexiest woman he'd ever seen. Just like that he forgot everything—his plan, the crummy game, the firing squad of a press conference that had followed—*everything* except pulling her close and tasting her right then and there.

The instant his lips touched hers, raw desire sliced through him, so sharp and sweet that his heart stood still. He caught her surprised gasp, and then she softened. Her mouth opened and she kissed him back. She tasted wild and sweet and intoxicating, like the ripe strawberries she spooned into her thick, decadent ice cream shakes.

Lust rushed through him and gripped his body in a tight squeeze that lodged the breath in his lungs. His testicles throbbed and swelled, and suddenly he couldn't taste her deep enough or fast enough. He tilted his head and sucked her tongue into his mouth.

Her hands slid up his chest and around his neck. Her fingers curled into the hair at the nape of his neck and she leaned into him. Her breasts pressed against his chest and her hard nipples burned into him through their clothing. He slid his hands around her waist to the small of her back and drew her even closer, as if he could absorb her luscious heat through the clothes that separated their bodies.

He cupped her round ass and pressed his growing erection into the cradle of her thighs. He fit perfectly and he knew beyond a doubt that they would be good together. So good that the notion scrambled his common sense and upped his body temperature to a dangerous level. One kiss turned into one hell of a long kiss. He devoured her with his mouth for what seemed like forever before the familiar ring of his cell phone finally penetrated the haze of lust that engulfed them.

Long, but not long enough, a voice whispered as he tore his mouth from hers and gasped for air.

His cell phone gave a few frantic beeps that indicated the call had gone to his voice mail, and reality sank in.

He'd deviated from his own plan and it had backfired. The whole point was to tempt her. Instead, he was the one ready to bust his pants at the moment.

And Babe?

Her eyes were closed, her full lips quivering just enough to tell him she'd liked the kiss. She'd liked it a lot. She had the dreamy look about her of a woman well satisfied.

Until she opened her eyes. He saw the surprise in the bright blue depths and recognized the mix of emotion pushing and pulling inside her.

No. Yes. Now. Wait. Whoa…

He recognized it because he felt the same things. Too many things for one friggin' kiss.

Even if it had been pretty damned terrific.

No more, he vowed to himself. He wanted her past the push-pull. He wanted her hot for him.

His body throbbed at the thought, and he swallowed.

Blazing hot. The sooner the better.

An Important Message from the Editors

Dear Reader,

Because you've chosen to read one of our fine novels, we'd like to say "thank you"! And, as a special way to thank you, we're offering you a choice of two more of the books you love so well, and a surprise gift to send you – absolutely FREE!

Please enjoy them with our compliments...

Pam Powers

Peel off Seal and Place Inside...

FREE GIFT
EDITOR'S SEAL · THANK YOU

What's Your Reading Pleasure...
ROMANCE? _OR_ SUSPENSE?

Do you prefer spine-tingling page turners OR heart-stirring stories about love and relationships? Tell us which books you enjoy – and you'll get 2 FREE "ROMANCE" BOOKS or 2 FREE "SUSPENSE" BOOKS with no obligation to purchase anything.

Choose "ROMANCE" and get **2 FREE BOOKS** that will fuel your imagination with intensely moving stories about life, love and relationships.

Choose "SUSPENSE" and you'll get **2 FREE BOOKS** that will thrill you with a spine-tingling blend of suspense and mystery.

FREE!

FREE!

Whichever category you select, your 2 free books have a combined cover price of $11.98 or more in the U.S. and $13.98 or more in Canada.

And remember... just for accepting the Editor's Free Gift Offer, we'll send you 2 books and a gift, ABSOLUTELY FREE!

YOURS FREE! We'll send you a fabulous surprise gift absolutely FREE, just for trying "Romance" or "Suspense"!

Order online at
www.FreeBooksandGift.com

THE EDITOR'S "THANK YOU" FREE GIFTS INCLUDE:

▶ 2 Romance OR 2 Suspense books

▶ An exciting surprise gift

YES! I have placed my Editor's "thank you" Free Gifts seal in the space provided at right. Please send me the 2 FREE books which I have selected, and my FREE Mystery Gift. I understand that I am under no obligation to purchase anything further, as explained on the back of this card.

PLACE
FREE GIFTS
SEAL
HERE

Check one:

| ROMANCE |
| 193 MDL EE39 393 MDL EE4M |

| SUSPENSE |
| 192 MDL EE4L 392 MDL EE4X |

FIRST NAME

LAST NAME

ADDRESS

APT.#

CITY

STATE/ PROV.

ZIP/POSTAL CODE

▶ DETACH AND MAIL CARD TODAY! ▶

© 1998 MIRA BOOKS

(ED1-HQN-06)

The Reader Service — Here's How It Works:

"I…" she started, her tongue darting out to sweep her trembling bottom lip. "What was that—"

"Let's go," he cut in, reaching for her hand and tugging her along after him. "We've got reservations."

"So THIS is Cody's favorite upscale restaurant?" Babe stared at the candlelit interior of Whiskey Creek, a western-themed bar and restaurant located a few blocks from the stadium.

"Actually, it's mine." He grinned and her heart skipped the way it had been doing every time he looked at her since he'd kissed her.

The kiss.

Her lips still tingled, even though an hour had passed. While she'd wondered if the heat she'd glimpsed in his gaze last night had been real or imagined, the kiss left no doubt that Brodie Jessup wanted her.

Bad.

She'd felt a momentary rush of joy at the realization before sanity had given her a good swift kick. If Brodie wanted her and she fantasized about him, then what the hell were they doing sitting here talking about Cody?

She meant to ask him. At the same time, a small part of her still feared that she might be reading more into the whole thing.

Okay, so it was more like a minute part, but it was still there. Still stirring her doubt. And so she decided to kick back and follow his lead. If he really and truly wanted her, he would kiss her again.

Unless he wants you to kiss him.

As soon as the thought struck, she pushed it aside. While Babe had nothing against aggressive women, she'd never been one to gamble on anything other than a sure thing.

If he *really* wanted her, he would kiss her again.

HE DIDN'T kiss her again.

Despite the fact that he had plenty of opportunity. They sat at a small secluded table in a far corner of the restaurant. The place was full, but none of the guests bothered them to hash over the day's loss or ask for an autograph. They wouldn't because they were angry and hurt by the possible move.

Babe didn't blame them and she might have felt the same if she hadn't been too busy feeling Brodie's thigh brush against hers whenever he shifted in his chair. Or his fingers play over hers when he reached to sample a bite of her steak. Or his mouth so close to her ear when he leaned over to ask her if she wanted more wine.

He didn't kiss her, but he didn't have to. She felt just as giddy when he simply stared at her mouth. Her nipples tingled as fiercely when he slid his arm around her shoulders. And when he licked a drop of wine that had dribbled down her finger, she all but came right then and there. The dark desire swimming in his intense green gaze told her he recognized her reaction, and he liked it.

By the time the evening drew to a close, she knew beyond a doubt that he wanted her, and that things truly had shifted beyond friendship. Last night had been about changing her mind. But tonight... Tonight was about the two of them and lots of kisses and s-e-x.

At least, that's what she thought until she found herself standing in the doorway of her apartment. She watched him step onto the elevator at the end of the hallway. His parting "See ya" echoed in her head.

She'd obviously been wrong.

That's what she told herself. But as she stomped around the apartment, shedding clothes and telling herself she didn't need him, anyway, she couldn't help but wonder why—*why*—he'd walked away. It wasn't as if she hadn't been more than receptive to his advances. She'd welcomed them.

She just hadn't initiated any advances of her own.

The truth crystallized as she stared into the mirror at her reflection and noted the flush to her cheeks and the glitter in her gaze. She looked like a woman who wanted to have hot, wild sex.

But she didn't act like one.

She hadn't acted, period. She'd played it safe, waiting for his next move. Afraid to make a move of her own for fear that she would fail. The way she'd been doing her entire life.

Before she could stop herself, she reached for the phone and punched in Brodie's cell number. It had been over an hour since he'd left and he was probably sound asleep and—

"Yeah?" his deep voice cut into her thoughts after the first ring.

"Can you come back?" she blurted. Without waiting for a reply, she rushed on, "I need you. I really need you."

Silence followed, as if he were waiting for more and she felt as if she were back in the ninth grade at junior varsity volleyball tryouts. As she'd sat there waiting for her name to be called to try out, she'd watched the other girls serve and slam and pass— her older sister among them—and she'd worried the entire time that she wouldn't be good enough. She'd been so worried, in fact, that she'd stood and walked out of the gym without even trying.

The same worry bubbled up inside her and before she could stop herself, she blurted, "I need you, that is, for a, um, trial run."

"Excuse me?"

"I think I've got enough for a full-fledged seduction, but I'd really like to go through the motions at least once before the real thing."

"You want to *practice* on me?"

"If you don't mind."

Another silence followed and she feared he would still refuse. Worse, she fully expected him to tell her which way to get off and just how far to go. She wouldn't blame him. It wasn't exactly, "I want you because you're my fantasy." But old habits died hard, and Babe had never been one to put herself out there.

Even if she suddenly wanted to.

"Please," she heard her own voice, soft and pleading, slice through the tension.

"I'll be there in a half hour."

4

WHEN BRODIE arrived at Babe's apartment, he half expected her to meet him at the door wearing nothing but a pair of ridiculously high heels, bright red lipstick and a smile.

She pulled open the door and the picture she made was even better.

His gaze swept from her pale blond hair pulled back in a loose ponytail to her toes and back up again. Her soft, fuzzy pink bathrobe was belted loosely at the waist. The edges parted just enough to reveal one creamy white thigh that tapered down to a shapely calf and trim ankle. Pink-tipped toes rested on the hardwood floor. She drew in a startled breath and her cleavage played a quick game of peekaboo with him. Bright, startled blue eyes met his, and his stomach hollowed out the way it had that very first day when they'd been kids and she'd climbed onto the fence to watch him work on his fastball.

At the same time, his reaction was different now. More potent. More dangerous. Because they were all grown up now. Where a warm sense of camaraderie had existed way back when, a blazing hot chemistry had now taken its place.

His chest hitched, his groin tightened and it took everything he had not to press her up against the nearest wall and sink himself into her hot, tight body.

But somewhere in the back of his head, he remembered that *she* was supposed to be seducing *him*. And so he held himself in check. His breaths came quickly and his heart raced as if he were about to step up to the plate and hit the ball out of the park.

"That was really fast," she blurted. "I didn't expect you for another fifteen minutes."

"I made every light." His gaze caught and held hers. "And broke every speeding law between here and my place."

"Oh." As realization hit and she seemed to note the hunger in his gaze, her voice softened. "*Oh.*" As if she'd just noticed her appearance, she lifted a hand to push at a strand of hair that had come loose from her ponytail. "I was just about to get dressed."

"I thought the whole idea was to get *un*dressed."

She grinned and the tension between them eased just enough so he could breathe. "If all goes well." She motioned behind her. "Come on in and have a seat while I get ready." She led Brodie into the living room and then disappeared down the hall.

He wasn't sure what he'd expected Babe's place to look like, but this wasn't it. She'd always been such a tomboy and so the cream-colored sofa strewn with pink throw pillows caught him off guard. A dark cherrywood coffee table supported a pair of crystal candleholders, along with several issues of *Cosmo* magazine.

But it was the copy of *Sports Illustrated* peeking from beneath the stack that brought a smile to his lips and eased the tightness in his muscles. He drank in the rest of the room and noted even more candleholders situated here and there. On the dark cherrywood bookshelf. The fireplace mantel. The big-screen TV that sat off to the side.

While the overall colors were ultrafeminine, the room itself wasn't overly girlie. No knickknacks or stuffed animals or overabundance of plants. It was tasteful and low-key and comfortable.

And even more, it felt warm. Familiar even.

Unfortunately, he was wound too tight to relax.

A fluffy rug in the same shade as the sofa covered the hardwood floor and cushioned his steps as he sank down into a nearby armchair to wait.

An agonizing five minutes later, the strike of a match sizzled in the air. He turned to see her standing in the living room doorway. She wore hot-pink short-shorts fashioned after the ones worn at Hot Buns. A Slammers' T-shirt shaped her voluptuous breasts. Her nipples pressed against the soft cotton and desire knifed through him. She wasn't wearing a bra.

He couldn't help but wonder if she'd left anything else off beneath the barely-there shorts.

A dozen images filled his head, along with the sweet scent of vanilla and cinnamon and something he couldn't quite name as she sashayed from candleholder to candleholder. She walked to the wall switch and turned the adjustable lighting. A soft glow of flickering light pushed back the shadows and danced off the pale walls.

"You're much too tense," she said a heartbeat before she came around to stand behind him. Warm fingertips closed over his shoulders. Her touch heated him through the thin material of his T-shirt and his groin tightened. "You really need to relax."

He meant to keep his eyes open. After all, he wasn't like most of his players who visited Miss Marla's House of Massage twice a week to be touched and pampered by a bunch of beautiful women. Brodie kept his head on straight and his mind on business, and if his shoulder started to ache he simply rubbed a tube of Icy Hot into his aching muscles and went on about his business.

Babe kneaded harder and his eyelids drifted closed. He had to admit, there was something to this whole massage thing. If Marla's girls could do even a fourth of what Babe was doing, it was no wonder the place attracted half the team on a regular basis.

Babe continued working on him, and his muscles screamed with relief for the next few minutes.

"You're loosening up, but you're still wound too tight. I think it's the clothes. You can't get the full effect with your shirt still on." Her arms came down and she tugged at the hem of his T-shirt.

He leaned forward and let her peel the soft cotton up and over his head. Cool air soothed over his heated flesh, but it did little to ease the fire that burned his body from the inside out.

"There," she breathed. "Now we can really work the kinks out." Her bare hands touched him. Her fingertips burned into his skin, and heat swamped his body. His breath caught and he seriously doubted his ability to breathe. But then she started rubbing and pressing and kneading, and the air eased from his lungs.

For the next fifteen minutes, her soft hands pushed and pulled and worked at his shoulders and upper arms until he all but melted into the chair.

"There's nothing like a full body massage to really get the blood flowing," she murmured. "To all the right places." Her hands disappeared for a moment before he felt them close around the back of his neck. They were warm and slick and scented with oil. "It's Miss Marla's special blend," she murmured as her fingertips slid across his skin, spreading the oil and massaging it in. His skin tingled and his nostrils flared with the fragrant, intoxicating scent.

"What exactly is that?"

"A mixture of base and essential oils. An essential oil is very powerful. It promotes vigor and lust. At least that's what Marla said. And she should know. She's an expert."

Babe said the last word directly into his ear. A heartbeat later, he felt the warm rush of her breath and the soft flick of her tongue along his earlobe. The sensation was subtle, but it sent a delicious ripple through his body that landed smack dab in his lap.

His blood rushed and his pulse raced and where he'd been relaxing a few seconds ago, every muscle in his body suddenly went on high alert.

"Easy," she breathed when his entire body stiffened in reaction to his growing hard-on. "Just smell and feel." Her hands slicked down his chest, spreading the oil onto his muscles and swirling the hair on his chest. Her palms rasped against his nipples and his breath caught. "It feels good, doesn't it?" She'd didn't wait for his answer. She came around him then and knelt before him. Her hands went to his chest again and he watched as her pink-tipped nails flicked his nipples, tugged and pulled until they were rock-hard nubs. Then her hands moved lower, down his abdomen. She toyed at his belly button a moment before following the dark funnel of hair to where it disappeared beneath his jeans.

Her glistening fingertips plucked at the button of his jeans and the opening slid free. She grasped his zipper, but it wouldn't tug down over the substantial bulge in his pants. He covered her hand with his and helped her ease the zipper down.

She caught the edge of his underwear and tugged it down until the dark head of his erection sprang forward. Her fingertips touched the smooth ridge and swirled around it.

He wanted to close his eyes and savor the sensation. At the same time, he couldn't look away. The sight of her mesmerized him. Her skin was such a stark contrast against his own, her pale white fingertips so soft and slick against the ripe purple head of his penis.

She pulled his underwear lower and stroked him, tracing the veins that bulged along his length until he sucked in his breath and his body tensed.

He touched her then, one hand on her shoulder while the other cupped her cheek and forced her gaze up to meet his. He had the insane urge to tell her he knew the whole pretense of a "practice" session was pure bullshit and that she wanted him, plain and simple. He'd heard it in the quiver of her voice when she'd called him earlier, seen it in the flash of pleasure in her gaze when she'd realized that he'd damned near killed himself getting to her as fast as possible. She might not want to admit it, but he knew.

Because he felt the exact same way.

The past few days with her had stirred deep, dormant feelings. A mix of emotion he'd felt as a kid, yet hadn't been mature enough to act on. The pleasure in having her near. The need to see her smile. The disappointment when he'd left for college while she'd waved to him from her front porch. The fear that he would never, ever see her again.

He barely resisted the urge to turn, press her into the sofa and plunge deep into her body over and over until she told him the truth. He needed to hear it in the worst way.

But then she licked the tip of his cock and sensation exploded in his brain. He forgot everything except the fire burning between them.

Her tongue traced a pattern around the bulging head as she cupped his testicles. She loved him with her mouth for several, heart-pounding moments, pushing him to the breaking point.

Need kicked in and before he could think, he turned the tables on her. He hauled her onto the couch, pressed her into the soft cushions and kissed her.

She hesitated, as if shocked and scared at the sudden tip of the scale in his favor.

"Wait." She twisted her head to the side and braced her

palms against his shoulders. "I'm supposed to be seducing you," she murmured.

"Mission accomplished." He lapped at her bottom lip.

"But I haven't done my striptease yet. Or the lap dance."

"You'll get your chance. Later. Right now, I need to kiss you before I lose my mind."

Desire fired in her gaze and her palms slid around his neck. He had a brief glimpse of her full lips curving into a smile before his mouth settled over hers.

Brodie pushed his tongue inside, stroking and sucking until she opened her mouth even wider and tilted her head to the side. He deepened the kiss and slid his hands under the material of her short-shorts. *Nothing.* The thought registered as his fingers pressed into the lush curve of her bare ass. Heat scorched his fingertips and ignited a flame that spiraled through his body and fireballed in his groin.

A soft moan vibrated from her mouth as she curled her hands up around his neck, her fingers insistent at the base of his skull as she held him close. Her legs shifted slightly apart. Her pelvis cradled the hard-on that was getting harder by the second.

He pulled her even closer and deepened the kiss, drinking her in like a player starved for water after a knockdown, drag-out game. But he couldn't get enough of her. She wasn't close enough and so he held her tighter. He couldn't taste enough and so he kissed her even deeper and longer and more thoroughly. His heart pounded and his nerves buzzed. He pulled one hand from beneath her and slid his fingers between her legs. Her essence drenched his skin as he traced the pad of his finger over the soft swollen tissue. She gasped.

He caught the sound with his lips and slid his finger lower. He pushed into her just a fraction. She moaned this time, and her fingers curled around his neck. She whimpered, begging for more, and he gave it to her. He pushed all the way inside in a swift motion that made her cry out.

The sound was enough to penetrate the passionate haze that surrounded him and he instantly stilled his movements. Resting his forehead against hers, he fought to catch his breath and gather his control.

He wanted her wild and screaming in ecstasy. There was no doubt about that. But not yet. Brodie wasn't heading for a home run until he'd touched all the bases.

Slow and easy, he withdrew his finger and ignored the way her body clutched at him, trying to draw him deeper. She shuddered when he pulled completely free.

Babe didn't want to open her eyes. Things had been going so well. He'd been out of control and past the point of return and now… He'd stopped.

Which could only mean one thing.

He hadn't been past the point of return. Because she hadn't pushed him over the edge, or driven him crazy, or seduced him to the point of wild, crazy sex.

"Look at me." His deep voice trembled in her ears.

"No." She caught her bottom lip and fought back the dread. "It didn't work."

"Babe."

"I knew I should have done the striptease. That was the clincher. Then you'd be out of your mind instead of stopping and—"

"*Babe!*" The desperation in his voice urged her eyes open and she stared up into his hungry gaze. Desire raged bright and fierce, turning his green eyes a deep, vivid jade.

Wait a second. Desire?

"You stopped," she said accusingly.

"I slowed down." He dropped a kiss onto her lips and murmured, "But hell will freeze over before I stop."

His words slid into her ears and her mouth went dry. Her thighs trembled, and warmth pooled between her legs. It was a reaction she'd felt before—she wasn't a virgin, after all—but never this intensely.

He kissed her again, slow and deep this time, and she found herself caught up in a wave of pleasure as he made love to her with his mouth until she clung to him and clutched at his shoulders.

Before she knew what was happening, he picked her up and started down the hall, his lips never once breaking contact with hers. Several kisses later, he slid her down the length of his hard, hot body until her feet touched the floor near her bed.

He pulled the clingy T-shirt up and over her head. Dipping his head, he caught one nipple between his teeth. He flicked the ripe tip with his tongue before opening his mouth wider. He drew her in, sucking her so hard and long that she gasped for air. A moan curled up her throat.

He stopped long enough to unfasten her short-shorts and peel the material down her legs. His fingertips grazed her flesh and made her quiver until the confining spandex fell to her ankles. She kicked it aside and stood before him completely naked.

Naked.

Every inch of her.

Inch after inch after inch…

She lifted a hand to cover herself. He caught her wrist midair and kept staring as if she were the sexiest woman on the planet.

A memory played at her brain, drawing her back to the ice-cream shop that first night when he'd offered to help her out. His deep voice played in her head. *You're round in all the right places and thin in all the right places.*

Yeah, right.

But there was no denying the sincerity in his eyes or the flash of appreciation as his gaze roved from her head to her toes, pausing at all the interesting spots in between. Her mouth. The curve of her neck. Her breasts. The dip of her waist. The smooth V between her legs.

"You're so damned beautiful, Babe," he breathed, the words washing away her anxiety and stirring a rush of confidence. "You're perfect. Just perfect."

As he stared at her for those next few moments, every insecurity that had haunted her throughout her life faded into a rush of sizzling heat. Suddenly, she didn't give a fig about being good enough or pretty enough or sexy enough. With Brodie staring at her with such reverence, she felt all three and then some.

He clasped her waist and backed her to the nearest wall. Pressing one hard thigh between her legs, he forced her wider until she rode him. The sudden intimate contact drew a gasp from her lips. His gaze hooked on her mouth and she knew he wanted to kiss her again.

He didn't.

Instead, he leaned into her, his hard, muscular thigh pressed against her, working her until dampness flooded from her body and his breathing came almost as frantic as hers. She slid against him, the friction making her eyes hot and bright.

He touched her then, sliding his hand into the wet, swollen folds between her legs. At the first touch of his fingers, a ragged moan curled from her lips and she shivered. She leaned back against the wall and her eyes drifted closed. She was almost there.... Almost.

"No," he murmured before he scooped her up and settled her on the bed. He shoved his jeans and underwear down with one swift push and stepped free. He paused to retrieve a condom from his pants pocket.

Babe watched him slide the sheath onto his penis. Her mouth went dry at the sight of him touching himself. Long, lean fingertips worked the latex over the ripe purple head and down the smooth shaft. Her heart thundered in her ears and she licked her lips, eager to taste him again.

He didn't give her the chance. He urged her backward onto the soft mattress and followed her down. He slid his hands under her thighs and urged them farther apart. And then he plunged into her, so fast and deep, that her heart seemed to stop beating for a long moment, before kicking back into gear and pounding forward even faster than before.

The feel of him so hot and thick pulsing inside her nearly made her scream with satisfaction right then and there. Her arms slid around his neck, her muscles clamped down around him and she closed her eyes to the delicious feel of being filled to the brim with Brodie Jessup.

It was her dream all over again, yet it was better. His body was even harder than she'd imagined, his skin more sizzling to the touch. She drank in his scent and ran her hands over his sinewy shoulders and the corded muscles of his back.

He withdrew and slid forward a second time. His hard length rasped her tender insides, creating a delicious friction that sent a dizzying heat straight to her brain. His body pumped into hers over and over, pushing her higher with each thrust. She lifted her hips, meeting him thrust for thrust, eager to feel more of him.

Harder.

Deeper.

Faster.

Her mind went numb and she exploded. Convulsions gripped her and she tightened around him, pulling him in as he plunged yet again and followed her over the edge.

Several breathless moments passed as she lay there and absorbed the implication of what had just happened.

Her seduction had worked.

That's what the sexual satisfaction coursing through her meant. Her body tingled and her toes felt numb and her breasts ached—all physical proof that her research had paid off.

And the sudden urge to curl up next to Brodie and feel his heart beat against her palm?

Heartfelt gratitude because he'd helped her live out her fantasy.

One night, she reminded herself. That's all this was. One hot, wild night. End of story.

She listened to the deep, steady sound of his breathing for several moments and tried to resist the pull of his warm body. Cool air whispered from the air-conditioning vent and goose bumps raced up and down her skin. She tried to summon the energy to reach down and pull up the blanket, but she felt limp. Spent. *Satisfied.*

Besides, it wasn't as if she had to resist him right now. She'd fantasized about one hot night, not one hot encounter. Her gaze shot to the clock on the nightstand. They still had several hours left together. With that thought in mind, she snuggled into the curve of his shoulder.

Even so, she wasn't resting her hand on his chest.

Not now.

Not ever.

Because even if she did have feelings for Brodie Jessup— which she didn't—she had no clue if he felt anything for her beyond the lust that burned so fiercely between them. And even if he did, he was leaving at the end of the season. The whole situation had heartache written all over it.

Tonight wasn't about getting her heart broken. It was about living out her fantasy and having great sex. Fantastic sex. Memorable sex.

Mission accomplished.

THEY HAD SEX again that night. And again. And in between, they ate ice cream and reminisced about the past.

"I had a big crush on you back then." She wasn't sure why she told him except sitting side by side in the dark, eating her favorite chocolate raspberry swirl ice cream, she felt so easy and relaxed, the words seemed to slip out of their own accord. "You had a cute smile." She slid a bite of ice cream into her mouth, but she wasn't nearly as overwhelmed by the rich taste as she was by the way his eyes glittered as he stared at her, into her, in the dim candlelight.

"You were pretty cute yourself." He dipped his spoon into the carton she held and scooped some of the rich chocolate.

"You were the only one who thought so. Don't get me wrong, I'm okay with myself, but I'm no beauty queen. I never was and I never will be. Not compared to Mickey. And I'm much too soft compared to Sandy."

"You're perfect, Babe." He leaned forward and lapped at a spot of chocolate on her chin before catching and holding her gaze. "Compared to anyone." His voice was deep and raspy and sincere. "In fact, I don't think anyone can compare to you."

A giddy warmth swelled in her chest and spread through her body, chasing away the small chill brought on by the ice cream. She spooned another bite and slid it into her mouth. "Well, I *am* pretty good in bed," she said once she'd swallowed.

"I don't know if I would go that far." He took the spoon and carton from her hands and set it aside. Then he reached for her. "Not unless you're ready to prove it."

"Again?"

He grinned as he leaned closer. "Again." And then his mouth captured hers.

BRODIE STOOD in Babe's kitchen early the next morning and read the headline that blazed atop the local newspaper.

ADIOS, SLAMMERS!
DON'T LET THE DOOR HIT YOU ON THE WAY OUT!

Christ, it was one loss, barely a few games into the season, and the town had already written off the team.

So?

Isn't that exactly what he wanted?

The question echoed through his head as he spooned the scrambled eggs he'd just made onto a plate. He added bacon and a few pieces of toast and set it on the small tray he'd unearthed from her cabinet. He poured a glass of juice and added it to the tray before he let his gaze drift toward the open bedroom doorway. He glimpsed the bottom half of the bed adorned with a shapely leg. His groin ached.

A practice run. That's what last night had been as far as she was concerned.

Thankfully. The last thing he needed was a clingy female at this point in his life. He was ready to forge a relationship with his father. Maybe.

Maybe not.

He ignored the doubt. He would gladly pack his bags when the time came and head for Las Vegas. Hell, he was looking forward to it, even if he didn't end up forging a relationship with the old man. Brodie's life had always been about baseball, and the Slammers were his team. If the good folks of Louisville wanted to give up on them this soon, so be it. Brodie would follow his team wherever they went. Happily.

That's what he told himself, but damned if the notion didn't bother him.

He tossed the paper into the trash beneath the sink, picked up the tray and walked into the bedroom.

It was barely six in the morning and Babe was still sound asleep, obviously spent after the past several hours. He didn't blame her. He felt exhausted himself, but in a good way.

Too good.

The notion stuck in his head as he swept his gaze the length of her. Her nostrils flared softly as she slept, her mouth slightly parted, her bottom lip full and plump from last night's kisses. He had the sudden urge to chuck the tray, press her back into the mattress and love her one more time.

One last time.

He'd already done that, he reminded himself. He'd kissed every inch of her body and licked and sucked until she'd come apart in his arms. Then he'd simply held her and listened to the sound of his own heart drumming a frantic rhythm despite the fact that he hadn't had an orgasm himself. Watching her had brought him enough pleasure. Feeling her. Tasting her.

One *night,* he reminded himself.

Already the morning sun blazed outside, pushing through the blinds to cast vertical shadows across the soft beige carpet.

Brodie gathered his control, set the tray on the nightstand and dropped a chaste kiss on her forehead. And then he turned and walked away before he let himself get distracted.

Because Brodie didn't get distracted. He stayed determined and focused and accomplished whatever it was he set out to do.

He always had and he always would. He just wished the fact didn't suddenly bother him so damned much.

BABE STOOD at her bedroom window and watched Brodie climb into his Jeep Wrangler. She swallowed the lump in her throat and vowed not to shed even one tear. This is what she'd expected. What she'd wanted.

She knew that, but there was just something about knowing he would leave and actually watching him do it that made her want to cry her eyes out.

This was a happy occasion, she reminded herself. She'd done exactly what she'd set out to do. Sort of. She'd had great sex. Spectacular. *Unforgettable.*

That was the trouble. Now she couldn't forget, much less imagine sex with anyone else. In her fantasies, or otherwise.

Babe walked back to the bed, sat down on the edge and stared at the tray he'd prepared for her. Oddly enough, the notion that he'd cooked for her made her want to cry all the more.

No, the notion that he would never cook for her again was what made her want to weep. Along with the fact that he would never touch her the way he had last night. Or sit in bed with her in the candlelight, scarfing down ice cream and talking.

Jeez, she must have been orgasmically deficient. That's why she was having such crazy thoughts. She'd gone so long without a really good climax that when she'd finally had one, it had short-circuited her brain.

That had to be the explanation. Because if it wasn't, that would mean she'd actually done something really and truly stupid—like fall in love during a one-night stand.

Babe had done no such thing.

No, she'd fallen in love with Brodie a long, long time ago, way before their one-night stand.

The truth echoed in her head as she stared at the breakfast tray, and she did the only thing she could do—she cried. And then she picked herself up and headed for The Sweet Spot to get on with her life.

Minus Brodie Jessup.

5

Four days later

BRODIE SPENT the next several days thinking about Babe. He didn't *mean* to think about her. *Hell*, no. He meant to keep his mind on pumping up his players and pushing them above and beyond during practice to avoid a repeat of the past game.

But just when he hunkered down behind the plate to observe Riley Kelleher's curveball—Riley was his star pitcher and had been with the team since day one—or sank into his chair to watch another replay of Saturday's ass-kicking, Babe Bannister slipped into his head.

She wore nothing but her fuzzy pink bathrobe and a hungry look that made him want to chuck everything and head back to her place.

For sex.

That's what he told himself.

What he'd been telling himself since he'd walked away from her Sunday morning.

The damned trouble of it all was that he didn't believe it any more than he believed little green men would land in the middle of the field and zap Cody Cameron back into shape.

The damned E.R. doctor had been way off base. Cody hadn't just bruised his toe. He'd suffered a hairline fracture. Which meant he wasn't getting back to work for at least another three weeks. Which meant there was the serious possibility that the team would lose the next game. And the next. And so on.

Unless Brodie could whip Cody's replacement into some

serious playing shape before they went up against the New York Yankees this Saturday.

That's what he'd been trying to do, but his heart simply wasn't in it.

Because losing is a good thing. It cinches the deal with Vegas.

That's what he told himself, but truthfully, Brodie had too much integrity to purposely sabotage the team for his own personal gain. Hell, he wasn't even certain he stood to gain anything with the move. Sure, it would give him the chance to see his father more often, but Brodie still wasn't sure he wanted that chance. When he'd been younger, he'd dreamt of it. But now… He knew who he was—a successful manager for a very successful team—and he didn't need any affirmation.

No, the restlessness deep inside him had nothing to do with his father and everything to do with a certain blond, blue-eyed, voluptuous ice-cream guru who'd been haunting his every damned thought.

Brodie stood in the Slammers' locker room on Thursday night and scrubbed his wet hair with a fluffy white towel before chucking it toward a large bin. It was barely a quarter past nine and the place was already empty. He'd been working the guys until ten every night since the loss, but he'd dismissed them early tonight. When he'd made the announcement, his players had hightailed it off the field in record time, probably fearful that he'd yell "Gotcha!" and drag them back out for a few more plays. And so Brodie was all by his lonesome with the exception of the stadium's night security.

Thankfully.

Brodie had reached his limit. He was wound so tight, he was *this close* to coming undone. He sure as hell didn't want to do it in front of his players. His job required he be in control, yet Brodie felt anything but. His muscles were tight. Awareness prickled his skin. Need pushed and pulled inside of him, urging him to forget the stack of game films sitting in his office and head over to The Sweet Spot.

He needed to see her in the worst way. To feel her. Just one more time. If he could just pull her close and sink into her soft, warm body, then he could ease the frustration welling inside of him once and for all.

Yeah, right.

He would want more. His head knew it even if his body didn't want to agree. The desperation driving him went way beyond anything physical. While Babe had felt softer and warmer and more right than any woman he'd ever been with, she was more than just the best he'd ever had in bed. She was the best he'd ever had, period.

He'd never met a woman he could talk to the way he talked to her. She knew him. His past. His present. And she understood him, both his determination when it came to his job and his love of the sport.

Hell, she shared it.

She felt the same passion and drive when it came to The Sweet Spot, which was why she'd taken a simple ice-cream shop and turned it into one of Louisville's must-sees. And she sure as shootin' loved baseball.

His gut clenched and his chest ached, and Brodie did his damnedest to ignore both. He had work to do. The Yankees were on a winning streak and he needed to review their past game films to see if he could find any weak spots in their plays.

He retrieved his clothes from the locker and set them on the bench. Pulling his T-shirt over his head, he leaned down and reached for his jeans. Once he'd pulled on the denim and buttoned his fly, he dropped to the bench. With stiff arms, he pulled on his boots and ignored the urge to howl. His friggin' life had been going so well until last week.

He finished tying his boots and pushed to his feet. Metal cracked against metal as he slammed the locker closed and headed for his office, which sat next door to the dressing area. He sank down behind his desk and popped the first film into the video player. Grabbing his remote, he settled back in his chair and hit the play button.

He tried to focus on the players, but Babe's image danced in front of him.

Christ, he missed her. He missed stopping off at The Sweet

Spot after practices. Over the years, he'd grown accustomed to her smile and her voice—and *her*. He wanted to see the sparks in her eyes when she vented about a difficult customer. He ached to hear the excitement in her voice when she told him about the latest recipe she'd cooked up in her kitchen.

He hadn't had a peaceful night since she'd first mentioned her damned seduction idea to him and he'd volunteered to help.

Not one.

The realization struck and the truth crystallized as he sat at his desk and watched the Yankees' pitcher throw yet another fastball. All this time, he'd convinced himself that her rich vanilla ice cream was his comfort food. The key to a decent, restful sleep. But it wasn't the ice cream that chased away the crazy loneliness that dogged him most nights. It was Babe. She made him feel good. Comfortable. Complete.

And he made her feel?

He didn't know, but he intended to find out. Because suddenly Brodie wasn't half as concerned with fixing his life—namely the relationship with his father—as he was with getting a life. It was time he stopped being so focused and determined and lonely.

Starting now.

BRODIE WASN'T SURE what he expected when he walked into The Sweet Spot a few minutes later, but he knew what he didn't expect—to see Babe standing behind the counter, wearing the Slammers T-shirt she'd seduced him with on Saturday night. The soft cotton hugged her full breasts and outlined the lace of her bra. He could only see her from the waist up, but his memory filled in the bottom half, complete with the short-shorts and shapely legs, and his groin gave an answering tug.

Even worse than what she was wearing, however, was what she was doing. He stood just outside the doorway and watched through the glass as she spooned glazed strawberries onto a square of the mousse/ice-cream cake she'd recently created. His memory stirred and her voice replayed in his head.

I'll serve him a sample of my latest creation. When he's over-

whelmed with the rich, decadent taste, I'll lure him back to my place with the promise of more.

Reality hit him like a fastball straight to his middle and his initial desire faded into a wave of anger.

He pushed through the doorway. The bell jingled and Babe's head snapped up. Her surprised blue gaze collided with his.

"You can't do this," he blurted.

"Excuse me?"

"You can't seduce Cody."

"What are you talking about?"

"This." He waved a frantic arm and tried to fight down the wave of jealousy and anger that rose inside of him. "No way. No how. *Hell*, no."

"This?" She actually had the nerve to look puzzled as she glanced at the counter. "But this isn't—"

"It's not happening," he cut in. "So you can just go back into the storeroom, peel off that getup and forget all about it."

"You think…" She shook her head as she glanced down at her shirt and then back at the piece of cake. "You don't really think—"

"I don't think, sweetheart. I *know*. And like I said, you can forget it. You're not doing it."

Her gaze narrowed as it collided with his. "Oh, really? Why not?"

Because I want you.

Because I need you.

Because I love you.

The truth was there in his head and his heart. But Brodie was a man who'd heard the words so seldom while growing up—and believed in them even less—and so when he opened his mouth, all that came out was, "Because I said so."

Her gaze widened before it narrowed again to dangerous slits. "Because *you* said so? Is that what you just said?"

"Yeah, but I—"

"And just who are *you* to tell me what I can and can't do?"

"I'm your…" *Come on, boy. Spit it out.* "I'm your, er, friend."

"My friends don't tell me who I can and can't seduce."

"Your boyfriend," he corrected. *Atta boy.*

He wouldn't have thought it possible, but her gaze narrowed even more. "The term *boyfriend* implies a romantic relationship. We had a one-night stand. No relationship involved."

"You have to admit, it was a pretty incredible one-night stand." He grinned, trying to turn the situation away from the dangerous path they were following. But it was too late.

Her eyes flashed blue fire. "So?"

"So you can't sleep with Cody Cameron."

"You're right. I'm not sleeping with him." She waved a hand at the cake. "First I'm going to seduce him and *then* I'm going to sleep with him."

He barely ignored the urge to pick her up, toss her over his shoulder and take her back to his place until she got the ridiculous notion out of her head. "It's been less than a week. The bed's not even friggin' cold yet."

"Actually, it's very cold." Colder than Babe had ever imagined since she'd rolled over Sunday morning to discover that Brodie had left without so much as a goodbye.

She'd known it was for the best, despite the goose bumps that had raced up and down her arms and the empty feeling she'd had in the pit of her stomach.

Better not to clutter things up with an awkward morning after. They'd had sex. It was over. End of story.

At the same time, she hadn't been able to stop thinking about the sex, or all of the in-between moments when they'd talked and laughed and simply been together.

She hadn't been able to stop thinking about him, period.

Nor had she been able to shake the fantasy that had haunted her every night since. Forget the *Why Not?* variety with its red-hot sex and breath-stealing orgasms. She'd been haunted by dreams of breakfast in bed with Brodie and cuddling up with him on the sofa and picking out furniture and…

Not!

"Look," he told her, "I didn't mean what you think I meant. It came out wrong because I'm tired and I'm not really thinking straight."

"You're damned right you're not thinking straight if you think you can just waltz in here after four days of nothing and start ordering me around."

"Just calm down."

"There you go again. I don't have to listen to you. I don't have to do what you say. YOU'RE NOT MY BOSS!"

"Christ, I don't need this right now." He wiped a hand over his eyes. "Look, I've got a stack of plays to go over. I'm going back to work." He turned toward the door. "You settle down and we'll talk later."

"We'll do no such thing."

His gaze drilled into hers for a brief, heart-pounding moment. "Oh, yes, we will."

"Says you. There's nothing to talk about." *Is there?* She wanted to ask, but the words couldn't seem to make it from her brain to her mouth. "Have a nice life."

"This isn't over," he said over his shoulder.

"It's over. Done. End of story. You go your way and I go mine." She picked up a spoon, dipped it into the dessert she'd made to take over to Janie's, and took a bite. "Mine is definitely sweet."

"You're not having sex with him." He looked as if he wanted to strangle her and kiss her at the same time. "He has a girlfriend."

"So?" she called after him as he pushed open the glass door. "What makes you think that's going to stop me?"

He gave her a last, parting glance. "You wouldn't do that. You're not the type to sleep around without any thought to the consequences."

"You've spent exactly one night really getting to know me, which means you don't know much."

"That's where you're wrong. I've spent a lifetime getting to know you."

His words stirred an ache in her chest, but Babe held tight to the anger stirring inside. She had to, otherwise she would give in to the hot tears burning the backs of her eyes. "You still can't tell me what to do." The hurt she'd been nursing since Sunday rose like a huge tidal wave and crashed over, picking her up and tossing her around until she trembled with its force. "I'm sleeping with Cody Cameron," she yelled after him as he pushed through the door. "You can bet on that, buddy."

"I'M NOT sleeping with Cody Cameron," she told Janie fifteen minutes later as she paced the storeroom of her friend's memorabilia store. "Of course, I'm not. I wouldn't sleep with Cody after what happened Saturday night. Jeez, I can't even fantasize about him anymore. All I think about is Brodie."

"Did you tell him that?" Janie said around a mouthful of Babe's new dessert.

"Of course not. And even if I was still fantasizing about Cody, I certainly wouldn't contemplate sleeping with someone who has a girlfriend."

Janie spooned another bite. "Did you tell Brodie that?"

"No, I told him I didn't care. But I had to say that because he was being a know-it-all. He took one look at me wearing this shirt and assumed I'd put it on to wow Cody." She shook her head. "The only reason I put it on is because it reminded me of *him*." Babe remembered the feel of Brodie's body pressed up against hers and the smell of warm male and just a hint of cologne. Her nostrils flared. "It still smells like him."

"Did you tell him that?"

"No, but I didn't exactly get a chance with him shouting orders at me. Just who does he think he is, bossing me around? I mean, he *is* the man I just slept with and it *was* pretty incredible, but he's never said one word whether or not he has feelings for me. I think he does, but he didn't say it and I'm not a mind reader, for heaven's sake."

"Did you tell him *that?*" Janie licked strawberry sauce from her spoon.

"No, I just acted like I was cool with the whole one-night stand thing. What else was I supposed to do? He's never said anything about wanting more. He's never even said if he *likes* me, for Pete's sake. Maybe he doesn't. Maybe that's why he got so mad and stormed off like that."

"Jealous to the point of forbidding you to sleep with someone? Yep, that definitely sounds like a man who doesn't like you."

"Why didn't he *say* he liked me?"

"Why didn't you *say* you liked him?"

"Because I don't." Her gaze collided with Janie's and understanding lit her friend's eyes.

"You *love* him?"

Babe nodded and watched her friend's expression go from stunned to frantic.

"*Why didn't you say something?*"

The question haunted Babe as she locked up The Sweet Spot for the night and headed home.

Why hadn't she said something?

Because Babe Bannister didn't step up to the plate when it came to something she wanted. She chickened out before she even gave herself a chance.

Her chest tightened as she stopped at a light and waited for it to change to green.

Yes, she played it safe in life, and so she'd played it safe with Brodie, keeping her feelings to herself for fear that he would reject her.

The thing was, she didn't feel safe at the moment. She felt confused and unhappy and scared.

But the fear had nothing to do with rejection and everything to do with the sudden realization that she might never meet a man who made her feel even one tenth of what she felt for Brodie.

A man who made her laugh and smile and scream in ecstasy. A man who'd starred in both her *Not!* and her *Why Not?* fantasies.

The only man.

The light changed and for the first time in her life, Babe didn't think. Or worry. Or second-guess herself. She simply acted.

She made a U-turn and headed back toward the stadium.

"HIS FASTBALL curves to the left."

The soft, familiar voice echoed in Brodie's head, and he whirled in his chair to see Babe standing in his office doorway.

She stared past him, her gaze riveted on the television screen.

"Just a half inch or so, but enough to throw off your batters if they're not prepared on Saturday."

"What are you doing here?"

"I thought we could talk. At least, I thought I could talk. I let you make some assumptions earlier that weren't exactly true."

"Such as?"

"That dessert wasn't for Cody. Cody hasn't been into the shop since he hurt his foot. Not that I would have made him one if I'd expected him. I made it for Janie. I always try out new things on her because I know she'll be honest with me. Callie, too. But she's been busy with Donovan, so I didn't want to bother her."

"So you weren't planning on seducing Cody?"

She shook her head. "I only wore this shirt because it reminds me of you." Her gaze caught and held his. "If there's anyone I want to seduce, it's you." She swallowed down the lump that jumped into her throat. "You were right when you said you knew me. You know me better than anyone. I don't have to pretend to be something I'm not with you. You see the real me and I like that. I like you." She shook her head. "That is, I, um, love you." Her gaze glimmered with feeling as she met his. "I always have."

The words should have sent him running the other way. He was a man who'd made it a point not to get too close to any woman, to open himself up, to risk getting hurt, to fall in love.

Oddly enough, he didn't feel any fear or hesitation. Instead, he felt pure joy and a rush of excitement that pushed him to his feet and urged him to close the distance between them.

"Babe." He murmured her name as he lifted a hand to touch her cheek, as if to convince himself that she was really here. Right now. With him.

Her skin was warm and soft beneath his fingertips. Real.

"When I thought," he started, only to shake his head as he remembered the rush of jealousy, followed by the fear… A fear far greater than anything he'd ever felt before. "When I thought about you and Cody and…Christ, it made me nuts!" *Because he loved her. Because he wanted to love. Because he wasn't afraid to love her.*

Babe stared deep into his eyes and saw the emotion that glimmered in the depths, and joy rushed through her. She knew deep in her heart that he felt the same way she did. It was there in the way he touched her, as well, his fingers playing over her cheek. Softly. Reverently. As if she were the best thing he'd ever felt. *Ever.*

But knowing the truth and hearing it were two very different things. Call her a hopeless romantic, but she needed more. "Because?" she prodded.

"Because the thought of you with anyone makes me want to slam my fist into the nearest wall."

"And that would be because?"

"Because I don't intend to share you with anyone. Not now. Not ever."

"Would you just say it then?"

He grinned. "I love you and I don't intend to let you go around seducing other men."

"Then how am I ever supposed to get really good at it?"

"I guess I'll just have to be your test subject." He stared at her, into her. Heat simmered in the deep green depths of his eyes and warmed her from the inside out. "So are you going to take me back to your place to whip me up something special and offer me a piece?"

"Actually," she said as she leaned up on her tiptoes and slid her arms around his neck, "you don't get just a piece. You get the whole thing. If you want it."

"I want it, all right, darlin'. More than you'll ever know."

And then she kissed him.

Epilogue

The last week of May

"I WANT TO LICK YOU from your head to your toes." The deep, husky voice slid into Babe's ears and every nerve in her body tingled in anticipation.

She smiled at the tall, handsome man who leaned over her as she stretched out on the worktable in her kitchen at The Sweet Spot. "You say that now because I'm covered in whipped cream, but what about when it's just me?"

Brodie's eyes glittered with lust and sincerity that made her chest tighten. "I'll still want to lick you, with or without the whipped cream."

"Is that so?" Joy rushed through her, a feeling she'd become all too familiar with over the past few weeks since she and Brodie had moved in together. To some, the move had seemed quick since it had only been a few weeks since what she'd come to refer to as The Saturday Night Seduction. But the thing was, they hadn't just fallen in love. They'd loved each other their entire lives. It had just taken TSNS for them to both realize it.

"So, exactly where do you want to lick me?" she asked him.

"Here." He lapped at the white cream that topped her right nipple. "Here." He suckled the left. "And here." His tongue dipped into her belly button, laving and stroking long after the sweet cream had disappeared.

"What about Vegas?" While the team had only lost a few games, they still had half the season left. A winning streak *could* up the revenue and keep them in town. Just as easily, however, things could take a turn for the worst and it would be bye-bye Louisville.

His gaze caught and held hers. "I'm not losing you, Babe. If the team moves, we'll work something out when the time comes."

She knew they would.

Because Babe didn't care half as much about her ice-cream shop as she did about the man leaning over her. She wanted to go to bed with him every night. And wake up to him every morning. And everything in between.

While only time would tell what would become of the Slammers, Babe knew with certainty what would happen in her own life. She and Brodie would live happily ever after, wherever, however, because she loved him with all of her heart, and he loved her. That's all that really mattered.

Dear Reader,

I am the most uncoordinated, unathletic person in the world. I can barely walk a straight line, much less play many sports with any skill or dexterity. And I'd rather go to a Broadway play than a professional ballgame any day of the week.

That doesn't mean, however, that I can't appreciate the *fine* way a well-muscled, powerful man looks in a team uniform.

Of all organized sports, I've always had a thing for baseball. Probably because despite being a team effort, it seems to be a very solitary sport in some ways. One man facing down a ball, one man standing on a mound, one man deciding whether to steal or stay put. Baseball requires a lot of personal judgment and attention to detail as well as sheer athleticism.

Hmm…brains and brawn…what's not to like there? So it was easy for me to create my fantasy athlete—ballplayer Riley Kelleher. And who doesn't fantasize that Plain Jane really does have a shot at winning the heart of a superstar?

I had a great time working with Julie Elizabeth Leto and Kimberly Raye on this book. Since they're two of my favorite Harlequin Blaze authors, not to mention friends, it was a double treat. Hope Riley and Janie's romance is a treat for you, too.

Now, turn the page and…play ball!

Best wishes,

Leslie Kelly

SLIDING HOME
Leslie Kelly

To Julie and Kim—it's been great "playing" with you.
And to the real "boys of summer"—
thanks for keeping the summer months extra hot!

1

Early March, three weeks before Opening Day

WHAT JANIE NOLAN knew about baseball could be summed up in three words: zip, zero and zilch. She'd never liked sports of any kind, being far too focused on what her family called her "causes" to much care if some guy hit a ball with a stick farther than some other guy hit a ball with a stick.

So the fact that she'd ended up running a sports memorabilia shop called Round The Bases, which was primarily focused on Louisville's Major League Baseball team, the Slammers, made as much sense as if she'd decided to become a stripper. And even with her very early-in-the-alphabet cup size, she'd probably *still* have had a better shot at a pole-dancing career than of preventing her brother's store from going under while he served in the military.

Aside from Janie's blood, sweat and tears, there was only one thing keeping the shop afloat, and that was the elderly man sitting across from her on the lawn of Bluegrass Retirement Village. Her personal walking baseball encyclopedia.

"You oughta be able to get six hundred for that," Edgar Smith said, rubbing his jaw as he eyed the framed, autographed game picture in his hand. "'86 Mets, game seven over the Red Sox. With the certificate of authenticity, six minimum, maybe seven."

Nodding, Janie jotted a note in her small, spiral notebook, which was already filled with information the man had provided. He'd been an absolute godsend. Without Mr. Smith's input, she would probably have sold her brother's 2004 autographed Red Sox ball for ten bucks to some kid on a Little League team.

"You're my guardian angel," she said, squeezing Mr. Smith's age-spotted hand before putting the picture in her bag.

"Hands off, girlie, he's mine. Wouldn't want to have to arm wrestle m'own granddaughter for a man."

Grinning, Janie eyed her grandmother, Anne Nolan, who sat beside Edgar on the blanket. Tart and spry at seventy-eight, Grandma Anne was her closest ally, and her only family other than her brother. Even if Janie didn't love the depth of character she'd always found in the elderly, she would have spent every minute she could here just to enjoy her grandmother's company.

"I'm not a man stealer," Janie replied, lifting her brow.

Man "repeller" would be more accurate, given her romantic track record. Three words would sum that up, too: zip, zero and zilch. The last time she'd dated anyone seriously was before she'd taken over the store, so she was going on a three-year-long dry spell when it came to sexual experiences. Unless vibrators, rich chocolate ice cream from her friend Babe's shop or the number of times she'd watched the Brad Pitt bare butt scene in *Troy* counted.

"Unlike Mary Moseby. She *is* a man stealer," Grandma said. "I think she hid my uppers so I couldn't go to the races last week."

Janie didn't ask why Mrs. Moseby was swiping another elderly woman's dentures. And why her grandmother—who'd moved into the retirement community after a heart attack two years ago—was attending horse races. Sometimes she was better off not knowing.

"I should be going," Janie murmured, glancing at her watch.

She wished she didn't have to leave. The three of them were enjoying their Sunday afternoon picnic on this lovely early spring day, talking about family and the latest scandal among the amorous elderly. And baseball. Always baseball.

All around them, families visited with their loved ones, kids darting around catching butterflies or playing tag while the adults chatted. It was a ritual, and Janie loved it. If life hadn't interfered, she would have been working at this place full-time rather than just volunteering on Sundays. But life, in the form of her ex-sister-in-law Beth, *had* interfered. When she'd walked out on Janie's brother Tom, Beth had done more than break Tom's heart. She'd thrown Janie's life a curve, too. Literally.

Grandma Anne frowned. "You sure you have to go, honey?"

"Yes. Tomorrow's the start of another long work week."

"You're a good sister, Janie, to do this for your brother. Giving up three years of your life…there's not many who'd do it." Grandma's tone was hard. She hadn't gotten over Tom's bone-headed decision to enlist in the National Guard to nurse his broken heart any better than Janie had. "That boy didn't have the sense God gave a mule when it came to his trashy wife."

Janie remained silent, not daring to agree for fear Grandma would go off on a tangent about her grandson's poor judgment. Though agree she did. Tom's reaction to his wife's abandonment had landed him in the Middle East. Not even the fact that he'd finally attained his dream of opening his own sports memorabilia shop could keep him from enlisting. He'd left not giving a damn about anything, and Janie and Grandma had lived in terror ever since.

Grandma Anne hid her terror behind anger. Janie hid hers behind the store. Keeping Round The Bases up and running was the only way Janie could feel as if she were doing something for her brother. As long as he had something to come home to…well, he'd come home. She refused to think of the alternative.

She'd work at the store for as long as it took. Her degree in geriatric social work would still be there in the future. As she often reminded herself, everybody got old eventually so it wasn't as if she was going to miss out on all the business.

Edgar tapped her arm. "Are you gonna bring me the jersey that fella says is a gen-u-ine Cal Ripken?"

"Next weekend."

"It's a date!"

Janie smiled at the pleasure on Edgar's face. The man lived for baseball and loved helping her. Grandma liked the arrangement, too, because Edgar was a catch among the geriatric crowd. Janie's need for help gave her grandmother a leg up on the other widows, who outnumbered the men two to one around here.

"Before you go, honey, would you mind dashing to my room and getting me the book on my beside table?" her grandmother said. "I think we'll sit out here and read aloud for a spell."

Rising, Janie brushed any stray grass off the back of her baggy jeans. "Of course," she said before heading inside.

Once in Grandma Anne's room, she spotted the book right away. Then she read the title: *Sexual Positions For The Ages.*

Janie gulped. Either her grandmother was playing a joke on her, or she was reading sex manuals aloud to her elderly boy-friend. Janie preferred to think it was a joke. Still, knowing Grandma Anne…well, anything was possible.

Determined to hand her grandmother the book and leave before any specifics were discussed—like which position was best on an eighty-year-old man's knees—*eww*—she headed outside. Striding toward the shady spot where she'd left the amorous octogenarians, Janie wondered whether she'd inherited any of her grandmother's sexual longevity. It was a serious concern, given her track record. Which was, er, uninspiring to say the least.

Yes, she'd started out with a bang, her first sexual affair being with a fellow college student—a musician—who'd introduced her to every naughty little thing a mouth could be used for. And she'd discovered she liked those things. *Really* liked them. Janie had, in fact, pretty much sixty-nined her way through senior year.

But when they weren't making it in her narrow dorm room bed, they'd had almost nothing to talk about. Eventually, even the sex hadn't been enough to make her put up with his laziness.

Since then, she'd been darn near celibate. Considering she was short, relatively flat-chested, always kept her long, boring brown hair in a ponytail and wore glasses—she liked to sleep late, and wearing glasses allowed her to spend an extra five minutes in bed every morning instead of putting in contact lenses—maybe that wasn't so surprising. A femme fatale she was *not,* even if she did like sex more than she liked to breathe. Now that she worked in a store where ninety percent of her customers were jocks who liked cheerleader types, the thought that she might meet someone who would see the sex-addicted female beneath the bookish exterior seemed to have flown right out into left field.

Oooh, a baseball analogy. Maybe she was getting good at this sports thing. "Or is it football?" she mused aloud.

Deep in thought trying to remember the basics of team sports, she barely noticed that her grandmother and Mr. Smith were no longer alone. She was just a few feet away, coming over the top of a small hill that hid them from view, when she saw they had company. *And what company.*

Janie froze. Because when she saw the man in the dark glasses sitting on the blanket she'd vacated five minutes before, she thought she was part of some undercover video show. A camera crew had to be nearby. They'd be ready to catch the moment when the skinny volunteer came face-to-face with a man who looked like he'd stepped out of the pages of some women's fantasy magazine.

Yeah. Good TV. The unsuspecting victim goes to retrieve a naughty book and comes back to find a sex god's perfect butt occupying her spot. Sounded like a great setup since it was so far from reality. Because guys like this—perfect, mouthwatering, to-die-for gorgeous guys—did not stumble across the paths of the Janie Nolans of the world. And they certainly didn't place their rock-hard tushes and firm thighs on their blankets.

No. The nonglamorous Janies of the world only met horny college students who'd be loyal to even plain girls if they sucked them off on occasion. Or beefy jocks who didn't notice them. Or nice teachers. Or store clerks whose clothes never fit right because they waited to purchase them at the deepest discount…like one man she'd dated. Guys who had never once been overpowered by uncontrollable lust, and certainly not by anything resembling love. Not where Janie was concerned.

She simply wasn't capable of inspiring that kind of emotion in a man. She doubted she ever would be.

And she most *certainly* would not with a strong, powerful specimen like this one, with his thick, sandy brown hair blowing loosely in the breeze, his stubbled, lean cheeks, and a sexy pair of lips that were curled in a playful grin. His long legs were stretched out in front of him as he leaned back, bracing his weight on his elbows. The position emphasized the thick muscles striping his shoulders and chest. More devastating was the way it tugged his khaki slacks tightly across his impressive lap.

Very tightly…and *very* impressive.

Gulping, she reminded herself to breathe. Not stare. *And lap leering is out.*

The man was laughing at something Edgar said, a low sound that warmed her from a few feet away. His amusement brought out two deep dimples in his cheeks. *Recognizable* dimples. Suddenly shaken out of her lap-induced dementia, Janie realized whom she was staring at. "Oh God."

It was Riley Kelleher, aka Riley the Rocket, aka the sexy, studly star pitcher who played for the Louisville Slammers and owned the heart of the city. Not just the women's hearts, either—*all* the fans adored him. The man was often called the soul of the team, with everyone taking pride in his prowess and his love of the game.

She'd seen his picture in the paper—especially a few years ago when he was going through a divorce that had shocked even the most jaded sports fan—but he was so much better-looking in person that she simply hadn't recognized him. But there was no doubt that one of the most sought-after bachelors—and talked-about playboys—in baseball was chatting up her elderly grandma.

"Janie! Here you are," Mr. Smith said as he spotted her.

Wishing she'd turned around and walked away, Janie trudged closer to the old man who said, "Isn't this a nice surprise? My grandson's come to visit. I've been wanting you two to meet."

Grandson. Janie's breath escaped her lungs in one giant gush. Good grief, no wonder Mr. Smith knew so much about baseball—his grandson was one of the stars of the sport.

Though Janie's dislike of baseball—and playboy baseball players, no matter how gorgeous—was matched only by her dislike of going to the dentist, she managed a weak smile. "Hi."

The pitcher, whose reputation as a stud off the field was as well known as his abilities on it, slowly tilted his head back and looked up at her. Janie shifted from foot to foot and clenched her hands together like a starstruck teenager in front of a member of some boy band. Which was *so* not her, considering she didn't hold sports figures up as heroes.

But being honest, it wasn't his status that had twisted her tongue into an incoherent knot in her mouth. It was his looks.

"So you're little Janie."

She stiffened. At five foot four, she'd heard her share of petite/little/diminutive comments. "I'm *just* Janie," she snapped.

He rose slowly, his muscular body moving with innate grace. When standing, he was only a head taller than she, probably of average height. Not too tall for her. Perfect, in fact.

Forget about it, he's perfectly *out of the question!*

He extended his hand. "Gramps has told me a lot about you, Just Janie."

"Funny, he never mentioned your name at all."

"Well, Riley likes to keep a low profile," Mr. Smith said.

The low-profile sex god was still standing there with his hand out, so Janie lifted hers, forgetting the book.

If fate had been kind, the manual wouldn't have fallen to the ground. If it had been at least decent, *Sex For The Ages* wouldn't have landed faceup at Riley Kelleher's feet. And if it had any heart at all, the man wouldn't have been able to read.

But fate screwed her again. Because as Riley bent over to pick up the book she'd dropped, he began to chuckle.

Oh, God, just let me die now.

She didn't know which was worse: him thinking she was the one reading the sex manual, or finding out her grandmother was.

"Uh, yours, I believe?" he said, his voice not disguising his laughter. He held the book out to her. "Interesting reading for a Sunday afternoon at the old folks' home."

Oh, great, now he'd done it. Before Janie could warn him of the fire he'd brought down on his head, Grandma Anne was on him. "Who're you calling old folks?" she asked as she struggled to her feet and grabbed the book. She wobbled on her pale, skinny legs, revealed by a pair of pink shorts that hung to her knobby knees.

"You pushed one of her hot buttons," Janie murmured, almost feeling sorry for the ballplayer, who suddenly looked sheepish.

"My apologies, ma'am. I mean, the retirement home."

"Community for the enlightened years," she snapped.

To give him credit, Riley didn't laugh at Grandma's haughty tone. Instead, he replied, "That's a perfect description."

Grandma Anne jerked her thumb toward her own frail chest and poked herself with it. "I came up with it myself." The power of her own thrust almost knocked her off her feet. Fortunately, Mr. Smith had slowly followed her up and was there to support her.

Not that a strong breeze wouldn't have blown him over, too.

Janie couldn't help it. She started to giggle, lifting her hand to cover her mouth so Grandma Anne wouldn't see.

"I think I'll take Annie to her room now," Mr. Smith said, frowning at his grandson. "She's had enough of an upset."

Saying goodbye to her grandmother and kissing her smooth, delicate cheek, Janie watched as Mr. Superstar suffered under his grandfather's glare. When the older couple had gone, he said, "Has she got a problem with being old, or what?"

"Or what," Janie said dryly. "She has no problem being old. She has a problem with anyone *telling* her she's old."

"Like it doesn't exist if nobody says it aloud?"

"Kind of."

"Sounds superstitious. Bet she's a baseball fan."

"Are they superstitious?"

"Not as much as the players," he said with a lopsided grin.

His grandfather hadn't introduced him as a famous baseball player, but Riley obviously expected her to recognize him. She didn't try to pretend otherwise. "Including you, Mr. Kelleher?"

He nodded. "I've been known to wear the same socks for ten games when I'm on a streak."

Janie wrinkled her nose. "Ew."

Laughing, he crossed his arms. "I have a washing machine."

With a challenging lift of her brow, Janie retorted, "Even when you're on the road?"

"There's always somebody to wash the uniforms on the road."

Her smile faded. Though she knew he almost certainly meant the Slammers had staff to care for the uniforms, she couldn't help thinking of all the other people dying to *help* the players on the road. Help them into the nearest bed, most likely. That was supposedly what had caused his nasty divorce.

She fell silent, wondering why he was still standing here talking to her when she was so not his type. He said nothing, either, watching her watch him, so Janie took a moment to notice the little things. Like the tiny curls of gold-tipped hair at the nape of his neck. The small lines beside his mouth that said he smiled a lot. And, oh, the way he smelled.

She loved man smell. Not heavy cologne, but that strong, musky scent that seemed to emanate from a hard, masculine body. Especially when it was aroused. Wow, would she like to smell this man when he was aroused.

Keep your nose to yourself, girl. Swallowing hard, Janie took a step back. This guy was completely out of her league. He had groupies, actresses and beauties after him all the time and would most assuredly not appreciate a social worker who was not in the least seductive sniffing him up.

He suddenly chuckled, as if remembering something. "She took it with her...so the spunky old lady was reading the sex book?"

"To *your* grandfather," she replied with a smirk.

Some of the color fell out of the handsome face. Janie almost felt sorry for him, knowing what was going on in his head.

"I could have gone my whole life without knowing that."

"Me, too," she said, watching the way his lips pursed a little when he winced. Great lips. Incredible mouth. Lord, it had been a long time since she'd kissed a man.

It had apparently been a long time since she'd learned how to hide her thoughts, too. Because suddenly Kelleher was pushing his sunglasses onto the top of his head, looking at her closely as if he'd caught her staring. "So do you volunteer here often?"

Tearing her stupid fan-girl gaze off his mouth, she focused instead on his eyes. And was lost. Spring-green and heavily lashed, Riley's eyes twinkled with humor and self-confidence. Not to mention knowledge. He *knew* how he was affecting her.

Her face grew hot. "Not as much as I'd like to."

"That's great of you. Not a lot of young people would give up their Sundays to make a bunch of strangers happy. I wasn't kidding. My grandfather has mentioned you dozens of times."

So, he didn't know Janie was also visiting her own grandmother. She didn't volunteer the information, not certain why she didn't want him to know. "Your grandfather's a nice man."

"He's a shark," he said with a laugh, his admiring tone saying he meant it as a compliment. "Old school all the way."

"Old school?"

"Tough, proud, honorable and honest."

Qualities Janie liked in a man. Qualities she wondered if Edgar's grandson shared. The tabloids hadn't made him sound like he'd lived up to the honorable and honest parts during his marriage. But in recent years he'd supposedly put his wild reputation behind him, and now took his game very seriously. Since he was a Kentucky boy who lived in Louisville year-round—unlike some members of the team—the local papers were always singing the man's praises.

"Anyway, sweetheart, I appreciate it. You're an angel."

Janie was a modern woman and a strange man calling her *sweetheart* and *angel* would normally have set her off. But Riley's soft, lightly Southern accent and nod of genuine appreciation made the words seem like harmless endearments. Which was why she melted inside again, going soft and weak, wanting to giggle like a kid, scuff her toes on the ground and simper.

Who was this man and how was he turning her into a mutant?

Whoever he was, she needed to get away from him. So without another word, she tore her gaze off his handsome face and broad shoulders. Still shaken, Janie swung around and bent down to pick up her blanket. It was only after she'd doubled over that she realized she was practically wagging her butt at the guy.

A quick glance over her shoulder revealed he'd noticed. He'd *definitely* noticed, and was staring. That sparkle was still in his eyes, and he made no effort to hide his amusement. And maybe…just maybe…a hint of appreciation.

She shoved the pleasure that thought gave her into the recesses of her mind. She'd take it out and play with it later, when she was alone. Not now, when Louisville's favorite son was probably thinking she was some sex-starved groupie like the ones who threw themselves at him every day. She'd probably imagined the appreciation, anyway, because no way should her tiny self in baggy jeans have inspired a reaction from a hunky superstar.

Quickly dropping to her knees, she rolled the blanket into a sloppy, lumpy ball that she clutched to her chest. Yanking her satchel, which contained this week's newly priced sports items, she rose to her feet and offered him what she hoped was an impersonal smile. "Nice meeting you. I've got to go."

He just stared, saying nothing. A long silence stretched out, during which Janie could have whirled around and marched to her car, confident that she'd just made a fool of herself in front of the sexiest man she'd ever seen.

But her feet wouldn't move. The longer he stared—so intent, so silent—the heavier her limbs felt. The laughter of the children faded into the distance, until she heard only the buzz of a passing bee…and the sound of her own breath. Finally, unable to stand the tension, she whispered, "What?"

"I'm trying to figure something out," he murmured, still focused entirely on her face.

"What's that?"

With an unapologetic shrug he admitted, "Which I want to see more—your pretty brown eyes without those awful glasses? Or your magnificent ass in something other than those hideous jeans."

Janie's jaw dropped open and she sputtered something. Her heart pounding in her chest, she tried to fathom it—he was flirting with her. Riley the Rocket *flirting* with *her*?

Before she could say anything, the man with the magic hands

on the field reached out and tilted her mouth closed. His touch was warm, the scrape of his fingers on her skin electric.

"Don't worry, darlin'." His voice sounded thick, less flirtatious, as if he didn't like what he had to say. "I may have a reputation, but I don't go after innocent little coeds like you." With a shrug that looked mournful, he muttered, "Damn, I know I'm gonna regret this. Someone musta shined my halo today."

And turning on his heel, he walked away, striding toward the building without a single look back.

2
___

Five weeks later, mid-April

RILEY KELLEHER had known from the age of seven that there was nothing he wanted more in the world than to play baseball. Well, in the fall of 1981, he *might* have wanted the brand new Pac-Man game for his family's Atari system more, but in terms of what he wanted to be when he grew up, there'd been no other career for him since *that* day. October 21. Yankee Stadium. Game Two of the World Series, Yankees vs. the Dodgers.

He'd walked in a typical kid who sighed whenever his talkative grandfather started reminiscing about his days in the minor leagues. He'd walked out a complete baseball junkie.

Before the first pitch, going to a World Series game hadn't seemed as exciting as getting out of school for a couple of days to take an impromptu trip to New York City with Gramps. The man had scored a pair of tickets in some magazine contest, and no one had been more surprised than Riley when he, the youngest grandson, had been the one chosen to fill the second seat.

Now, of course, he understood. Gramps had seen it in him long before Riley had recognized it in himself: he'd been born with the gene. The game was in his blood in a way some people would never understand.

His grandfather had been thrilled. He'd told him so as they'd left the stadium, wide-eyed and full of excitement about the Yankees victory. Gramps had discovered the baseball gene in himself at the age of seven, too, when he'd watched Lou Gehrig oust Babe Ruth as the Yankees' power hitter by nailing four home runs in one game.

Riley's relationship with his grandfather had changed right then and there. Even now, twenty-five years later, he could still close his eyes and recapture the sounds, the smells. He could also remember the sudden rush of a surprisingly adult realization about just how much the Second World War—and a Nazi bullet—had cost Edgar Smith. Not simply some of his mobility, but also, most likely, a place in the majors. A spot in history.

Which was one of the many reasons Riley so loved his job. He was living the dream for *both* of them.

"Now don't you forget to ice that shoulder down," his grandfather said as the two of them walked toward the entrance of the retirement home one Sunday in mid-April. Edgar had, as usual, attended that day's Slammers home game, sitting in the private skybox reserved for players' families.

"I'm fine. That shoulder stretch during the bottom of the eighth was strictly to psyche out Rodriguez."

The old man's eyes gleamed his approval. "We're on again for Tuesday?"

Riley nodded, already back in his routine for this season, which included his grandfather in the stands during every home game. His parents and brothers had flown in from Texas for Opening Day a couple of weeks ago—and would probably do so a few more times this summer, but Gramps *never* missed a home game.

Riley didn't want to think about what would happen if the team moved.

Signing with the Slammers and moving back to Louisville from Houston—where he and his family had moved when Riley was in high school—had been the perfect way to take care of the old man, who'd refused to move with them. Riley had never regretted making that choice, though he missed his parents and brothers. Still, being a successful ballplayer had a few perks...not the least of which was the money to buy a lot of airplane tickets for a lot of loud, boisterous family vacations.

A sharp spasm shot through his shoulder, which did, indeed,

desperately need some work. Riley flinched a little, then surreptitiously rotated it, planning to head back to the Slammers complex as soon as he left here. If he'd gone for a rub down immediately after the game, his grandfather would have insisted on taking a cab back home, something Riley would never allow.

Gramps obviously noticed. "'Psyche out' or not, you take care of that arm, boy,"

"I'm fine," Riley insisted

"You're no twenty-year-old, anymore." Gramps's blue eyes twinkled, so Riley knew he was trying to get a rise out of him.

Keeping the laughter out of his voice, he gave it right back. "And you're no eighty-year-old, anymore."

His recently-turned-eighty-one-year-old grandfather gave a phlegmy chuckle. "Like they say, there may be snow on the roof, but there's still a fire in the hearth."

Riley didn't point out the obvious: the "roof" was almost completely bald.

"Ah, look who's here," Gramps said, sounding pleased.

Riley followed his stare to see an elderly woman standing at the door, a smile of greeting on her face. He recognized her instantly…Gramps's girlfriend. The one who read him sex books.

Closing his mind against *that* image, he couldn't help looking around, thinking of the pretty volunteer he'd met here a little more than a month ago. He had no idea why a petite, twentyish young woman would so occupy his thoughts, but she had. Every time he'd come to visit, he'd kept an eye out for her.

He'd never asked Gramps about her. As if Edgar knew Riley was interested, he'd been closemouthed about his young friend. Gramps had never *completely* abandoned the idea that Riley was an off-the-field playboy. He'd likely have panicked at the thought of his grandson targeting an innocent young volunteer.

Riley wasn't targeting her. He just wouldn't mind seeing her again, without the glasses. And in a much tighter pair of jeans.

Strange that he couldn't stop thinking about *Just* Janie. He'd certainly seen more beautiful women. God, in his line of work, he had females throwing themselves at him all the time, and a

piece of ass was never more than a wink away for any player who
wanted one.

Riley had gone through a phase of being one of those players.
Briefly. It'd been right after his very ugly, very public divorce,
when he hadn't given a shit about anyone or anything. Except
his family, and the game.

Not anymore, though. He'd gotten it out of his system. Especially once he'd realized he'd turned into the kind of person his
ex-wife had been. He, at least, had waited until *after* their divorce.
She hadn't waited much beyond their honeymoon.

From betrayed husband to playboy to…well, loner. That's the
way his life had gone. So maybe that was why the image of
sweet, sassy Janie had popped into his head on more than one
occasion in recent days. Maybe it was the smile, the laugh. The
big heart. Hell, maybe it was even the blush. He couldn't recall
having met a woman who blushed since he'd gone pro.

"Annie and I are going to our poker game now," Gramps said,
smiling at his lady friend. "Can you take this to my room for me?"

Without waiting for an answer, Gramps shoved his Slammers
pennant, noisemaker and a big plastic tub used for holding un-
shelled peanuts into Riley's hands. The tub came with free refills.
No matter how many times Riley offered to have a caterer bring
a full spread into the skybox, his grandfather never wanted
anything more than his peanuts and exactly two ice-cold beers.
Riley paid the stadium staff to clean up the shells, since, after
all, there was no point eating peanuts at a ballpark if you couldn't
toss the shells to the ground. Since they all knew and loved the
old guy, nobody seemed to mind.

"Have fun you two," he said. "Don't fleece anyone."

"What fun's that?" his girlfriend asked with a wink.

Laughing, Riley watched them walk away, then headed to
Gramps's room. This upscale place offered its residents as much
independence as they could manage, but had medical care at the
push of a button if they needed it. The doors to the suites of rooms
were usually kept unlocked for such care. So Riley didn't even
pause when he reached Gramps's, he simply pushed on in.

And was greeted by the sight of a female, on all fours, sticking out from underneath his grandfather's bed. Presenting him with a very nice—very *familiar*—view.

Oh, boy. He definitely recognized that feminine backside, and couldn't prevent a low groan of appreciation. Yeah, *definite* appreciation. Which could mean trouble all around.

Knowing she hadn't heard him enter, he murmured, "Hi."

Janie, the very woman he'd been thinking of just moments before, jerked so hard that she struck her head on the underside of the bed. The *thunk* told him it had been hard. Her string of muttered curses told him it had hurt.

So much for the "sweet little thing" image. Somehow, he liked the idea that she had a naughty side. "You okay?"

She wriggled out from under the bed, backward—Lord, have mercy—then swung her head around to look at him over her shoulder. When she recognized him, she jerked again, lost her balance and started to tumble sideways onto the tile floor.

Riley dropped the items in his hand. Lunging forward, he instinctively slid in as if Mike Piazza were above him, reaching for the catch from the third baseman during a bases-loaded forced run. He was on the floor beside her before her hip, or any other body part, could painfully land on anything harder than his lap.

Which was exactly where she ended up.

"You," she muttered, staring at him owlishly from behind those same thick glasses.

He grinned. "Me. You're not real graceful, huh?"

Her brow pulled down. "And you're not terribly polite."

He shook his head. "Well, here I thought I just saved you from takin' a painful tumble."

She looked down, obviously just acknowledging the fact that he'd dived to the floor and she was now pretty much lying on him. Fitting very nicely against him, truth be told, with her soft hip and thigh cradled between his legs and her curvy little ass doing tantalizingly wicked things against his groin.

"I'm sorry. You did. I just meant, you startled me, bursting in like that," she mumbled as she slid away.

Bursting? If she didn't get off him, that could be what his jeans would soon be doing.

Shaking off his increasingly heated thoughts, he rose to his feet, knowing Gramps would never forgive him if he seduced—then drove off—one of his favorite new people. *So hands off.* He could almost hear the old man barking the order in his head.

He obeyed, though he did offer her *one* hand, to help her up. She was so slight, one pull brought her up with an *oomph.*

She appeared embarrassed as she glanced down and brushed away some dust from her loose clothes. A strand of her hair had worked its way out of her ponytail and it fell forward, curtaining her eyes. Riley couldn't resist reaching out to brush it back. The moment his fingers touched her cheek, she gasped. But she didn't move away. She simply stared at him, as if silently asking what the hell he was doing.

He didn't know. Couldn't have explained it if he tried. So he merely dropped his hand. "Speaking of being startled," he said, "what were you doing under there, anyway?" A disturbing thought made his mouth pull tight. "Please tell me you weren't tracking down any more, uh, *self-help* books."

A soft trill of laughter escaped her curved lips. When she laughed, dimples appeared in her cheeks and her eyes sparkled behind the glasses. Another sizzling flash of heat shot through him. It was accompanied by a further tightening of his jeans. Even the image of his grandfather's frown wasn't enough to relax the muscles in the southern half of his body.

"What if I were?" she asked, sounding flirtatious. "Are you looking for something like *that* to read?"

A sex manual? Uh, no. Considering the way he was feeling about this particular female, he probably could have written one himself. Stepping closer, he murmured, "Do you think I need one?"

He thought she'd step back, back down. She didn't. Instead, her lips pursed, almost warning him that she was taking the challenge and upping the ante. "I don't know. I guess it depends on whether you shined up that halo again today. Did you?"

He would have laughed if he could have forced the sound out

of his tight throat. Halo? Man, the way he was reacting to her right now, he might as well have a pitchfork behind his back.

Cool it, a voice in his head said. *She's not your type.* This time, he recognized the voice as his own, not Gramps's.

Knowing he needed to stop this before he did something stupid like kiss the laughter right out of Janie's pretty mouth, he glanced around for a distraction. The items he'd dropped when diving to cushion her fall were good enough. Bending over to pick them up, he gave himself a few seconds to get a grip.

"Thanks for, you know, trying to make sure I didn't get hurt," she said softly, obviously realizing he really had been trying to protect her a few minutes ago.

He shrugged, depositing the peanut container and other items on a table beside the bed. "No problem. So, you never answered my question. What were you looking for?"

"You're probably not going to like hearing this," she said, suddenly sounding amused, "but I'm looking for a pearl earring which might have been lost, uh…*here.*"

He stopped her, throwing one hand up, palm out. "That's far enough. I don't want to hear another word. What, do they serve raw oyster gruel in this place?"

One of her fine brows arched up over an eye. "Gruel? Reading Charles Dickens lately?"

"Sorry. I guess this is a bit upscale to be the workhouse."

A wicked glint appeared in her eyes. "Nice to know you can read more than the sports page."

He caught the insult and couldn't help grinning. She did have a wicked streak. He liked it. A lot. "I think can even manage to count to a hundred."

"Because that's your batting average?"

Clutching his chest, he let out an exaggerated groan. "Now that hurt. My grandfather didn't tell me that mouth of yours was a lethal weapon."

"Locked and loaded."

He'd like to see her mouth locked and loaded. Locked on his. Loaded with his tongue. Or other parts of his anatomy.

Her face grew pink, which was when Riley realized she'd had the same flash of mental imagery he'd had. She was blushing.

Damn it, that sweetly embarrassed look was such a turn-on when contrasted with the saucy, sexy comebacks this girl was capable of throwing around. It was also a double-edged sword. The color in her cheeks was attractive as hell, but also served as a reminder that this was no experienced groupie he was messing with. She was young and fresh, and Gramps's second-favorite female. He needed to keep his horny thoughts—and hands—off her.

Which was why, as difficult as it was, he managed to say, "Well, it was nice to see you again. Thanks for everything."

She opened her mouth, her lips quivering a bit, as if she had something to say. Something she wasn't sure *how* to say.

Riley wasn't ready to hear it. If she said one more even flirtatious thing, he was gonna be tempted to push her against the wall and taste that mouth, sample that sweet, sassy tongue.

"Bye, Just Janie," he said, giving her the same friendly, flirtatious smile he gave every female fan from eight to eighty.

Then he strode out of the room. He only hoped she didn't correctly interpret his quick footsteps down the corridor and realize he was practically running away.

3

Five weeks later, late May

"OKAY, MISSY, it was your idea to go after our fantasy men, so don't you think it's time to get down to business?"

Janie didn't even turn around at the sound of Callie Andrews's voice as her good friend invaded the stockroom of Round The Bases. Instead, she brushed the dust off a shoebox full of trading cards. An old woman had brought them in earlier, asking fifty dollars for the lot to get them out of her late husband's closet. Judging by the dust, they'd been there a long time. Janie had no idea if she'd paid too much or too little, but she'd figured they had to be old and therefore worth something.

Besides, the woman had looked as if she needed the money, and, as her family always reminded her, Janie was a pushover. Hadn't she been the one who'd taken every blanket in their house and given them to the needy during her junior year of high school? Her father had muttered under his breath all that winter about the cold he couldn't shake, while also beaming over his daughter's kindness.

And she'd never forget his expression the time she'd volunteered the whole family—and their turkey—to a homeless shelter the year before her parents had died. Somehow, the memory of their good-natured grumbles but secretly proud smiles made the memory of that last Thanksgiving even more special than all those that had preceded it.

"Did you hear me?" Callie asked, her smooth tone holding amusement, as if she knew Janie had been avoiding her.

"I heard you," Janie said. She didn't turn around, not wanting to see Callie's disappointment that she hadn't gone through with the plan to seduce someone connected with the Slammers.

Seduction—wild sex, heat and eroticism—had been filling her mind since the March day when Janie had first met Riley Kelleher. The man had filled her nighttime dreams and her daytime fantasies. She'd never been as instantly affected by a man, *never.* And his being a baseball star had absolutely nothing to do with it, Janie had no doubt of that. His smile, his laugh, his incredible eyes and amazing body—well, Riley could have worked selling peanuts at the stadium and she'd still have wanted him every bit as much.

"It's been over two months since we sat in your stockroom and you came up with the idea to seduce our fantasy guys. To have one wild fling, even if we had to act like groupies to get it. You've done nothing about it," Callie said, not giving up.

Janie hadn't expected her to. Callie was nothing if not determined, probably one reason all their businesses—Callie's four-star restaurant, this store and Babe Bannister's ice-cream shop—were thriving. Callie was a great businesswoman and kept a steady stream of customers coming to this sports-themed complex, despite the lingering fears that the Slammers might leave town.

The team had been winning throughout the month of May, and the fans were standing by the Ross family, especially since opening day when team owner Donovan Ross had revealed the reason he'd used the Slammers as collateral on a risky loan. Still, there was that uncertainty, especially since the team had lost their last few games.

"Stop pretending you're fascinated by that dusty old box of cards when I know you have no idea who any of the players on them are. Let's make a plan for you to seduce your fantasy guy."

Janie sighed. Seducing her fantasy guy had sounded all well and good back in March after that first time she'd met Riley Kelleher. When he'd flirted with her, admitted he was attracted to her. That he liked her eyes. Not to mention her backside.

She'd ridden that high—even while being annoyed that he'd

pegged her as a college-age kid—for days. She'd thought about him almost nonstop, wondering what might have happened if she'd told him she *wasn't* some coed, but a fully adult twenty-five-year-old. One who really enjoyed *very* adult activities.

She'd also been wishing she'd been wearing something sexier or even some makeup. On the day she'd met Riley, she probably hadn't touched so much as a tube of lipstick in ages. So if he'd been interested when she was looking her *worst,* what might happen if she made a real effort to attract him?

That was what she'd been thinking the night her two best friends, Callie and Babe, had barreled in to talk about the possibility of the team leaving Louisville. That rumor had *really* gotten her emotions in a tangle. Between fretting over Tom losing his store, and her guilt over the flash of happiness she'd felt at maybe being free—*plus* the Riley incident—she'd been a mess.

The wine hadn't helped. Instead, it had made her open her big dumb mouth to her two closest friends to admit what she'd been thinking: What would it be like to seduce a fantasy man from the team before the team left? To be, just once, the flavor of the month for a dreamy stud who probably wouldn't even remember their affair, but who might give her a lifetime of hot memories?

She'd said the words without truly planning to, but she certainly hadn't shocked them. She, Callie and Babe had shared many late-night bitching sessions about men, and had poured their hearts out to each other about *all* the anxieties in their lives. Callie's long-buried, troubled past. Babe's uncertainty of her place in the world given her father's passion for baseball…and desperation for a son. And Janie's worries about Tom and her never-far-away sadness over the loss of her parents. So admitting she'd been having lusty thoughts about an unnamed member of the Slammers organization hadn't exactly been breaking news.

Her friends—obviously as romantically unlucky as Janie—had thought it was a great idea. Unlike Janie, however, they'd actually had the guts to do it. And look where it had gotten them. Both of them were blissfully happy, Callie back with Ross

Donovan, her ex-husband, who owned the team. And Babe cozying up to the manager.

But Janie...well, Janie had chickened out.

Because while part of her suspected Riley had been interested, that didn't mean he wouldn't turn her down. Even going into it with eyes wide-open, knowing it would be about nothing more than a wild, never-to-be-forgotten one-night stand, her pride could still be savaged by a casual rejection.

The second time she'd run into Riley Kelleher—a month later in Mr. Smith's room—had convinced her to forget the whole thing. Because, that day, she'd flirted, dropped some sexy hints and laid down some serious innuendo. And the man had practically run away in terror. How totally depressing.

She was a flavor all right. Vanilla. Strictly plain, boring and unseductive. Just Janie. Just vanilla.

"I should've gone for a bat boy," she muttered as she put the lid on the box, resecured it with a crusty rubber band and shoved it on a crowded shelf.

"What?" Callie asked from behind.

Janie swept a strand of her brown hair back into its ponytail. Then, knowing she couldn't explain her reluctance to someone as strong as Callie, turned around. "Nothing."

"It's not nothing. I want to know why you backed down."

She backpedaled. "Attendance is great, the team will bounce back again. It may have been a big scare for nothing. If Donovan pays back the loan to that Vegas slimeball in time, the Slammers won't go."

"Which means you'll still be here painting fantasies in your head five years from now when you should have leapt on them."

She couldn't deny it. Because Callie was absolutely right.

"Who is he, anyway, your dream guy? Tell me that much, and I'll help you figure out how to get him."

Ha. Callie, with her perfect face, great figure and sexy red hair wouldn't have to do more than wave. Janie, on the other hand...well, it would take some real effort, if not a complete makeover. "I don't really want to say."

"I'm here, armed with three spoons and some Riley Ripple."

Janie couldn't help flinching as Babe Bannister entered, carrying sinfully delicious ice cream, vanilla swirled with ripples of chocolate fudge and raspberry. This flavor, named after the Slammers star pitcher, was her new favorite.

Sometimes, she had to admit, vanilla could be very, *very* good. Especially when it was…rippled.

The thought made her go soft in warm contemplation. But remembering she wasn't alone, she forced herself to straighten up. She knew she'd been unsuccessful in disguising her reaction because a second later, Callie let out a loud "Aha!"

Oh, rats.

"It's Riley Kelleher," Callie exclaimed.

"No, I said it's Riley Ripple," Babe clarified.

"Her fantasy," Callie said over her shoulder.

"You fantasize about my ice cream? That's great."

Janie could only grunt.

"Her dream *man,*" Callie said, laughter in her eyes. "Riley Kelleher is Janie's seduction target and I now understand why you haven't done anything about it. Goodness, Janie, when you decide on a conquest, you do aim high. The star of the team?"

"I know, I know. He'd never even consider…"

Callie put her fingers over Janie's mouth. "Don't you even think that. You're lovely and he'd be damn lucky to get you."

Babe's nod set her blond curls bouncing and made her curvy figure jiggle in a way that her new boyfriend probably loved.

Janie didn't wiggle. Ever. Not if she jumped up and down. Not even if she stood on her head. Or in a wind tunnel.

She grabbed the ice cream. "Forget it," she said as she dug in, the chocolate and raspberry creating a cacophony of sinful excitement on her tongue. Much like Riley would, she imagined.

Not happening.

"I won't forget it," Callie said, looking her over. "You know what? I like this idea. You might be just what Riley needs."

"A skinny fan-girl?"

Callie pinched her. Actually grabbed her arm and *pinched* her with her strong fingers. "That's enough of that."

Rubbing her arm, Janie began to laugh. "Okay, Mama."

"If I were your mama, you'd stop trying to hide your looks."

Babe, digging out a big spoonful of ice cream, nodded her agreement. "She's right, you know. You're exactly Riley's type."

Janie cast a doubtful look down at her unimpressive curves. "Uh-huh." Then she licked her spoon, unable to stop thinking of Riley. And ripples. All those yummy, muscular ripples.

"I mean it," Babe said. "He needs a nice, normal woman with class. Brodie says Riley's a good guy, despite his reputation and his bad press from a few years ago."

Callie backed her up. "I've known him since Donovan first bought the team. Riley went through a total dog phase after his divorce. But since then, he's just been a great guy who ignores the skanks who follow him around."

Well, she wasn't a skank. There was that. But she was not at all convinced the man wasn't a player. She'd seen Riley's magnetism up close and personal. No way could he be that good with women if he didn't get a *lot* of practice with them.

"What does it matter whether I'm his type or not?" she muttered. "All I wanted from the man was a one-night stand. Hot sex. Because there's no way on God's green earth I'd ever let myself actually fall for someone like him."

Callie frowned, looking almost disapproving. "I just said he's not a bad guy, despite his past."

"Dogs and new tricks…ever heard of them?"

"Second chances, ever heard of *them?*"

"Okay, forget you being his type," Babe said, cutting them both off. "You're right, you said all along this would be a wild fling. Just because Callie and I batted out of the ballpark and found true love doesn't mean you have to, or even *want* to."

She did. She just wasn't fool enough to think it would be with someone like Riley Kelleher.

Babe continued, "So, you can just have a couple of amazing booty calls with the pitcher, then go on with your life."

Janie couldn't help laughing. "Booty calls, huh?"

Callie rolled her eyes, but also smiled. "I still say you two are a great couple. But if booty's all you're after…"

"It is." Janie wouldn't even allow herself to consider going after more. Not a woman like her. Not with a man like Riley. She was a plain Jane. And he was a superstud.

Uh-uh. It'll never happen.

Sighing heavily, she admitted, "I'd be lucky to get a call for a beer, much less booty. In case you haven't noticed, I'm not exactly the gorgeous, seductive, *booty* type."

Maybe once she had a man naked she was. Her few previous lovers had always seemed…pleasantly surprised by her enthusiasm. But *getting* a man into bed wasn't her strong suit.

"You're lovely," Callie said as she reached for Janie's ponytail holder and tugged it free, sending her long hair tumbling. She lifted it and started piling it on Janie's head, leaving a few tendrils draping down over her shoulders. "As for seductive? Well, honey, I know all about making yourself *that*."

Babe was tugging Janie's glasses off her nose. "I know a little something about makeovers myself." Then, without warning, they both dove for their handbags and grabbed bottles of makeup, tweezers and containers of eyeshadow. Janie could only sputter as they began to smear and spread, highlight and pluck.

Unable to do anything but sit still for fear one of her eyeballs would get poked out, she put up with it for a few minutes, then tried one more time to protest. "Guys, I can't…"

"Yes, you can!" they both said as they each took an arm and spun her around. They were watching while she caught a glimpse of her reflection in a mirror hanging over her desk.

And at that moment, spying the exotically made-up woman with the upswept hair, the shadowed eyes and the full, reddened lips, Janie began to wonder if they might be right after all.

4

A few days later

RILEY HADN'T thought much about the fact that he hadn't been laid in ages until he noticed the brunette in red. The woman was sitting a few tables away at Diamond, his favorite restaurant. He'd watched her come in, her nicely curved body nicely displayed in the sparkly cocktail dress that revealed a mile of leg. Not to mention a mouthwatering hint of delicate cleavage.

Riley's heart had skipped a beat when she'd entered the place. It'd skipped another when he heard the soft, lyrical sound of her voice talking to the hostess as she'd approached.

She was a beauty, but a quiet one. A classy, petite, perfectly formed feminine package, and she'd made every masculine cell in his body come to attention. Instantly.

For some reason, he'd felt a flash of recognition, as if he knew her. But he knew he didn't. He'd definitely have remembered a woman as sultry as this one.

Sipping his beer, he'd ignored the voice in his head that tried to convince him his celibate streak ought to end, because she *had* to be meeting someone. But as the minutes had stretched on, no one had joined the woman. He couldn't believe any man would stand her up, but it looked as if that's what had happened.

Since she was seated facing him, he surreptitiously noted the slender neck and her high cheekbones. Her delicate face was almost heart-shaped, framed by a mass of rich brown hair. Highlighted with streaks of gold, her hair was pulled back except for a few long curls brushing her shoulders.

Then there were the eyes. Wide-set, big and brown, like dark chocolate. With her lush red lips the color of ripe raspberries, he couldn't stop thinking of the ice cream the shop around the corner had named after him. And how much he wanted to lick her juicy lips and to taste that creamy vanilla skin.

"Enjoying your evening, Mr. Kelleher?" a smooth voice asked.

He shook off his study of the stranger and glanced up to see the owner of the place. Rumor had it she was about to remarry Donovan Ross. "Yes, thanks, everything's wonderful, as usual."

"I was glad to hear you'd be dining with us," Callie Andrews said. "Though I do wonder why you never bring anyone with you."

He hadn't been tempted to bring anyone anywhere—into this restaurant, into his *life*—for a long time. So why he couldn't stop focusing on the brunette, he had no idea. "Can't get a better steak in Louisville," he said, speaking to Callie, though his attention was glued to the female four tables down.

The female who suddenly looked up and caught him staring.

Riley almost looked away. His first instinct was to break the visual connection and let his attention casually roam over the other diners in the restaurant. Evade. Avoid. Walk away.

That had been his strategy for some time now. Evade emotional traps. Avoid potential complications. Walk away from anything that could be construed as genuine personal interaction.

Even *sexual* interaction was something he didn't think about too much these days. Sure, in the first year after he and Bronwyn, his first wife, had split, he'd taken solace in the arms of any attractive woman he'd wanted. But it hadn't helped. He'd quickly realized he was being stupid…as selfish and self-indulgent as his ex had been. So he'd gotten back on track, determined to remain private, unattached. *De*tached. Except for his family, he'd let no one come close. It just wasn't worth the risk.

It had worked. Pretty much.

He and the stranger continued to watch one another. Riley noted the way her eyes flared and her mouth opened as she sucked in a quick breath. Her pink tongue darted out to moisten her lips, and a slow flush of color rose from her neck up her cheeks. Not a flush of embarrassment…their staring hadn't disconcerted her. But a warm rush of heat. As if she'd sensed he'd been undressing her in his mind, considering letting go of his rules and his self-imposed exile from anything resembling romance.

Then she smiled. A tiny smile…a welcoming smile. A come-here-and-buy-me-a-drink-and-I'll-make-your-night-divine smile.

Oh, man, he was in trouble.

"So what have you been doing with yourself?" Callie asked.

"We've been on the road a lot."

"Don't I know it," she mumbled.

Smiling, Riley lifted his beer mug. "Been missing Donovan?"

"Desperately." She quickly glanced side to side, as if afraid she'd been overheard. Lowering her voice, she added, "But don't tell the big jerk I said that. His head'll swell too much to fit through the door." The sparkle in her eyes told him Callie wouldn't have her ex-husband any other way. That she adored him.

A sharp stab of want hit Riley in the gut. Damned if he was a jealous man, and he didn't covet Donovan Ross's fiancée. But maybe, deep down, he coveted that feeling Ross must have when he looked at the woman he loved and *knew* she loved him just as much.

He'd never had that.

Oh, he'd loved, but as for being genuinely loved in return? Well, he didn't know if any guy in his position could ever be sure of that. Because most women they met were after a notch on their own player's scorecard. Or a big fat alimony check, like the one he wrote out every month, which was the real cherry on the sundae since *he'd* been the wronged one in the marriage.

The judge hadn't cared. And the media hadn't bothered to question Bronwyn's claims that Riley's off-the-field playing was responsible for the breakup of baseball's favorite sweethearts.

Those closest to him—his parents, brothers, good friends— knew the truth. To hell with the rest of them. He'd long ago realized people would believe what they wanted to believe.

Shaking off the memories, he glanced at the stranger again. She was sipping red wine, which left her lips ripe with color.

"She's very attractive, isn't she?"

He should've known the restaurant owner would pick up on his not-so-subtle interest. "Yeah," he mumbled.

"Want an introduction?"

"You know her?"

"I might. Shall I…fix things up?"

"Got a second career as a matchmaker going?"

She shuddered visibly. "Donovan would never forgive me."

"Then it's just as well I'm not looking to be fixed up."

"Suit yourself. If you like dining alone…." Walking away, she left him with nothing to do but look into the depths of his drink. Or at the woman across the room.

She was definitely a more interesting subject, and apparently she felt the same way about him. Because again, she caught him watching her and after a quick, nearly imperceptible shift of her eyes and quiver of her body, met his gaze boldly.

But that tiny flash of hesitation told him something. Right at that moment, Riley got it. This woman hadn't been stood up. The tightness of her lips, the tremble in her hand, betrayed her nervousness and he finally figured out her game. She'd come here, dressed like that, to one purpose: to pick up a man. *Any* man. And he was the man she'd chosen.

He could almost visualize what would happen if he accepted the hot, unspoken invitation in the brunette's eyes. He'd smile as he walked to her table. She'd invite him to join her. They'd share another drink and talk about nothing while whispering a million silent, erotic promises.

They might make it through dinner…or they might give up any pretense and walk out before their food arrived. Their hands would clasp, fingers entwining as they left the building, knowing what was about to happen. Her leg would brush against his, a delicate touch of near innocence that was utterly sinful.

They'd make it to the parking lot before they kissed. Riley's hands would be buried in her soft hair while he roughly explored the depths of her mouth with his tongue. They'd share breaths, share heat, share an almost indescribable excitement.

Once inside his car, they'd pause for another intense, more private kiss. And if they were lucky, he'd have the strength to start the car and drive to his place—or hers—to finish what they'd started. Maybe they wouldn't be able to wait, though, and his cramped car would do for some quick, hot, fabulous sex.

He'd played this scene before. Not recently—not for a few years. But it had happened in his early days with the Slammers.

You're not that guy anymore.

No, he wasn't. He'd long since realized meaningless sex was not the way to eradicate the memory of his failed marriage. And that, as strange as it seemed, *he* was being used, too, by women who never wanted Riley the person…just Riley the pitcher.

He didn't hate them for it. Hadn't his wife, the woman who'd pledged to love and honor him until death, wanted the sports star, too?

Not the man. Never the man he was inside.

So he'd changed. He wasn't one of the players *off* the field anymore, despite the rumors. And he didn't care. Life was good now without women. Which made it hard to understand why he couldn't stop thinking about the brunette.

"You know what," he murmured to his waitress as she came to deliver his dinner, "I've changed my mind. Can you box that up?"

The waitress jerked her head up and down, as obsequious to one of the star players in this town as most other people.

Like the lady in red?

That cinched it. He wasn't certain the woman had recognized him, but it was possible. And he sure didn't want any obsequious woman willing to do anything to say she'd made it with a sports star. He'd been there, done that. So as soon as the waitress came back with his food and check, he handed her some cash and stood to leave. His stride didn't slow as he passed the stranger, though he was unable to resist giving her an appreciative nod, if only to thank her for the distraction she'd provided.

Once outside the main dining room, however, he realized he'd forgotten his dinner. "Damn," he muttered. Because he was *hungry.* And because he'd look like a loser going back in there to get it after playing Mr. Cool and Confident while escaping.

"Problem?" the hostess asked.

He could ask her to retrieve his bagged dinner. Or he could walk out and hit a drive-through on the way home. In the end, however, he decided on a third option. "I just decided to go into Fever Pitch for a while," he told the woman, smiling as he crossed the vestibule to the quiet bar, which served light food. Not his nice medium-rare steak, but it'd do.

Anything would do, as long as it got his mind off the temptress he'd just walked away from.

"THIS WAS the stupidest idea on the face of the earth."

Janie didn't bother keeping the disgust out of her voice. There was no point. Callie had witnessed the entire humiliating scene that had just unfolded in the restaurant. There was no way the other woman, no matter how loyal, could deny the truth: Janie had given it her best shot. And had been completely shot down.

"He was interested."

Snorting, Janie reached for her wineglass. "Right."

"He could barely keep his eyes off you."

"Sure managed to keep his hands off."

As the owner of Diamond, Callie enjoyed a lot of privileges. Like being able to ignore the rest of her customers and sit at Janie's table. "Janie, he was so into you. Maybe he was just unsure…needing you to make a more obvious first move."

More obvious? Good grief, the only way she could possibly have been any more obvious was if she'd stripped off her dress and flung it at the man. "*Riley* and *unsure* are two words that do not belong in the same sentence."

Callie frowned. "I can think of one: Riley wanted you badly but you are unsure of that *fact.*"

She didn't give an inch. "Riley wanting me badly is, I am *quite* sure, *fiction.*"

"Why are you convinced you don't have a shot with him?"

"Why are you so determined to think I do?"

Callie leaned closer, staring so hard at her that Janie wondered if she had a splash of wine on her cheek or something. "I am determined to think that," she said, her voice low and no-nonsense, "because ever since you first mentioned who your mystery man was, I *knew* you two would be perfect together."

Knew it? Janie barely knew whether she'd be able to get her newly cut, newly highlighted hair back up into this style again after tonight. Much less who her perfect man was.

But her friends really had tried to help her, and, despite what had just happened with Mr. Slammer Stud, Janie was feeling pretty good about herself. Maybe she wasn't sexy enough to garner the attention of a sports superstar, but, for the first time in a long time, she felt capable of holding her own with a normal man.

Okay, probably *not* her customers, the jocks who wanted big-boobed blond bimbos, either. Still, she looked good and felt *almost* capable of trying to pick up a man for some much needed sexual release. A normal man. Teacher. Accountant. Salesman.

Yawn.

It was no use. There was only one man she wanted. But she wasn't brave enough to go after him again, not in this lifetime.

"This can work. I know it."

"Thanks but no thanks," she murmured, giving Callie a weary smile. "Though I do appreciate everything you and Babe did." Remembering one particular part of her makeover—a visit to a woman's salon earlier today—her smile faded, dissolving into a shudder. "Except the, uh, painful waxing. I will get even some day for this afternoon's experience."

Callie bit her bottom lip, trying to hold back a grin. "Janie, honey, I didn't suggest *that* thorough a wax job."

"Yeah, well, I wish you had been a little more clear with that Brazilian woman before you let her drag me back into the torture chamber. She could give tips to the mob on making people talk." Janie shifted in her seat, still not entirely accustomed to the feel of her, um, bareness. There wasn't much left down there, other than what her torturer had referred to as a "landing strip." It felt strange against the skimpy-to-the-point-of-nothingness panties she was wearing.

"I hear some women get off on just the process of having it done," Callie said with a shrug.

Oh, right. How arousing…having her hair ripped out by the roots while being fingered pretty damned intimately by another woman. "Look, I don't think Angelina Jolie could convince me to swing to the dark side sexually, so I'm quite sure a three-hundred-pound Brazilian woman named Consuela couldn't."

Callie snorted.

Finishing her wine, Janie pushed her chair back from the table. "Thanks again for everything. But I think I'll go and turn back into my real self before I change into a pumpkin."

No, it wasn't midnight. But it didn't matter. As much as Callie and Babe had played fairy godmothers, Janie hadn't ended up with the handsome Prince Charming. She wasn't Cinderella.

She was still Just Janie. And despite her best efforts, still very vanilla.

UNFORTUNATELY, his dinner in the bar did not do a damn thing to eradicate Riley's hunger. Physical…or sexual. It didn't change a thing. By the time he finished his burger, an hour after he'd left Diamond, he'd decided he was a total moron. He'd let his unexpected reaction to a woman drive him out of his favorite restaurant, away from a juicy steak that had most likely turned into a congealed, artery-hardening mess by now. "Asshole," he muttered before he paid his tab and left.

It had been a long time since a woman had so disconcerted him…had left him questioning his decisions. Ever since his first sexual experience back in high school, he'd never questioned his choice to accept or decline an opportunity. So why couldn't he stop thinking he'd made a mistake this time?

For half a second, while passing the entrance to the restaurant, he considered stepping inside to see if the brunette was the kind who liked to linger over a long dessert and coffee.

Chocolate and raspberries.

But he thrust the idea away. He'd look ten kinds of fool. Besides, she'd been pretty set on leaving with someone and he didn't particularly want to see who she'd chosen in his place.

Having been invited by Callie Andrews to park in the alley out back to avoid some of the more persistent Slammers fans— or critics, given their recent six losses in a row—Riley headed down a quiet rear hallway. Digging his keys out of his pocket, he couldn't help wondering how his night might have ended up if he hadn't grown something of a sexual conscience.

He was so focused on the slew of delightful possibilities flashing through his brain that he almost didn't notice the crash. But it was followed by a loud, feminine scream.

Hell, that shriek could startle a man out of contemplation of a *Penthouse* centerfold, so it certainly interrupted his own rather mild visualizations. "What now?" he mumbled, turning around. No one was in the hall behind him, but he had just passed a door marked Round The Bases: Deliveries. Pulling it open and sticking his head in, he said, "Hello? Everybody okay?"

No response.

Probably the noise had come from the restaurant, but just in case someone was hurt, he stepped inside what appeared to be a stockroom. Shelves laden with jerseys, Slammers caps, coozies, pennants and seat cushions surrounded him. And right in the middle of it, covering the floor, was a mountain of big yellow foam hands with index fingers sticking up.

He saw the hands, which proclaimed Slammers Are #1, during every game. But he'd never seen them moving by themselves, undulating on the floor like a big yellow serpent.

Suddenly a head popped out of the pile, and he realized it wasn't the *hands* moving. It was the woman beneath them.

At least, he assumed it was a woman. Since he could only see the back of a thick head of dark hair, he couldn't be sure. But given the shapely figure outlined by a tight pink T-shirt and jeans that worked its way out from beneath the yellow mountain, he figured he was right. That was confirmed when a feminine voice muttered a very foul word. He bit his lip to hold back a laugh.

"Slimy salesman. Oh, sure, we needed a thousand of these things," she said as she sent a bunch of the hands flying in all directions. "I'll tell you where you can shove your dumb…"

Clearing his throat and raising his voice, he said, "Hello?"

The woman immediately jerked her head around to stare at him. Which was the exact moment he recognized her.

"You," he whispered, completely shocked. He hadn't known what to expect, but it definitely had not been this. Because the cursing, dusty little jeans-wearing package was the same dark-eyed angel he'd seen an hour ago sitting four tables away.

Riley smiled. Things were suddenly looking up. Fate, aided by a box full of foam hands, had given him a second chance. And maybe now he would go ahead and act on his devil-red hunger for the woman who'd been wearing the devil-red dress.

5

SMILING, Riley watched the flustered woman analyze his presence. She, of course, recognized him, too. *He* hadn't changed his entire persona in the hour since he'd left Diamond.

While they stared at one another, those big eyes of hers reached saucer diameter. "What...?"

"I heard a scream," he explained, raising his hands, palms out, so she wouldn't feel threatened. "Are you all right?"

She nodded. "I'm fine, thanks." Frowning at the mess, she added, "My stock attacked me."

"Kinda gives new perspective to the idea of roving hands."

Her eyes twinkled. "I've known guys who seemed to have more appendages than an octopus before, but this was a bit extreme."

Lips twitching, he stepped closer. Though tempted to ask her if she needed a hand, he modified his offer. "Need some help?"

"Thanks for not asking me the obvious."

"Busted," he said with an apologetic shrug. "I almost did."

"I probably would have slugged you if you had."

Since the woman probably only stood about five foot four, he didn't consider that much of a threat. But the fierce look on her face was so damned adorable, he didn't dare laugh at her. He'd learned growing up with his petite mother—who could silence any of her six-foot-plus sons with one frown—not to question the power of an upset woman.

Hiding his amusement, he looked around, wondering why she'd been "attacked" *only* by the hands. Everything else was stacked just as haphazardly. She was lucky the shelf of replica trophies hadn't landed on her head. "Got a little overstock here?"

Her succulent lower lip stuck out in a weary pout. "I think my inventory reproduces at night when I leave."

"Which is why you're here working so late? Trying to prevent any…procreation?" His voice softened on the last word, and he heard his own intensity as a whole litany of images returned to mind. The ones he'd been picturing when he'd considered taking her up on her sultry, unspoken invitation at dinner.

He couldn't help eyeing the foam hands. That yellow mountain might be a mess to clean up, but he'd bet it was very soft.

The woman sucked in a deep, audible breath, and her lips parted as she licked nervously at them. She'd heard his hesitation and correctly interpreted it. Something deep and basic passed between them—an acknowledgement of the brief connection they'd shared earlier in the evening. The realization that they were both feeling the same heated awareness. Maybe even a silent admission that something was going to happen.

Something exciting. Something erotic. Something amazing.

He hesitated, wondering why he was feeling none of the reservations he'd felt before about indulging in one night of erotic sex with a seductive stranger. Because right now, he wanted more than anything to taste her lips and feel that slender body pressed against his own.

She rose, kicking a few #1 hands out of the way. He didn't waste time watching her feet, however, not when her tight jeans were much more interesting. As was the shirt she wore, which highlighted the indentation of her waist and the softness of her arms. It also emphasized the delicate swell of her breasts.

Riley forced himself to lift his gaze, not wanting to make her uncomfortable, though she'd certainly been inviting stares at dinner. But since she was just as attractive all the way to the top of her head, he sank deeper into hot water.

She'd not only changed her clothes, she'd also brushed her hair out so it hung in a thick, loose curtain around her pretty face. She appeared younger than she had before, softer, though every bit as attractive. And he was reacting to her every bit as strongly as he had then.

There was still that tiny hint of recognition that told him he'd seen her before, but damned if Riley could place her. So he forced the thought away…no way would he have forgotten those lips. That face. That incredibly hot little body.

Finally, he couldn't help confronting her on the obvious. "You look different than you did earlier."

Her bottom lip quivered, but she said nothing. That quiver reminded him of the hint of uneasiness she'd displayed in the restaurant. It also reminded him that there was much more to the woman than a shapely figure highlighted in either a sexy dress or a sexier pair of jeans.

"I changed back into my work clothes."

Which didn't explain why she'd been dressed like a siren at the restaurant. As far as he knew, Diamond's dress code was dress casual. Not dress sexy. "Did you enjoy your dinner?"

"More than you did, I think," she said, tilting her head back with one brow arched in challenge.

"Touché."

"Why did you rush out, leaving your food behind?"

He answered her challenging question with one of his own. "Why did you leave and come here—*alone*—when you so obviously wanted to spend the night in someone's bed?"

She sucked in a quick gasp. "That's very…"

"Rude?" Crossing his arms, Riley leaned a shoulder against a shelf laden with trading card albums.

"I was going to say personal. But rude works, too."

"Maybe. But it's true. So, honey, why don't you tell me what you were up to tonight? I think I'd very much like to know."

Riley didn't know why he was enjoying baiting the brunette— maybe because he was so confused about who she really was. The sultry woman in red? Or the cute, flustered young woman facing him?

To be honest, he wasn't sure which he *wanted* her to be. But he still had to know. Had she been trying to pick up the Slammers star pitcher? Or Riley Kelleher, the man?

He'd like to think it was possible she hadn't recognized him, even though she worked in a sports shop. Maybe he was reaching—grasping for what he wanted to be true—but it was at least *possible*. God, he hoped it was possible.

"Tell me, what did you want?" he asked, his voice lowered to a near whisper. Then, stepping closer, he added, "And why did you leave without *getting* it?"

JANIE COULDN'T BELIEVE Riley was standing in the back room of her store, now, when she was at her absolute worst. All the primping, trimming, polishing and highlighting she'd done with Callie and Babe's assistance had been for nothing. Her makeover hadn't gotten her what she'd been seeking: Riley in her bed. No, it'd simply gotten her Riley in her stockroom.

Of all the bad luck—and lousy timing—why did the man she'd so glaringly failed to seduce have to be the one to find her looking like a brainless twit in a pile of banana-yellow foam hands?

"You didn't answer my question," he said, his voice low and too intense for her peace of mind. As if he already knew the answer…that she'd been trying to entice him. The fact that she had failed so spectacularly kept her tongue behind her teeth.

"Maybe I'll go first and answer a question for you," he said when she didn't reply. "If you'd come into Fever Pitch, I can practically guarantee you wouldn't have gone home alone."

She blew out a disbelieving breath. "Because there were a bunch of drunk, desperate guys in there?"

He straightened, his shoulders tensing as he eliminated the space between them in two long strides. "I meant because five minutes after I walked away from you, I was telling myself I'd made a huge mistake."

Janie sucked in a breath, surprised by the heat—the raw honesty—in Riley's voice. Not to mention the look in his eyes. That was attraction she saw there. The same attraction and interest he'd revealed briefly during dinner. Only now, it was magnified a million times over by his closeness. "Really?"

"Yeah," he admitted, stepping even closer so his trousers brushed against her jeans.

Attraction? No. That wasn't the right word. This was desire. There was no denying it, the man was looking at her through heavy-lidded eyes, his breathing slightly erratic.

It was heady, knowing he truly did want her. *Had* wanted her. And Janie didn't quite know what to make of it. Considering her own body had gone completely molten the moment he'd come near, she couldn't focus on anything but how good he smelled. How good the man would taste. How utterly amazing he would feel.

"Now tell me the truth. Why did you leave alone?"

Because you walked away from me.

The words were there, in her brain, but there was no way she was going to say them. Any more than she would admit that she'd started wearing her clothes a lot tighter, just on the off chance she'd run into him again now that she'd let Callie and Babe make her over into a baseball-star-attracting studette.

She didn't need to say a word, because his eyes narrowed. "You weren't going to settle for just anyone, is that it?" He lifted a hand and traced a fingertip across her jaw, then down her throat. His touch was simple yet potent, leaving her skin burning.

Stepping closer, until she could feel his breath on her face and the brush of his body against hers, he added, "Only me."

She couldn't deny it.

"You don't seem like the easy type." He sounded confused.

That got her vocal cords working again. "Definitely not."

"But you were trying to pick me up. And when I left, you dropped it."

Definitely right.

He stared intently at her eyes, then dropped his gaze, taking in the extra tight shirt and painted-on jeans that Callie had convinced her to buy. His jaw flexing, he murmured, "You know, you look familiar. I just can't imagine you're someone I would have forgotten meeting."

Oh, if only he knew. How little the man must have truly looked at her the two times they'd met at the nursing home. It had only been six weeks since he'd last seen her. And she hadn't changed *that* much. Just her clothes. Hairstyle. Contacts. Makeup.

Okay. Maybe she had changed a bit and could give him a break. "Now, back to my question," he said, a note of urgency—and, if it didn't seem so crazy coming from a superstar, maybe even vulnerability—in his voice. "Tell me why you were after me."

His words were a cross between a firm demand and a sweetly purred plea. And the genuine depth of interest in his tone reminded her of why she'd come up with the crazy seduction scheme to begin with. Because, whether she'd had the confidence to admit it, deep inside, she'd knew she'd been right all along. There was something between them. Heat. Awareness. Attraction.

He might not have acted on it. But that didn't mean it did not exist. "We're standing here like this and you really need to ask?" she said, leaning closer, falling deeper into the magnetic well of sensation between them.

His hand moved to the hollow of her throat and he traced the back of his fingers across her collarbone. Janie hissed, wanting more. Wanting to press into him and invite him to touch her much more thoroughly. Wanting his hands and his lips and his tongue and that mouthwatering ridge of arousal she could feel, hard and huge, against her hip.

She moaned as her nipples hardened against the cotton of her shirt. The sensual reaction wasn't caused merely by his touch, his crazy-sexy whispers or the feel of his warm breath against her cheek. But also because of her certainty that everything she'd fantasized about was real.

Riley Kelleher wanted her. Badly.

Riley glanced down, obviously able to tell she wore nothing beneath her shirt. His jaw tightened and his breathing grew more labored. For a second, Janie thought he was going to give up the talk and proceed directly to action. But she wasn't that lucky.

"I know why you want me *now*," he admitted, his mouth so close his lips brushed her temple, hinting at a kiss she could almost taste.

God, she was so lost.

"I want to know why you wanted me *then*, from the minute you walked into Diamond tonight. If you weren't out to pick up any guy who made you hot—only *me*—tell me why. I need to know."

She was losing the fight to keep her sanity with every feather-light breath, each delicate caress on her skin. Losing thought and reason and discretion. Which was why she finally leaned up and said, "Would you please just shut up and kiss me?"

His eyes flared in surprise. Having him this close, and knowing she might never have the chance again, Janie wasn't going to let him back away. Not without sampling, at least once, that incredible mouth. So she took a kiss. Stole it, seduced it from him, whatever it might be called. Twining her hands in his thick hair and curling her body against his, she pulled him down until their mouths met. Licking at the seam between his lips, she sighed as he parted them to meet her tongue in a wet exploration.

Riley had stiffened ever so slightly when she'd surprised him by making such a blatant first move. But he quickly relaxed, as if he could resist no more than she could. He dropped his arms to her waist, tugging her closer.

Lord, the man was *so* aroused. So big. The realization sent a flood of desire through her, making her weak. She moaned into his mouth as that thick ridge in his pants pressed against the juncture of her thighs. He responded by lifting one of her legs in his hand, tilting her hot, damp center directly against him. The pressure from her tight jeans and her swollen sex—smooth and vulnerable—made her arch harder.

He shifted a little, his lips moving away from hers for a second, as if he might end the kiss. She was in no way ready to let it end, knowing, deep down, that she might have only this moment. This one brief, delightful moment when she could believe she was about to have a wild, steamy affair with a man who literally took her breath away.

She just couldn't let him stop kissing her, couldn't let his brain reengage. "More," she moaned. "Please, more."

A throaty laugh told her he wasn't nearly finished, either. His words confirmed it. "Much more."

Riley returned his mouth to hers, this time taking control of their embrace. He slowed things down, capturing her frenzy and turning it into a lazy seduction of thrusts and licks, as if he found her utterly delicious and couldn't get enough of her taste.

Janie honestly couldn't remember an experience in her life as pleasurable as this one. With his broad chest pressed against hers, one hand dropping to cup her bottom with sexy familiarity and his glorious mouth kissing her as if he needed her tongue to go on living, she gave herself over to it. To this perfect, heady, purely sexual feeling, knowing there was nothing she wouldn't do to make love with him, here and now. Even with the knowledge that come morning, he would think of her as just another groupie and would never want to see her again.

This was what she'd wanted all along, wasn't it? To be the flavor of the month...of the *night*. Only she would not be vanilla. Tonight she'd be something much more tasty and decadent.

Tasty. Oh, God how she wanted to taste him. Before proceeding to stroking him, feeling him, riding him.

"You smell amazing," she whispered against his lips, her head filling with his masculine scent. Her body was reacting, growing even wetter as she recognized the familiar—delicious—physical aromas of desire, sex and carnality.

He moved his mouth from hers and tasted his way across her jaw, licking, sucking, biting lightly. "You, too."

He wasn't pulling away. Wasn't ending things. So she went a step further...taking more. Daring one more touch, wondering how far she could go before he remembered minor details such as the fact that she'd never answered his questions. That he didn't know her full name. And that they'd met before.

Resting her hands on his shoulders, she kneaded the thick muscles of his strong arms. "You're like a rock wall."

He laughed softly, shifting so he could scrape the tips of his fingers across her belly. "You're very...*very*...soft."

His touch was electric. Sizzling.

Reaching for the top button of his shirt, she slid it free, then kept unbuttoning. Janie sampled every bit of slick, salty skin as it was revealed. Nibbling a path down the well-defined muscles, she detoured to suck lightly at his flat, male nipple. His muscles quivered with every touch of her lips.

"Have I told you I love man smell?" she asked with a wicked sigh as she breathed him in. "Yours, in particular?"

"I don't believe so," he said, sounding far away. Risking a quick peek up, Janie saw his head was back, his eyes closed, as if he wanted to savor everything she was doing to him.

Which, as far as she was concerned, was her cue to do more. So when she reached the bottom of his dress shirt, unbuttoning the last button and tugging the fine, silky material free of his trousers, she didn't even hesitate. Instead she pulled her leg out of his strong grip and dropped to her knees.

Fortunately, those foam hands were nice and cushiony.

"Whoa...we can slow down." His voice was throaty. Surprised.

Looking up at him, Janie licked her lips, letting him see her want. And her intentions. "You really going to stop me?"

One of his brows shot up. "Depends on what you want to do."

What she wanted to do? Well, that was easy. She wanted to devour him, lick him up like a big, fat lollipop. Which was probably easier to say with actions than with words. So she reached for his belt buckle and slowly unfastened it.

He reached for her shoulder. "Darlin', I mean it. We could go back a few steps."

"Uh-uh." No way she was going to slow down, to give him a chance to reconsider. To start talking again. Not before she'd tasted him, imprinted his hot, musky flavor in her brain and sucked on that powerful ridge straining against his zipper.

"Let me," she whispered, wondering if he realized she was begging...not just trying to seduce him. "Please don't stop me."

"You're joking, right?" he asked with a laugh that sounded more like a groan.

That was all the permission she needed. Janie didn't look up anymore, completely focused on touching, tasting...*taking*.

Her hands didn't even shake as she reached for his waistband, though she moaned when her fingers brushed against his huge erection. Or maybe he did. Maybe they both did.

She sucked her bottom lip into her mouth, watching wide-eyed with her heart pounding loud enough to drown out every sound except her own choppy breaths. Then slowly, carefully, she unbuttoned, then unzipped his pants, tugging them—and his black boxer briefs—down to his lean hips.

"Oh, God." She gasped at the sight of his sex—long and erect—jutting mere inches from her face. Her lips. Her tongue.

"I'm dying here," he groaned, twining his hands in her hair. But he didn't tug her close, didn't try to force her in any way.

Which made her want him even more.

Janie smiled, moving closer. "Don't stop me," she mumbled, meaning it. She wanted to take him all the way. Wanted to suck him until he exploded into the back of her throat, then arouse him all over again so he could screw her into mindless oblivion.

But right before she touched her lips and tongue to that smooth, vulnerable skin, he muttered, "Can I at least know the name of the woman who, I suspect, is about to make me feel really, *really* good?"

She didn't look up, didn't think, barely even paused. "It's Janie," she muttered. "Just Janie."

Then she closed her mouth over the tip of his thick, delicious erection and sucked him into her mouth.

6

WITH A VELVETY smooth tongue and two petal-soft lips wrapped around his cock, Riley couldn't concentrate on much of anything except the pleasure. The wetness. The suction and the licking. The sweet coos of delight she made, as if she were getting off on this every bit as much as he was.

Then her hands got involved, stroking him, lightly running her fingers over his balls, cupping his ass. And all the while taking him deeper and deeper into her mouth, as if she wanted to drink him down, swallow him dry.

He'd never experienced anything like this. Never. Not with his ex, not with past girlfriends, not with any woman he'd picked up for a mindless lay. He'd never felt completely *savored* like he did right now, with this sexy little woman who looked like an angel and sucked like a professional.

"This is amazing," he whispered, closing his eyes and dropping his head back, his entire body nearly shuddering with delight. "*You're* amazing, Janie."

Janie. *Janie?*

Suddenly reality kicked him in the gut. Because everything came together.

Riley's eyes flew open. Blinking a couple of times, he tried to focus until the ceiling tiles came into view. The little bit of blood not centered directly in his dick finally flowed into his brain and it shifted into gear.

"Hell," he said, instantly stiffening everywhere else he wasn't already hard as a rock.

Looking down, he realized what he should have known from the start. This woman on her knees giving him the best blow job he'd ever had was the sweet nursing home volunteer he'd met a couple of months ago. His grandfather's darling. The one he'd figured for a twenty-year-old. "Stop," he croaked.

She heard, but must have thought he was stopping her for another reason—because he was close to finishing. Any other woman he'd been intimate with would have stopped at that. With this one, it was like waving a red flag in front of a bull. She stroked faster, sucked harder, not letting him pull away, practically demanding that he let himself go.

He wasn't a damn saint and the urge to come nearly overwhelmed him, especially because she seemed to *want* him to explode right in her mouth. But something was wrong here—this whole thing was not what it seemed.

So even though he felt certain his head was gonna blow off, Riley finally managed to get the message across by putting one firm hand on her shoulder and another on her cheek. And with great reluctance, he put an end to one of the most sinfully pleasurable interludes he'd ever experienced.

THOUGH FOR A SECOND Janie wondered if Riley Kelleher had stopped her so he could plunge into her and lose himself inside her aching body, one look at his face told her she was wrong.

With a groan that sounded as though it had been ripped from deep within him, he yanked up his trousers and stepped away from her. As if a few inches weren't enough, he shuffled backward, putting a good two feet of space between them.

Staring at one another, they both heaved in a few deep breaths. Janie slowly rose to her feet, keeping herself from lunging back into his arms by digging her nails into her palms. Riley tilted his head back and thrust his hand through his thick hair, visibly trying to grab some control.

She didn't want him controlled. She wanted him helpless with desire. Overwhelmed, just as he'd been a few moments before.

But it was too late. It was gone. The intensity, the need…it had left him.

She'd failed. Janie had enjoyed every second of what she'd just done to him, but he, apparently, had not. The most erotic foreplay she could think of hadn't made him rip her clothes off with pure animal passion. So short of ripping her clothes off, herself, she wasn't quite sure how to push him over the edge.

The knowledge that the most intense oral sex she'd ever attempted hadn't been enough was deflating, to say the least. Especially because she'd liked it so much.

"I know you," he eventually muttered. "My grandfather…"

"Yes."

"You're *that* girl."

"That *woman*," she clarified.

Finally meeting her eyes again, he looked her over, studying her intently. "I didn't recognize you."

"I know."

His body stiffening almost imperceptibly, he said, "Was that the point? Me not recognizing you?"

Janie couldn't deny it, not while her head was still spinning and her chest still heaving. "Yes. That was the point."

Her honesty seemed to surprise him. His brow furrowing in confusion, he asked, "Why?"

"Maybe to make sure you realized I am not a *girl*."

He nodded slowly. "I get the picture." Then, his eyes narrowing, he added, "I obviously didn't see you for who you *really* are, is that it?"

She merely nodded, willing him to see her now. See the woman who wanted him so desperately.

"So having made your point, are we done?"

Done? Good grief, she was nowhere near done with everything she wanted to do with this man. Not that she was ready to admit that out loud. One outrageously stolen intimacy had about used up her bravado for this evening.

"You paid me back for thinking you were a little innocent student or something. Now we're even. Is that right?" His voice sounded tense, almost angry. Whether he'd wanted her or not five minutes ago, he most certainly did not now.

Janie didn't under any circumstances want him leaving here thinking she'd been messing with his head. Neither, however, was she ready to yank her shirt off and ask him to lick her breasts like two scoops of ice cream.

Two scoops altogether…not each. Because she was definitely single scoop size on either side. Or maybe even less. Kid's size.

Which gave her even *less* incentive to rip her shirt off, because all of a sudden she remembered who it was she was trying to tempt here. Mr. Baseball Star who could probably open his own silicone factory with all the stacked women who threw themselves at him on a daily basis.

Who the hell had she been kidding with this whole seduction thing? Even after the most intimate sex act she could perform while fully clothed, the man was looking at her as if he wanted to throw her off a building.

"Helloooo?"

Janie shook her head, hard. "I'm sorry," she whispered.

Suddenly it seemed a whole lot worse for Riley to think she'd imagined herself able to seduce him than to have him think she'd been playing some kind of payback prank on him. So, while already mentally painting a big yellow "chicken" stripe up her back, she added, "I guess I just heard one too many 'little Janie' cracks and I decided to make sure the world—" *you* "—saw me as the woman I am."

Riley stared into her face, as if assessing her honesty. It took every bit of strength Janie had to hold his gaze, not blush or blink or do that shirt-ripping-off thing.

Kid's size. Sample cones.

She kept her shirt on.

Eventually, Riley sighed and gave her a short nod. "Well, consider the point made." And without another word, he turned and walked out of the stockroom.

Leaving her with a bit of her pride intact, but the rest of her completely empty.

ON MONDAY MORNING, Riley left his newly purchased historic Victorian house in the Old Louisville district, planning to head straight for the airport. The trip was good timing. Like many other buildings in the area, his was undergoing renovations, and he really didn't want to be around for the jackhammering.

He was already distracted enough, thanks.

The Slammers were playing a series out west this week, and

he needed to get his head back on straight before stepping onto the field. He had no business dwelling on anything except his game. *Winning* his game. Which meant shaking off this string of bad luck that had kept him from having a decent play in weeks.

He knew he couldn't blame every loss on bum luck. Riley had had some shitty streaks in the past that couldn't be blamed on anything except a sore shoulder, a lapse in concentration or a stupid late night out. But this time felt...different. Because he had never felt better physically, and his life seemed pretty good right now.

So losing for no reason, well, this time, he feared, it just came down to chance. Like his teammate Beau Léglise liked to say in his thick Louisiana accent, "Sometimes the field, she is a flawless diamond, and sometimes she's a damn white line in the dirt leading straight to hell."

Exactly. Just bad luck that he'd been following that tricky white line in the wrong direction. It would require all his focus to get past the losses.

But his mind didn't seem to want to cooperate. Because ever since Saturday night, a slim little brunette had been doing tap dances in his brain and he couldn't shake himself loose of thoughts of *her.* The cute nursing home volunteer who'd turned into a sultry temptress, and then a tease.

Just Janie. The woman who right this minute was standing behind the counter of Round The Bases, looking utterly frustrated as she talked with a big, hairy guy in a cowboy hat.

"What are you doin', jackass?" Riley asked, not sure if he was speaking to himself or the stranger paying such obvious attention to Janie inside the store.

He idled his car, which was double-parked right outside the shop. This was bad. He was watching through the front window like some kind of pathetic stalker.

Drive away.

But he couldn't. Not yet. Because she looked so sweetly sexy, yet so...tense, somehow. He realized why when the big guy in the stupid hat, which looked as if it had come straight off of J.R.'s head, leaned far across the counter and got right in her face.

Though he pointed to something behind her, the man looked down, as if trying to peek down Janie's tight tank top, which scooped low to reveal the curves of her high, pert breasts.

Riley stiffened, his fingers clenching the steering wheel.

Janie wasn't dressed in her loose, baggy, nice-young-volunteer getup. She wore a pair of tight-as-sin white pants with the tank top, and her hair was curled and soft around her face. No glasses, either. So he was obviously seeing the temptress from Saturday night, not the angel from the retirement home. And she was definitely getting attention from the man who leered as Janie turned around and bent over to grab something off the shelf behind the counter.

She's a tease, not some virgin. Maybe she likes it.

But Riley knew better. Knew, deep down, that whatever had driven Janie to behave the way she had Saturday night, she was not the type of woman who sought out the attention of just any big, burly guy. Especially when she was alone with him.

Especially when he touched her.

Because when Janie rose and handed the customer whatever it was he'd asked for, the man didn't let go of her hand. She tried to pull away, her body growing tense, but he didn't release her.

A shocking rush of anger burst through Riley, so powerful and strong it made him shake. Jerking the steering wheel to the right, he crammed his small sports car into a parking space, nearly clipping the front fender of a sedan but not caring. He leapt out, thrusting his keys into his pocket, and ate up the sidewalk in three long strides. Yanking open the door to Round The Bases, he moved toward the checkout counter.

It took him less than two seconds to process Janie's expression—concern. Maybe even fear. And one second beyond that to notice that the burly asshole had now grabbed her other hand, too, and was trying to convince her to come out from around the counter and go to lunch with him.

"Get the hell away from her."

The stranger had obviously been so focused on what he was doing that he hadn't even realized Riley had entered the store. He spun around, fast, hopping about two feet away from the counter and the suddenly very relieved-looking woman behind it.

"Wha…"

"Get out. Now," Riley ordered, hearing the rage in his voice, knowing if the man resisted he would have to hurt him.

"Why don't you mind your own business? The gal and I were just having a friendly conversation."

"I'm not your friend," Janie said, her voice shaky but also stern.

"You *can* be."

A roaring began to build in Riley's head, his whole body was taut and expectant. On alert. Ready. "I don't want to have to tell you again. Leave. Now."

The other man's chin jutted out. "You don't work here. If the princess wants me out, she can tell me herself."

Janie didn't hesitate. "I want you out."

Good girl.

"Please leave," she added. No waver in her voice now. She was calm, determined. "I don't want to see you in here again."

The man's face mottled red, either with anger or embarrassment. If it was anger and he made one wrong move, Riley was going to pound him. Game or no game.

Clenching his fists, he stepped closer, knowing the other guy was taller, but also seeing a roll of flab around his middle. He could take him. No doubt about it.

"Screw it," the man said with a disgusted sneer. "So much for trying to be friendly."

"I have enough friends," Janie said, holding it together.

"Well, I hope you have enough customers, too," the man said, suddenly sounding petulant. "Because I'll never be one again." Then he grunted and started walking toward the door.

Riley didn't step out of his way, he merely crossed his arms, leveling a steady gaze on the other man to make sure he didn't think about changing his mind.

Suddenly, the guy recognized him. He stopped, looked Riley in the eye and mumbled, "You're…"

"Yeah."

They each paused. Staring. Assessing. Then the jackass in the cowboy hat smirked. "How about an autograph?"

Riley merely shook his head in disbelief. "You've gotta be kidding me."

And the guy left, muttering a few choice curses. Guess he was not only a former shopper of Round The Bases, but now also a former Slammers fan. *Tough shit.*

Once he had gone, Riley walked a few feet closer to Janie, who had come out from behind the counter and now stood watching, her eyes wide, her mouth open in a little circle.

"You okay?"

She nodded. But he didn't believe her. So without giving it much thought, he opened his arms, and she walked into them. She shuddered once or twice, but didn't cry or break down. Instead she just stood there, her arms wrapped around his neck, her curves fitting perfectly against his body. Just as if she belonged there. Just as she had Saturday night.

"You really should have someone else here with you for security," he said softly as he stroked the small of her back.

Sniffing a tiny bit, she slowly stepped out of his arms, her face flushing red.

There was that blush again. On the face of a woman who'd been sucking on him as if he was a big, sweet piece of candy less than forty-eight hours ago.

Shaking her head, she said, "I was ready to protect myself."

Raising a curious brow, he watched as she lifted her hand, which was clenched into a fist. Though he could see she had something clasped in her fingers, she didn't seem able to unclench. That was when he realized how rattled Janie was. He didn't begin to assume it was because of his presence—or the fact that she'd just been in his arms again, as though she'd never left them—and chalked it up to the asshole who'd just left.

Moving slowly, so he wouldn't startle her, he reached out and touched the tip of her finger with his own, slowly tugging it back. Then he moved to the next finger, and the next, until her fist opened and a roll of pennies tumbled off her hand and fell to the floor.

They both looked down as the coins thunked, and Riley was

unable to prevent a disbelieving groan. "What were you gonna do, buy him off with a half a dollar?"

Her chin shot up. "I was ready to hit him."

With her small fist and fifty cents' worth of copper. His lips twitched.

"Don't laugh at me. My brother taught me to fight. That fist would have gone right in his Adam's apple, giving me enough time to get to the door."

Okay. So she had the right idea and she hadn't been fooling herself that she could actually go toe-to-toe with a two-hundred-fifty pound attacker.

"And then," she added, "I would have been outside screaming bloody murder. I'm not stupid, you know."

"Never doubted it for a minute, honey, but you do sometimes seem to get in over your head."

Her jaw dropped. "I don't know what you're talking about."

Selective memory. He could remedy that with one hot, possessive kiss that would clue her in to exactly what he meant. One reminder that she'd been playing with fire less than forty-eight hours ago and damned if they hadn't both nearly gone up in flames.

"I mean, you obviously aren't always careful about the men you play these games with."

Direct hit. She flinched. "I'm not a game-player, Riley."

"Could have fooled me."

"I wasn't playing you. I…"

"Yeah? You what?"

Her mouth opened, then closed. Until finally, sounding almost helpless, she admitted, "I just wanted you. That's all. No games, no paybacks. I just wanted to sleep with you for the sheer physical pleasure of it."

He stared at her for a long moment, assessing the truth of her words. He knew she wasn't lying to him. At last Janie was being honest about her feelings, her desires.

She'd wanted him. And God knows he'd wanted her.

But there was still a voice of doubt in Riley's mind that wanted to know *why* she'd been so desperate. Why she'd wanted him so badly. Why she'd showed up at Diamond the other night, dressed to seduce him, then gone about doing exactly that.

He *had* to know why. Had to know if she wanted *him,* Riley, the man. Or just another notch on her baseball players' card, like so many other women he'd met.

Payback and revenge? Sex and conquest? Or sweet, simple desire between two people who had been hot for each other from the moment they'd met?

He had to know.

"Janie?" he said, speaking softly, wondering why his own question suddenly seemed so damned important. Why his heart was pounding like it did when he was about to throw a three-two pitch to a power hitter.

But before he could ask it, the door to the shop opened and a group of teenage boys burst into Round The Bases. Laughing, shouting, and, as to be expected, immediately recognizing him.

Despite what had just happened with the ass in the cowboy hat, Riley *always* made time for his fans, particularly the younger ones. During the off-season, he spent a lot of time speaking at schools and athletic centers, encouraging kids to pursue their dreams. He'd received many letters from parents who thanked him for inspiring their sons to stay on the right path, and he always found time for them. Today was no exception.

So instead of challenging the woman with the lovely brown eyes to be honest about what she really felt, what was going on inside that pretty, sexy head, he found himself signing autographs and watching Janie grow more and more distant. Until she froze him out completely.

7

"WHY HAVE YOU BEEN coming here every night this week?"

Janie stared at her grandmother, not surprised by the question. It was Thursday night, less than a week after Janie had shared those wild, arousing moments with Riley Kelleher, and just a few days since their conversation at the store. She had visited the "home for the enlightened years" every evening since Monday. Mostly to make up for not having come Sunday.

She and her grandmother were sitting in the community room, trying to talk over the cackles and cutthroat game-playing of the bridge group at the next table, so she raised her voice to respond. "Don't you like me coming more often?"

"Well, of course I do, but you look like you're going to fall over. You work until six, come here until eight. Why not just wait until Sunday, honey. Edgar and I wouldn't mind."

"Where is Edgar?" she asked, gazing around the crowded room, surprised she hadn't seen him yet.

"He's lying down." Grandma Anne frowned. "Doing that a lot lately. I don't think he's feeling well, but he won't admit it."

Janie hated to think of the man being sick, and not just because she liked him so much. Nor was it because she suspected her grandmother loved him. But because she *knew* Riley did.

Riley. He was the reason she'd been coming here at night, rather than waiting for the weekend. The Slammers were on the road, down another two games—continuing their disappointing downward spiral after the winning streak that had given them all hope during the month of May. Janie had been paying attention to the Slammers schedule because the last thing she wanted to do was run into their star pitcher. Not while she was still so embarrassed about what had happened between them last weekend.

Riley would be gone through Saturday, and she imagined the first thing he'd want to do on his return was visit his grandfather. Which meant Janie was not about to risk showing up here on Sunday.

It wasn't the intimacy they'd shared that had her trying to avoid him. It was her dishonesty. She'd lied to him, thinking it would make her feel better later, would save her dignity.

She'd been wrong. Janie had never been a liar, so right now she was feeling pretty much like pond scum. Especially after Monday, when he'd been so protective. So amazing.

She'd tried to come clean then, admitting she'd simply been acting on her desire. But she hadn't been totally honest. Hadn't told him of the scheme she, Callie and Babe had come up with to seduce someone associated with the Slammers. She somehow suspected he wasn't going to like that, even if the idea had been prompted by Janie's instant reaction to Riley and nothing else.

"Tell me the truth, honey, why are you coming out here at night all of a sudden?"

"Maybe so she can avoid running into *me?*"

Janie's whole body jerked in shock as a very familiar voice spoke from behind her. His tight tone gave her a good hint about Riley Kelleher's mood. *Not good.*

Taking a deep breath, she turned in her chair, looking over her shoulder. As always, the man's incredible face and body zapped her brain cells into slow motion. But not so slow that she didn't notice the way his weary expression was emphasized by the tiny lines of fatigue on his brow.

"Hi," she murmured.

"Why would she be avoiding *you?*" Grandma Anne asked, her voice sharp with curiosity.

"You'd have to ask her," Riley replied evenly, though he never took his eyes off Janie. "Maybe she can explain her enjoyment of payback games to you."

Okay, yes, definitely still angry.

Grandma snorted. "Boyo, that's some imagination you've got. My granddaughter doesn't know the meaning of the word payback."

"*Granddaughter?*"

"That girl's picture is in the dictionary beside the words *bleeding heart.* Hasn't she put her whole life on hold for her mush-brained brother?"

Janie wished one of the players from the bridge game at the next table would screech in triumph, anything to drown out the sound of her elderly grandmother singing her praises to a man who loathed her.

"Is that so?" he murmured. "And here I thought she was the type who likes to get even."

Grandma Anne snorted. "She's a sweet-natured angel. Janie wouldn't so much as slap a man who pinched her behind."

Even while Janie groaned inside, she saw Riley's lips quivering.

There was no doubt what he was thinking. Grandma's words had reminded them both of their former encounters. When he'd pretty much come to her rescue with that jackass in the store on Monday.

And Saturday. Oh, yes indeed, Saturday.

She certainly hadn't slapped *him* when he'd touched her so intimately. Curled up against him like a vine around a trellis was a better description of her reaction.

The memory made her shift in her seat, as if she could still feel the man's hand cupping her bottom and his body pressed against hers. The perfect way his rigid erection had fit against her tight jeans…and how much better it would have fit if she hadn't been wearing those jeans. The glorious way he'd tasted and smelled.

She'd thought about those things many times during the five nights since they'd had their carnal interlude, but this was much more potent because Riley was watching her, his eyes glittering. He was remembering, too. Remembering *all* of it, not just his anger at her perceived game-playing.

"Time for me to go take my medicine," her grandmother said, rising to her feet with a speculative look. She winked broadly at Janie, obviously having decided that Riley was a potential romantic interest. Potential train wreck was more like it.

As soon as her grandmother was gone, Janie stood and grabbed her purse. "I need to go, too."

She should have known Riley Kelleher wouldn't let her get away with that. He fell into step beside her, escorting her to the door, walking with that natural confident athleticism that women found so irresistible.

Not me. No sir.

Ha.

"Admit it…you're here now so you can avoid me this week-end," he said as he held the door for her, then followed her out into the hot night.

"Don't flatter yourself." Her retort was weak and held no bite, so he had to know she was lying. "What are you doing here, anyway? I thought you were on the road."

"Been keeping track of my schedule?"

"Is there anyone in Louisville who doesn't?"

He shrugged. "No game tomorrow. I don't have to be back in California until Saturday."

He'd hopped on a plane and returned to Kentucky for one night. She leapt to the obvious conclusion. "Is Edgar okay?"

"Oh, yeah, he's fine. The doctor says he just has a cold, but other than that, he's in perfect health."

Had he truly flown back to Kentucky for an old man's cold? Or, maybe, for something else? Janie didn't want to even let herself think it had anything to do with her. Still…

"So you're an angel who wouldn't slap a man who grabbed your behind, huh? I guess that's lucky for me, considering I helped myself to a nice handful."

Feeling her face grow hot, Janie was glad for the lateness of the hour. The streetlights casting pools of illumination in the parking lot certainly wouldn't reveal her blush.

But somehow, he knew. Damn it, the man *knew* he'd flustered her. Because he stopped, took hold of her upper arm and turned her to face him. "What's the matter? Embarrassed to be reminded of your little prank?"

She shook her head, wondering again just what kind of soap Riley used that made him *smell* like that. Like the ocean and heat and sex. Mercy, he smelled good enough to eat. Again.

"Or maybe your grandmother was right, and it was no prank," he said, his voice low, thick with intensity. He waited, asking her for an explanation with just the firm touch of his hand on her arm and the confusion evident on his shadowed face.

Janie could no longer deny it. "I was telling you the truth on Monday," she admitted, her tone barely above a whisper. "Yes, I went into Diamond specifically because I knew you'd be there. Not to get even, like I let you believe Saturday night, because I was so embarrassed that you *didn't* rip my clothes off and dive on me…after." She swallowed, then went on. "It was simply because I wanted you. Wanted you from the minute you made that comment about my ass the first time we met. Okay? Happy now?"

He released her arm, staring intently into her face, his green eyes glittering in the near darkness. Embarrassed, disconcerted, confused as hell, she spun away and started walking toward her car, absolutely determined never to make a fool of herself in front of the man again. "I've got to go. Take care of yourself. Break a leg in Saturday's game," she muttered.

His groan alerted her to her faux pas. Wincing, she peeked over her shoulder. "Uh, isn't that what they say in baseball?"

"I think that's for actors," he said, shaking his head as he followed her. This time, the hand he put on her shoulder wasn't firm, not tight at all. In fact, he was gentle, carefully rubbing the side of his thumb on her collarbone, fingering a strand of her hair. "Don't really want to think about 'breaking my leg' when I'm on the field, Just Janie."

His touch was so soft. So sweet. So incredibly arousing.

"Let me ask you something," he said.

Strip naked and dance with me in the moonlight? Sure. Okay.

"You don't know a single thing about baseball, or sports in general, am I right?"

She nibbled her lip and shook her head. "Not really."

"So, what the hell are you doing working in a sports memorabilia shop? Who would hire you?"

"I wasn't exactly hired, I volunteered to help," she explained, containing a sigh of disappointment. She wished he'd move his hand away so her heart could start beating again if they were going to talk about something as mundane as the store.

Who was she kidding? She wanted his hand moving *down*. Side to side. Around in circles. One right after the other.

"Volunteered?" he asked.

"My 'mush-brained' brother needed someone to run the place while he's serving his time."

Riley's brow shot up, though he still grinned. "In prison?"

She had to laugh. "No, in the Guard."

"Whew. I'd hate to think you have some violent brother who's gonna come after me when he gets out of the big house."

Curious, she looked up at him. "Why would he do that?"

"Maybe I'm about to give him a reason." He didn't take his hand—now delicately brushing her neck—away, hinting at more. So much more. And she was on fire for it, even though she kept trying to remind herself she was unable to seduce this man.

"So have you ever even been to a game?"

Subject change. *Brain, reengage.* "No."

"You've never heard the blissful sound of a bat cracking against a fastball that was supposed to end your playoff dreams and instead brought an entire stadium to its feet, then?"

His words painted a vivid picture, and she heard the passion in his voice. "No, I never have. Maybe I should go to a game." *Before the Slammers leave town,* she mentally added. But she didn't want to add to the pressure the star pitcher had to be feeling to turn the team's recent losing streak around.

He shook his head, one side of his mouth curling up. "You work in a store called Round The Bases, but how much do you know about rounding the bases, Just Janie?"

She liked the way he said that, as if whispering an endearment. It took any sting of criticism from his words.

"I know you know a lot about certain positions," he added.

Janie hadn't realized the rapidly changing conversation was becoming about much more than sports until he came closer, sliding one foot between hers so their legs touched. Moving his fingers up the side of her neck, he twined them in her hair. "You know something about first base, don't you, sweetheart?" He leaned in, kissed her temple and breathed in her scent.

Oh, *oh,* she was in trouble here. Because she'd given him an opening, room to squeeze past her last shaky remnants of control. She might very well be about to make a fool of herself again.

Then she thought about it and took a calming breath. She wasn't the one doing the seducing this time, right? No, indeed, she was just standing here, minding her own business, while the sexiest man she'd ever met whispered wicked innuendo in her ear.

"You must know *something* about the excitement building as you race toward second," he said, his voice nearly a purr. "Your pulse pounding as you wonder just how far you're gonna go. If you'll be stopped there or if this time you'll be going farther."

"Oh, God," she whispered, his words making her weak.

"And, honey, oh, rounding third. It's amazing. Being close, *so* close, to the ultimate goal, you can almost *taste* it."

She closed her eyes, whimpering, picturing exactly what he wanted her to picture. She might not know anything about the game of baseball, but she sure as heck knew the sexual analogies associated with it. And what she'd done to him in the stockroom Saturday night definitely qualified as a triple play.

"There's nothing like it," he added, moving in until the front of his T-shirt brushed against her sleeveless blouse. Her nipples puckered into two throbbing points beneath the fabric.

"And please, darlin', tell me you understand the pure pleasure of sliding home."

Closing her eyes, she pictured it. Him, sliding…into her.

She wanted it. Desperately. Fears of rejection, fears of looking like a pathetic, boring little nobody simply couldn't compare to the hunger she felt.

Now was her chance. Time to put up or shut up. To play ball, or get off the field.

The choice was surprisingly easy. Janie was ready to play. Ready to take a swing again, even if she missed.

Somehow pulling a few brain cells together, she managed a sultry comeback, loaded with innuendo. "I can appreciate it from the perspective of the plate," she whispered, "you know, the one on the bottom…the one being slid into."

He groaned. Janie felt his reaction, the sudden strength of a fully erect man pressing with delicious possibilities against her hip. And she began to wonder if everything she'd been fantasizing about having but thought she'd lost her chance to have might indeed be hers for the taking. Here. Now. Tonight.

Finally, right when she'd begun to fear Riley was about to laugh and say he'd merely been repaying her for her perceived game-playing, he whispered, "As long as we both score, angel, does it really matter who's on top?"

RILEY HAD GIVEN IT about ten seconds' thought before deciding not to deny himself what he wanted. No, he hadn't started their sassy, sexy game of verbal ping-pong with the intention of getting between Janie's sweet legs, but damned if that wasn't the way he was going to finish it. And she knew it.

Somehow, her admission earlier that she'd wanted him from the first time he'd flirted with her made it okay. She wanted the man who'd liked her ass. Not the guy on the trading cards.

Which was about the best news he'd had in weeks.

"Let's go," she said, her voice shaking. He suspected it was more from excitement than from nervousness. The way her eyes sparkled and her lips quivered told him she was as on fire as he was, ready to do what they'd both wanted to do from the minute they'd met. Have wickedly hot, pulse-pounding, roar-to-the-moon sex.

Her affirmation that she wanted it as much as he did stripped away any last, lingering questions about what he was doing. Sliding his hand to her cheek, he tangled his fingers in her thick hair and tugged her close for another drugging kiss. Her tasty mouth opened in welcome and she squirmed into him, wrapping her arms around his shoulders.

The kiss was good. Better than good. He didn't want it to stop, not even long enough to get in the car to drive someplace where they could get rid of their pesky, inconvenient clothes.

Without letting their mouths part, Riley lifted her, groaning at the way she instantly parted her legs, wrapping them around his waist. He supported her slight frame easily, feeling the heat of her even through their jeans.

"Honey, I don't know if I'm going to make it to the nearest bed," he managed to mutter when she rubbed herself against his cock, letting out a groan of pleasure.

"Isn't this your car?" she asked, pressing hot, feverish kisses along his jaw.

Laughing at her desperation, he replied, "Yeah, but there are an awful lot of lights around here."

She shook her head, looking desperate as her gaze darted over the parking lot. About a dozen cars were parked in various spots. Cars whose owners could be coming outside at any time.

"Where do you live?"

"Not close enough," she said with a groan. Then a tiny, wicked smile widened her swollen lips. "Wait. I have an idea."

So anxious to have her he didn't even ask her what that idea was, he let her wriggle down. The moment she was out of his arms, he wanted her back there. But she was quick, dashing around his car to a small sedan on the other side of it. She opened the trunk, lifted a blanket from inside, then slammed the lid down. Almost racing back, she didn't even pause when she reached him, simply grabbing his hand and tugging him along after her.

Riley started to laugh, caught up in the excitement and the outrageous sense of mischief. "Where are we going?"

"To the place we met."

He understood. Stumbling to keep up with her, he watched as the circles of light cast by the overhead streetlamps began to disappear. They reached the lawn and continued to stride across the moist grass. The brightly lit windows of the closest building were a few hundred feet away, and when Janie led him over a small rise, then down the other side, those lights disappeared, until they were enveloped in darkness.

"You can't see this spot from the building, which is why I was caught completely by surprise that day."

That day. The day he'd seen an adorably cute young woman whose creamy cheeks had flooded with color and whose smile had eclipsed the sun. A laughing young woman spending her Sunday afternoon volunteering to read to the elderly.

Oh, right, *she* hadn't been the one reading the sex manual. But the concept was the same. She'd appeared to be just a nice, friendly, nurturing female who'd had a fabulous ass and a pair of eyes that positively glowed with life. And she'd appealed to him instantly, even when he'd figured her to be too young and inexperienced for him.

The thought made his steps slow. "Just how old are you?"

She looked at him over her shoulder. "Twenty-five."

Whew. Definitely legal. And judging by the way she kissed, the way she'd rubbed her tight nipples against his chest, the way her long, slender legs had wrapped so instinctively around his waist, she definitely wasn't inexperienced. She hadn't seemed that way Saturday night.

The thought of those legs and that kiss and that incredible mouth made his heart trip over itself. He wanted to see her. Taste her. Touch her. Wanted her open to him under the moonlight. Months of celibacy had his entire body on alert, on edge, but he didn't regret them. Because tonight, he suspected, was going to have been worth the wait. "This is far enough," he muttered, coming to a stop.

Not arguing, she spread out the blanket, then turned to stare at him. The starry night brought flecks of gold alive in her hair and made her eyes sparkle with warmth. Want. Desire.

But she didn't move. She simply stood there, watching, as if suddenly uncertain.

Riley wasn't uncertain of a damn thing. He hadn't planned

this, hadn't intended on meeting someone who made him feel crazy-hot but also incredibly alive every time he saw her, but it had happened. And for tonight, he was just going to enjoy it.

Reaching for her again, he pulled her close, his hands going to her waist to tug her shirt free of her jeans. He needed to feel her warm skin. She helped him, yanking the blouse up, as if desperate to be rid of it. Riley barely noticed it hitting the ground; he was focused on staring at her. Slender. Soft. Creamy. Her delicate breasts were utterly perfect, small but beautifully curved, tipped with tight, dark nipples that he immediately wanted to taste.

"You're the prettiest sight I've seen in a very long time," he muttered through a tight throat. Skimming his hands up her sides, he hissed as the tips of his thumbs brushed the skin just below her pebbled nipples.

"Oh," she moaned, arching into his hands so he could cup each tender mound. When he caught those sensitized tips between his fingers, she moaned even louder. "That feels incredible."

"I can't wait to taste you," he muttered hoarsely as he kissed his way down her jawline, then her throat. He nibbled a path across her collarbone, feeling her shake in his arms.

Riley pulled away long enough to tear his shirt off, but didn't trust himself to go further. Because right now, his jeans were the only thing keeping him from plunging into her and losing his mind to pleasure.

"More," she whimpered. Janie ran her nails lightly over his shoulders, making him flex and clench in reaction. "You're so big for a baseball player."

He laughed softly, then tugged her down until they both knelt on the blanket. Janie arched back, silently telling him what she wanted. And without a warning, he gave it to her. Hungry, ravenous, he covered her breast with his mouth and sucked hard. She shook, but steadied herself by twining her fingers in his hair and holding him even closer.

"Riley…" she moaned, her voice holding a hint of desperation. The way she rocked her hips against him told him why she was so desperate. Her arousal was visible on her face. Her eyelids were heavy and her breathing ragged. He could also inhale deeply and catch the intoxicating scent of aroused woman. The need to feel that moisture overwhelmed him, and he reached down, until he could slide his hand between her legs.

"You're hot."

"I'm dying."

"Don't die yet, honey, we've got a long way to go."

"I know," she said with a moan. She reached for her own waistband, quickly unsnapped and unzipped, and tilted closer, as if she didn't want to waste the time it would take to push her jeans out of the way before having him touch her more intimately.

Riley closed his eyes, focusing on the sensations—her sighs of pleasure, the breeze blowing a hint of coolness across their bodies on this hot June night. The warmth of her supple skin as he slid his hand down her soft stomach, to the elastic edge of a pair of silky panties.

"So soft," he muttered as he moved lower, his fingers tangling in a minuscule, warm thatch that was the last obstacle between his hand and her wet folds. He wanted to explore that much more thoroughly. Close up.

His quick suspicion that she had recently had one of those wax jobs he'd heard about was confirmed when he moved just a little farther. Past that small, soft nest, to the softer, completely bare lips of her drenched sex. "Oh, man."

He was dying to taste her there, to drink from her.

Her eyes flew open and she nibbled her lip. "It's, uh, different. You don't like…"

"Hell, yes, I like it," meaning every word. He stroked her, soaking his fingers in her creaminess, then using the moisture to caress her hard little clit until she was panting. "I was just imagining how sweet that's going to taste on my tongue."

Her sigh of relief was so loud it made him laugh. "You approve of that idea?"

"I've been fantasizing about you doing that to me. Among other things."

Oh, yeah, here's to that. And other things.

Remembering how she'd so gotten into what she'd done to him Saturday, he decided to see how she liked being on the receiving end of some intense oral sex. So without saying a word, he pushed her jeans down, helping her wriggle out of them, and her panties. By the time she'd finished kicking them away, Riley was lying flat on his back on the blanket, ready to gobble her up.

Her eyes flared as he reached for her and tugged her to him. She tried to lie down, then began to shake when he instead lifted one of her legs and draped it across his neck, bringing her vulnerable, feminine flesh into full, glorious view.

"Riley..."

"You're beautiful."

He wished it were brighter outside, since the starry, moonlit sky only gave him a tantalizing glimpse of her bare, glistening sex. But since looking at her was only the start of what he wanted to do, he quickly thrust the regret away. He tugged her closer so he could taste that smooth, plump skin and suck her sensitive clit between his lips.

She squirmed. "Riley!"

"Shh," he murmured, holding her hips in his hands, keeping her positioned where he wanted her. "I'm real busy right now, Janie honey." He was. Busy nibbling her bare lips and licking into her creamy crevice. Busy devouring all that juicy sweetness.

And devour her he did, until she was moaning, then whimpering, then crying out to the sky in utter satisfaction.

8

JANIE HONESTLY didn't know how she managed to remain upright during Riley's thorough, blissful oral lovemaking. She only knew that within minutes his tongue and mouth had coaxed her into a shattering climax and still the man continued to kiss, lick and taste her as if she were a banquet.

She also knew one more thing: she was going to start making a standing appointment at the waxing place. Because oh, *mercy*...

"That was amazing," she said with a deep, sated sigh.

But now she wanted more. Wanted to be filled by him. To take him, love him until neither one of them could move anymore. So sliding down his body, she stared into his eyes and smiled. "Thank you. But I think you're done."

He laughed softly. "Honey, I've barely gotten started."

"Me, either."

Straddling his hips, she quickly unfastened his jeans, then tugged them down. When he was gloriously naked, she paused to appreciate the muscular ripples of his powerful body. "Ripples," she murmured with a smile. "I love ripples." Then she slid back up, rubbing herself against his muscular legs and his hip, taking pleasure from the firmness of his body against her dripping flesh. Especially one firm part of his body, which she caught between her thighs and rubbed ever so lightly against.

His every muscle tightened, the cords in his neck standing out. And, if it were possible, his rigid sex grew even larger between the cheeks of her bottom.

They stared at one another, saying nothing for a moment. Janie knew Riley was feeling the same, irreplaceable sense of anticipation that came only from savoring something you knew was going to be utterly magnificent.

"This is gonna be good, isn't it Janie?" he asked softly, reaching up to cup her face. He rubbed the rough edge of his thumb across her jaw. "We're gonna be good."

She had no doubt he was talking about a lot more than sex. And somehow, even though this was their first time and they hadn't known each other that long, something told her he was right. They were going to be good together.

"Yes. We are." And they both smiled.

As much as she wanted to lower herself onto all that male heat right this moment, Janie wasn't stupid. "I have a condom in my purse," she said, reaching for it.

He laughed softly. "I have one in my jeans pocket."

"Well, aren't we the responsible little citizens."

"Thank goodness," he replied, looking up at her with a wicked glint in his eye as he caught her breasts in his hands. "That means we can play twice as much."

Twice. That'd do…for a start.

Janie had a hard time locating the condom because Riley made it awfully hard to concentrate on looking. He kept stroking her, licking her nipples, teasing her by gliding his member back and forth across her wet opening.

"Stop," she whispered with a groan as she finally found the protection, "or I won't be able to wait to get this thing on."

His laugh was evil, but he stopped. Taking the small packet out of her shaking hands, he ripped it open, then sheathed himself. "Done. You taking over again?"

He was still laughing, she could hear it in his voice. Which made perfect sense because Janie wanted to laugh, too. To laugh and howl and make love and roll around in the moonlight.

She felt…joyous. Not just sexed-up, but very, very happy.

"I guess," she murmured as she rubbed herself against him, quickly wetting the latex covering his sex. "But, well, to be honest, ever since you made that comment about sliding home…I've been thinking how much I'd love to be slid into."

She'd never imagined a man could move so fast, because suddenly Riley was flipping her onto her back and holding himself over her, his lean hips between her parted thighs. "I can't think of any slide I'd rather make."

"Not even into home plate?"

"Uh-uh."

"Game Seven of the World Series?"

His laughter made his chest rumble, the wiry hairs there teasing her nipples. "Right this minute, honey, not even that."

Then his laughter faded and he slowly began his slide.

Riley's green eyes shone and Janie couldn't tear her gaze away from them. Her mouth fell open in a little gasp as he edged into her, filling her inch by devastating inch. His restraint was going to kill her soon because she was dying—ready to explode—with the need to feel him buried to the hilt inside her.

"You feel incredible."

Wrapping her arms around his neck and dragging his face toward her, she licked his lips, then murmured, "So do you, Riley. Now *please* hit one out of the ballpark and *score.*"

With a groan of helpless delight, he did as she asked, thrusting home, filling her so that she cried out at the pleasure of it. "Thank you," she moaned, wrapping her legs around his hips.

"Oh, don't thank me yet, that was just the first pitch."

Pressing her lips to his, Janie kissed him deeply, letting their tongues meet and mate. She savored his taste even as her body savored his invasion. Her hips moved to meet every thrust, and each time he filled her, she gasped against his mouth.

They weren't laughing anymore, but Janie still felt joyous—happy—as they thrust and stroked and loved well into the night.

And well into her heart.

THE SLAMMERS won their game in California on Saturday. Then they won the next two at home. And four out of five on the road.

Riley would have chalked the turnaround up to another twist of the sport, but, deep down, he suspected his own game was better because *he* was so much better. Happier. More fulfilled.

It was as if he'd suddenly started seeing something really good in his life and wanting everything else to be just as good.

Janie. It was all because of Janie.

After that first amazing experience on the lawn of the Bluegrass Retirement Home, he'd followed her back to her apartment and had spent the night in her bed. Every other night he'd been in Louisville since then had been spent there, too.

She amazed him. Her bright smile, her enthusiasm, her big heart—they'd all been obvious from the first time he'd laid eyes on her. But what he hadn't suspected until he'd really started spending time with her was just how smart she was, and how much fun she could be. In bed and out of it.

He'd never known a woman so open to trying anything—from the gator tail he'd persuaded her to sample at his favorite downhome restaurant, to the batting cage where she'd proved herself to be just about the most uncoordinated person he'd ever met. To the wild sexual adventures that left him breathless and insane.

They also made him rethink that coordination thing…because the woman had some incredible moves.

She was insatiable. She was delightful. And he couldn't get enough of her. If he could have brought her with him on the road, he would have done it, no matter how much it would have pissed off Brodie Jessup, his manager. But he couldn't, and the reason he couldn't was the one thing he and Janie couldn't agree on.

"How long are you going to keep this up before you collapse?" he asked as he entered the stockroom of Round The Bases. It was eight o'clock…thirty minutes *after* she was supposed to have met him at Diamond for dinner. He hadn't had to even think about where she might be before coming to find her.

She jerked her head up, pushing her glasses back up her nose with the tip of her index finger.

Riley liked the glasses. They gave her a sexy, brainiac look. They also went well with a plain, wraparound skirt she had, which she'd worn without anything underneath when they'd gone to the movies one night. No one would ever have guessed that he'd been fingering her to orgasm throughout the film.

"Oh, God, I stood you up, didn't I?" She sounded distressed.

"Yeah."

She leaped out of her chair, nearly knocking it over. "Riley, I am so sorry. I just had to get a handle on this order. Now that you guys are winning, business is booming again. I swear, sports fans are so fickle."

Crossing his arms and leaning one shoulder against a shelf loaded with sweatshirts, he shook his head. "So should I start losing so you can get a decent meal for once?"

She walked over to him and put her hand flat on his chest. "Not on your life, mister. I don't want you doing anything that could mean the team leaves Louisville."

He hoped she said that because she didn't want *him* to go anywhere. Not because of this business—which he was beginning to think of as the ball and chain around her slender neck. Because even if the team did move, which was, he'd heard, no longer a real threat, he had no intention of ending things with Janie.

It was too soon to be thinking about long-term stuff like love and marriage and all the crap he'd told himself he'd never have again. Lately, however, he *had* been thinking about it. *Allowing* himself to think about it…for the first time in ages. He'd even started talking to his family about Janie, enduring the big-brother ribbing he'd never fully escape and the delight of his parents, who'd been certain he'd been too badly burned to ever even consider remarrying.

He just didn't know if she was thinking the same things.

"Come on, let's get out of here. You've worked late every night this week. You're exhausted."

She certainly looked that way. Her brown eyes were shadowed by dark circles, and her face was pale and drawn. Suddenly suspecting there was more to her condition than just a lot of hard hours at work, he asked, "Is there something else going on? Something you're not telling me?"

She literally fell into his chest, burying her face in the crook of his neck. As always, her soft curves melted into his body until they felt like one person. "Tom's tour of duty was extended. I have no idea when he'll be coming home."

Tom. The brother. The one who'd dumped his responsibilities on his sister and allowed her to put her life on hold for him indefinitely. Riley knew he should admire the man for risking his life for his country, but right now, he really wanted to punch his lights out for what he'd done to Janie. "I'm sorry, honey, I know you've been feeling overwhelmed."

"Overwhelmed…and guilty for being resentful at how overwhelmed I am."

He got that. "You're human. And don't you think it's time to come up with some other options? Like, maybe hiring someone to run this place while you get on with your life?" *With me?*

"I'm barely covering expenses as it is," she replied, stepping back and wrapping her arms around her waist. "No way can I afford to pay someone a salary."

"You're not paying yourself?"

She shrugged. "Enough to get by. Not precisely a salary."

Angrier than he'd been before, he immediately said, "Why didn't you tell me, Janie? I'm a damned millionaire."

Stiffening, her lips pulled into a tight frown. "I'm not taking your money."

Her tone and the stiff set of her shoulders told him there would be no arguing with her. Janie wasn't the type of woman who'd let a man take care of her—even if he wanted to. She was the caretaker…she'd apparently *always* played that role, given what she'd told him about her family. First for her brother when their parents died, even though he'd been the older one. Then for her elderly grandmother when her health had gotten precarious.

So who took care of Janie? He'd like it to be him…but he knew her well enough to know that wasn't the answer, at least not financially. Emotionally? Well, that was another story. He hoped.

"I'm not handling things very well these days," she admitted. "Everything's changed. A few years ago, I knew what I was doing and where I was going. By now, I'd have been throwing myself into my career as an advocate for the elderly, working nine to five, dating a boring doctor instead of a to-die-for sports star who was supposed to just be a one-night fantasy."

He liked the to-die-for part. But the rest… "One night?"

She reached under her glasses and rubbed her eyes. "Seducing you was supposed to be a fling. One chance to be a flavor-of-the-month for a sexy athlete before the Slammers left town. Only, all three of us ended up getting a lot more than we bargained for."

Riley stiffened, his whole body going on alert. He didn't know exactly what Janie was talking about. But he damn sure didn't like it.

She didn't even notice. "Callie's back with Donovan and Babe's with Brodie Jessup." She looked at him and her lips curved up. "And look at me. Plain, vanilla Janie, having all kinds of wild sex with the most sought-after bachelor in baseball."

Hearing a pounding in his head, Riley realized his pulse was bursting through his veins as the full implication of her words rolled through him. He'd been under the assumption that Janie had seduced the guy she'd met on the lawn of the retirement home that day in March. Not the "most sought-after bachelor in baseball."

Through his tight jaw, he managed to ask, "What do Callie and Babe have to do with this?"

"They were here with me. The three of us were together when we hatched the plan to *get* our fantasy men—men associated with the Slammers—before you left town." She yawned, then turned to her desk and began clearing it off for the night. "That was when things looked bad for the team." Smiling at him over her shoulder, she added, "From what Callie says, though, things have really turned around. With the mayor challenging all civic-minded businesses to purchase five-year leases on skyboxes, Donovan will have plenty of capital to pay off his loan."

She kept talking, but frankly, she'd lost him after the words *plan* and *fantasy man*.

Janie had schemed to get Riley the Rocket into bed. She'd laughed about it with her girlfriends. Planned. Plotted. Then shown up in the restaurant next door in a devil-red dress to seduce the guy on the trading cards.

Not the man.

He turned to leave, not trusting himself to say a word. Because either he was going to explode in a rage, asking her if she'd ever once stopped to think about the fact that he was a human being before dressing herself like a sex queen and silently begging him from across a crowded room to screw her brains out. Or else he was going to push her onto the floor and have angry sex with her without saying a single word.

Either way, their relationship was going to be severely affected. So he was better off leaving to cool off. Now. Before he said something he was going to regret.

She finally seemed to realize something was wrong. "Riley? Is everything okay?"

"I've lost my appetite," he muttered, walking toward the door. "I'll talk to you later."

"What are you...you're leaving? But I thought..."

"Yeah, well we both obviously thought wrong. I thought you wanted a man you were attracted to. Not a pro-baseball-player notch on your bedpost."

He heard her gasp as he yanked the door open. But it didn't stop him from walking right out, not sure he would ever return.

JANIE'S MOUTH wasn't the only thing that dropped when Riley stormed out of Round The Bases. Her heart did, too, landing somewhere in the vicinity of her stomach. Because for the life of her, she could not figure out what had happened.

He'd stormed out, completely misreading her feelings for him...because she'd been late for dinner? Because she hadn't accepted his financial help? *Why?*

She strode across the floor, knowing she had to go after him. But something wouldn't let her do it. Until she knew why he'd come to such a stunningly wrong conclusion, might going after him just make things worse?

"What is it?" she muttered, looking around the jumbled stockroom. "What did I say? What did I do?" Whatever she'd done, it had been serious. Because before he'd roared out, Riley had looked very upset. "Not upset," she whispered. *Devastated.*

She just didn't know why.

Trying to figure it out, she couldn't help thinking about the first time they'd been in this room together. She so vividly remembered that night a few weeks ago when he'd first found her here. When they'd first kissed. When they'd first been so incredibly intimate. The way he'd wanted her, needed her, hungered for her. The way she'd pleased him.

It had been miraculous, but it had just been the start. Those memories were burned into her psyche and had become a part of her. Just as *he* had become a part of her.

Yes, it had been much faster than she'd have expected. But it had happened. Riley had taken up residence in her heart. She'd fallen in love with him against all of her own mental promises not to.

He, unfortunately, didn't appear to feel the same way. Not judging by the way he'd stormed out of here.

"From fantasy man to near stranger," she muttered as she kicked one of those stupid hands out of the way.

And suddenly it clicked. His words made perfect sense in light of *everything* that had happened that night—not just the physical pleasure and heat. She remembered his words, his demands to know what she'd been after...why she'd been trying so hard to seduce him, and *only* him. Even before he'd figured out who she was and had gotten so angry thinking she'd been playing a revenge game, Riley had been incredibly curious. Demanding to know *why* things had happened the way they had. Not dropping the subject until she'd taken control of the conversation with her lips and her tongue.

When they had finally ended up together that night at the retirement home, it had been *after* she'd admitted that all along she'd wanted the guy who'd flirted with her the day they'd met.

Oh, God. With everything she and Riley had shared over the past few weeks—everything they'd talked about regarding his marriage and the people who were always trying to get whatever they could from him—she knew how vulnerable he was on one topic. He was a generous, giving, sexy, playful man, and there wasn't much he wouldn't do for the people he cared about as long as he knew they saw him—the man, not the ballplayer.

"Oh, baby," she whispered, truly horrified at what she must have made him feel. "I'm so sorry."

"For what?"

Shocked by a male voice that had intruded on her self-recrimination, Janie held her breath. Slowly, she looked toward the door. Riley stood there, one hand on the doorjamb and the other on the knob. He looked ready to walk away with one wrong move. One wrong word.

She wasn't about to make the same mistake. "Riley, I'm sorry if I made you think you were nothing but a challenge to me."

"Wasn't I?"

Though part of her wanted to burst into denials, she settled for a simple shake of her head. "I wasn't kidding that night when I told you I wanted the guy who complimented my ass." She didn't smile, didn't try to flirt her way out of this one. This was way beyond anything sexy innuendo could cure. She was confronting the first major obstacle in a relationship that could be the most important one in her life. "I wanted the gorgeous man who dove onto a dirty floor so I wouldn't get hurt. The one whose lap was so inviting. So tantalizing."

His eyes flared. And maybe, just maybe, his shoulders relaxed a tiny bit. "Oh, yeah?"

She nodded. "Yeah. In case you don't know it, I don't much care for baseball players."

One of his brows lifted, but he remained silent.

"And I really *detest* playboy baseball players."

His cheek twitched. "I'm not a playboy."

"I know." She stepped closer, her hands clenched in front of her waist. "I know you're not, but I thought you were. And before I met you, I simply couldn't stand you. Anyone like you."

"Okay." His gaze shifted, his green eyes focusing on the foam hand half concealed beneath a cluttered shelf. "Well, you sure picked an interesting way to show it when you decided to seduce *someone like me*."

She moved closer, finding the strength to reach up and cup his cheek in her hand. "I'm telling you here and now, the whole stupid idea to try to seduce a fantasy guy came about because of the incredibly hot, flirtatious man I met while visiting my elderly grandmother. And for *no other reason*. You were the man I wanted. It was always *just you*."

He didn't relent entirely. "Convenient that the guy from the old folks' home happened to be somebody famous, huh?"

"Community for the enlightened years."

He didn't smile, but something warm and intimate flashed in his eyes. Which was when she knew she was getting to him.

"I don't know if I can do anything to convince you of this, but you are anything but a notch on a scorecard. I don't give a damn about scorecards, Riley. But I do give a damn about you."

"That's *all* you give?"

All? Oh, no, that wasn't all. She'd already given her heart and felt ready to give her soul—the rest of her life—to the man. Though she wasn't at all certain he was ready to hear that, she knew it was time to tell him, anyway. "No, that's not all. I'd like to give you more." She stepped closer. "I would like to give you my heart, Riley, if you want it."

Her fingers hovered a few inches above his chest, just a breath away from his heart, which she so desperately wanted to claim. But she wasn't sure, she couldn't say whether or not her feelings for him were reciprocated.

Until he smiled. And suddenly everything was all right.

"You mean it?" he asked, catching her fingers in his. "It's the man you want, not the guy on the trading cards? Because I'm not going to be there forever. I'm already thinking a few years down the road when this shoulder has finally had enough."

"What do you think you'll do?" she asked, distracted for a moment.

"I've done some on-air stuff for the networks," he replied. "And I've been made to feel really welcome. I like talking about baseball almost as much as I like playing it."

"Sounds perfect for you." Her voice said she meant it. "And

Riley?" She gestured toward the cellophane-wrapped albums on the shelves, full of shiny new cards. "I have enough trading cards. I want the man." Swallowing hard, she admitted, "I *love* the man."

That seemed to be enough. Because suddenly Riley was stepping in to meet her halfway, catching her in his arms and pulling her up against his big, hard body. His lips met hers and they exchanged an intimate kiss, full of sweet longing and promise.

"I love you, Janie," he murmured when he pulled away long enough to draw in a deep breath. "I never imagined feeling this way, and I didn't expect it to happen so fast. But it's true."

She started to smile, then to laugh, flooded with warmth and images of a future filled with possibility. "I love you, too."

He kissed her again, hotter, wetter, arousing her the way he always did. "You really need to get a bed back here."

She agreed. But before she could respond, Riley took care of the matter. Sweeping one arm across the pile of foam hands on the shelf, he scattered them across the floor. He sent a dusty shoebox full of trading cards down with them, but she didn't care. All she cared about was the soft, cushiony yellow mound at their feet. Janie almost purred at the realization that she was going to have him, again. No matter how long she lived, she'd *never* tire of making love with this man. And now that they'd both exposed their deepest, most vulnerable feelings, she knew their physical connection would be stronger—more powerful—than ever.

Tugging him down with her, she laid on the foam, looking into his eyes with all the emotion she felt for him.

Only to find him looking elsewhere. His attention was focused on something a few feet away. "Riley? Hello? You forgetting something here?"

His jaw had dropped. He asked, "Janie, where did you get that box?"

The cards. He wanted to talk trading cards when she was ready to get naked and wicked with him? If she didn't feel the big erection pressed against her hip, she might be offended. "I bought it from an old woman who was cleaning out her house."

"It can't be," he whispered. *"Can't* be."

"What?"

Shaking his head and not answering, Riley reached for the box. The rubber band had given way and a number of cards bagged in plastic were scattered around it. Riley flicked through them, making sounds of disbelief, then lifted one from the pile. He brought it to his face, let out a groan of shock, then rolled onto his back. "This can't be happening."

"What? Is it one of *yours?* If so, throw it away. I don't want the player on the trading cards."

She reached for the thing, but he grabbed her hand. Sitting up and dragging her with him, he said, "Janie, I don't think you want to throw this away. As a matter of fact, I think you want to go to that phone and call an auction house."

An auction house? She wasn't following.

He sounded dazed. "Unless I'm crazy, I think I'm holding a 1909 T206 Honus Wagner in my hand."

Okay. That was good. Maybe. "And?"

Finally giving her his full attention, he said, "Do you know who Honus Wagner was?"

She shook her head.

"He got his start as a shortstop right here in Louisville in the late 1800s. The man was the first spokesman for the Louisville Slugger. Legend says he demanded that production of his trading cards be stopped in 1911 because he thought they were pushing tobacco products."

"Good for him. I approve. Now, can we talk about something else? Like getting naked?"

He took her by the shoulders and stared into her face. "Honey, this is good for *you.* Stopping his cards meant they were very scarce. Very rare."

She was starting to get it.

"This card isn't mint but it's in excellent condition."

"So it's worth a lot?"

Grinning, he gave her a slow nod. "Uh, yeah. Mint gems of this baby have sold for upward of a million dollars."

Now it was Janie's turn to gasp. Her jaw dropped in shock and her heart started hammering. "You're not serious."

"Oh, I'm so damn serious." Then, grinning like a kid on Christmas morning, he grabbed more of the plastic wrapped antiques. "This is unbelievable. Eddie Plank. Ty Cobb." Slowly picking up another card, his hand started to shake. As did his voice. "T'll give you thirty thousand dollars right now for this 1936 World Wide Gum Lou Gehrig. It would mean a lot to Gramps."

"Thirty…." Her head started spinning. It was too much to believe. Too much to take in. "You're not making this up to try to get me to take money from you, are you?"

He dropped an arm over her shoulders to pull her onto his lap. "Honey, I couldn't make this up. This is like digging up a pirate's buried treasure. You're sitting on an incredible find in the trading card world. One that could make you rich." His expression grew serious, "One that could make this store pay for itself—and for a manager—so you can get on with your life."

With him. Oh, getting on with her life with Riley sounded better than anything.

Starting to believe it could really be happening, she narrowed her eyes and carefully touched the cards. "I need to track down that woman who sold them to me so we can renegotiate our deal. This could mean the world to her."

He hugged her, then kissed her jaw and her neck. "I love that about you. Your freshness, your honesty. Your integrity."

Grinning, she lifted a saucy brow. "My great ass?"

Riley dropped his hand down her body in a slow, smooth caress, cupping her bottom and lifting her higher on his lap. Janie slid one thigh over his legs, sighing in pure satisfaction at the perfect way their bodies aligned. "That, too."

Their mouths met in a sweet, wet kiss that went on and on. Then Riley leaned back, drawing her down with him. But before she lost herself completely, Janie quickly reached for the cards and tucked them safely back in the box.

"Ah, Just Janie, that's something else I love about you," he said, laughter in his voice. "You're always so sensible."

She ground against him. "Always insatiable, too."

He nodded and began drawing her clothes off, piece by piece. "Yeah. And I wouldn't have you any other way."

Epilogue

From the Louisville Ledger, August 7, 2006

IN A disappointing end to a thirteen-game winning streak, the Louisville Slammers lost the first game of a double-header last night in New York, but came back to win the second game. The team, currently in third place in the division, seems assured of a playoff spot, despite a short run of losses and injuries that seemed to weigh the Slammers down in late May.

Team owner Donovan Ross reacted to the loss with his typical philosophical good humor. "Isn't this exactly the kind of situation where you're supposed to say you can't win them all? I think we're okay with that…as long as we win the rest."

The team has had a tremendous run so far this season, thanks largely to the support of the fans and the business community of Louisville, who literally stepped up to the plate to ensure the Slammers would remain here after this season. Ross confirms this. "Yes, it is true, the threat of the team moving is over. I expect Louisville to enjoy Major League Baseball for many years to come."

Though the owner declined to answer detailed questions about the threatened takeover and move, insiders say Ross and his wife, restaurateur Callie Andrews Ross, worked tirelessly to ensure the team's security. Ross says, "I want to express my personal thanks to all the season ticket holders, the sponsors, the reporters and every guy on the street who walked up to the box office and shelled out his hard-earned money to support this team. We couldn't have done it without you."

From the city that gave the world the Louisville Slugger, what else would one expect?

Stability is highly overrated….

Dana Logan's world had always revolved around her children. Now they're all grown up and don't seem to need anything she's able to give them. Struggling to find her new identity, Dana realizes that it's about time for her to get "off her rocker" and begin a new life!

Off Her Rocker

by Jennifer Archer

HARLEQUIN
Next™

HN53
Available August 2006
TheNextNovel.com

Page-turning drama...

Exotic, glamorous locations...

Intense emotion and passionate seduction...

Sheikhs, princes and billionaire tycoons...

This summer, may we suggest:

THE SHEIKH'S DISOBEDIENT BRIDE
by Jane Porter
On sale June.

AT THE GREEK TYCOON'S BIDDING
by Cathy Williams
On sale July.

THE ITALIAN MILLIONAIRE'S VIRGIN WIFE
On sale August.

With new titles to choose from every month,
discover a world of romance in our books written
by internationally bestselling authors.

**Hidden in the secrets of antiquity,
lies the unimagined truth...**

Introducing

a brand-new line filled with mystery
and suspense, action and adventure,
and a fascinating look into history.

And it all begins with DESTINY.

In a sealed crypt in
France, where the
terrifying legend of
the beast of Gevaudan
begins to unravel,
Annja Creed discovers
a stunning artifact
that will seal her destiny.

*Available every other
month starting
July 2006, wherever
you buy books.*

GRA1

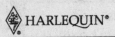

HARLEQUIN®

American ROMANCE®

IS PROUD TO PRESENT A
GUEST APPEARANCE BY

QUILL
BOOK
AWARD
WINNING
AUTHOR

NEW YORK TIMES bestselling author
DEBBIE MACOMBER

The Wyoming Kid

The story of an ex–rodeo cowboy,
a schoolteacher and their journey to the altar.

"Best-selling Macomber, with more than
100 romances and women's fiction titles
to her credit, sure has a way of pleasing readers."
—*Booklist* on *Between Friends*

The Wyoming Kid is available from
Harlequin American Romance in July 2006.

Silhouette® Desire®

**Introducing an exciting appearance
by legendary
New York Times bestselling author**

DIANA PALMER

HEARTBREAKER

He's the ultimate bachelor…
but he may have just met
the one woman to change his ways!

Join the drama in the story of a confirmed
bachelor, an amnesiac beauty and their
unexpected passionate romance.

**"Diana Palmer is a mesmerizing storyteller
who captures the essence of what
a romance should be."—*Affaire de Coeur***

**Heartbreaker *is available from Silhouette Desire*
in September 2006.**